"I don't think we should," she whispered. "I have to be a virgin for my husband. . . . It means a lot to me."

"Don't be dumb. *You'll* have to show *him* the ropes."

"You're repulsive."

"Might as well learn from the master." He kissed her breast.

Amy erupted, pushing violently against his shoulders.

He grabbed her straining hands, easing her back. "Hey, cool it. Settle down. Virginity's no big deal. Just do what other girls do."

"And what's that?"

"Lie."

YEARBOOK

A NOVEL BY

David Marlow

A FAWCETT CREST BOOK • NEW YORK

YEARBOOK

THIS BOOK CONTAINS THE COMPLETE TEXT OF THE ORIGINAL HARDCOVER EDITION.

Published by Fawcett Crest Books, a unit of CBS Publications, the Consumer Publishing Division of CBS Inc., by arrangement with Arbor House Publishing Company

ISBN: 0-449-23551-3

Alternate Selection of the Literary Guild

Printed in the United States of America

10   9   8   7   6   5   4   3   2   1

For Amanda

"Oh, no! It was not the airplanes.
It was Beauty killed the beast!"

Last line from 1932 RKO film,
King Kong

THE VENTURE

1958

September

1

Guy Fowler arrived at the top of Edson hill at 8:45, took one look, and knew he was never going to live through the day.

Monday, the twelfth of September, he made an entry in his mental diary: *My last sunrise.*

Hordes of strangers milled about the flagpole, forming cliques of varying sizes. A busy ant colony, they exchanged perfunctory greetings after a long summer's separation.

Weathered bricks and white colonnades reflected neither warmth nor welcome in their cold intimidation.

Two upper classmen, Marlboros drooping, poked each other. One pointed to Guy and remarked, "Will you just look at that? I swear, they get smaller every year."

As Guy walked by, doing his best to appear inconspicuous, one of the boys blew a puff of smoke in his face. "Tell the truth, sonny. You really a *sophomore?*"

Guy looked up and pulled an imaginary string atop his head. "No," he said, "I'm a ventriloquist's dummy!"

Amused, the tall boy let him pass.

Relieved, Guy lowered his head and walked under the arch and through the metal doors into Waterfield High.

Down in the girls' locker room, beautiful and bouncy, giggling and gossiping, a voluptuous Ro-Anne Sommers zipped herself into her snug red and yellow outfit and looked at the ID bracelet she was wearing: CORKY.

She sat down on the low locker bench to make a major decision. What to do? Cheerleading regulations stated most clearly: *No jewelry while jumping.* Still . . . she wanted all new girls at the assembly that morning to know damn

11

well, right from the start—Corky Henderson is spoken for. All mine. Hands off!

Ro-Anne dotted a few thick plops of white cream down her long legs and replaced the bottle inside her locker. She gently massaged the expensive moisturizer into her still-tanned skin.

"Finish up, girls!" Marlene, captain of the cheerleaders, clapped hands three times.

Ro-Anne made sure her braceleted wrist was behind her back as she took her place in line. Once certain Marlene hadn't noticed her indiscretion, she relaxed. Who cared if she broke a tiny, silly rule, anyway? Pretty girls can get away with murder.

At 8:55, Amy Silverstein carried her five-foot-nine frame into the *Eagler* office. She begged Leonard Hauser to let her off the hook. The last story she cared to cover was the sappy assembly for new students.

"Tough titty." Leonard yawned from behind his desk. "Someone's got to do it. Who else has your wit, your style, your deathless purple prose?"

Amy held up a thin, open hand. "Talked me into it! But I promise, once they start teaching those brats the alma mater, I'm leaving. I refuse to get nauseous before lunch. Cafeteria food will do that for me, as is."

Leonard peered up at Amy through thick eyeglasses, wondering as he did every time he saw her just how she had managed so well to miss out on nature's blessings— a girl whose hair was not just curly, but kinky; a complexion not just troubled with acne, but riddled; teeth not just crooked, but wired top to bottom, with marionette rubber bands which restricted movement as they were suspended from teeny hooks. Then there was the matter of that nose.

A regular baked potato.

"You're my star reporter!" The editor-in-chief, no perfection of nature himself, clicked his teeth.

Amy recognized Leonard's appraising look. Rather than pretend it wasn't there, she met it head on, saying as she walked out the door, "You bet, Leonard. Lois Lane with pimples!"

There was no one else in the boys' washroom as Guy rinsed his hands for the third time. He pulled a paper towel from the metal bin and heard all over again the dining room conversation of less than an hour ago.

"He's so creepy, Dad," Butch had complained, not knowing his younger brother was listening at the door. "Throws just like a girl. Honest. He's always picked last. Always."

Guy now regretted having eavesdropped. He also regretted the rest of what he'd overheard.

"I don't care." His father attacked a stack of pancakes. "One of you has to walk Guy to school. Just this first morning."

"Not me!" His sister Rose smiled sweetly through maple syrup lips.

"Not me!" Butch held up buttered fingers of protest. "Anyone who doesn't know we're related might mistake us for friends."

Guy's father swallowed a whole sausage link, tapped an impatient finger against his empty mug, looked from son to daughter and poured himself more coffee.

Birdie, Guy's mother, collected dirty dishes. "What Guy needs from all of you is a little encouragement. He's just sensitive is all."

"Sensitive?" Nathan protested, as if it were a dirty word. "Neither of my sons are sensitive, thank you, and Guy could learn to play ball like anyone else. He's just one of your late growers. He'd be fine, Birdie, if you'd get him away from those goddamn hobbies. And stop giving him money for the movies every time they change the program. . . ."

Guy discarded the recent memory with the soiled towel and looked out the bathroom window onto an empty athletic field. He inhaled deeply, hoping to calm down, hoping the month would change back to August.

There was a disturbing quality to the day. Not quite a

summer warmth, not yet an autumn crispness. A transitional season with no name. Something in the air which suggested an uncertain future Guy was not yet ready to face.

As he turned to leave he caught his reflection above the row of sinks. He stared several moments, sizing himself up with regret.

The mirror told the tale.

Fifteen and pencil thin. Still the smallest kid on the block—in the neighborhood. Fifteen and still the owner of a high-pitched, Mickey Mouse voice. Just turned fifteen and alone, still a stranger not only to the rest of his robust family, but to himself.

He could almost understand Butch and Rose's reluctance to accompany him to school. Hell, he didn't want to be seen with himself, either.

Three hundred hands crossed three hundred hearts, pledging loyalties.

Dr. Potter—educator, disciplinarian, idealist—stood on stage, behind a podium. American flag to his left, New York State flag to his right, the principal spent seventeen minutes explaining what it meant to be educated. Eight student leaders sat clumped together behind the good doctor, pretending to listen.

Amy sat in the last row of the auditorium, taking notes in a fast scribble. She loved Dr. Potter. He never caught on to the tongue-in-cheek manner in which she summarized his pompous remarks. He always thought Amy's barbs were valentines. Such was the power of her press.

Dr. Potter concluded his welcoming address, and those of the audience still alert applauded politely. "I now turn the program over to Ken Crawley, your Student Council President!"

In dark gray flannel suit, spanking white button-down shirt and skinny black tie, Ken Crawley smiled his way to the podium and looked out over a sea of constituents, counting votes. After an extensive greeting and a promise to clean up the hallways, he introduced the other student leaders onstage. In turn, he announced, "Senior class president and captain of our Eagles' trophy-bound football team . . . Corky Henderson!"

Corky rose to his feet, waved and conquered.

The girls wanted him.

The boys wanted to be him.

Tall and uncommonly handsome, charming, popular and powerfully built, Corky Henderson stood onstage, way up at the top of the totem pole, coolest of them all. Each short wave of his carefully parted dark hair was thicker than the next. His green eyes smiled at his appreciative audience and his dimples deepened with good reason: barely eighteen and already a legend.

Squealing in the wings with the other cheerleaders, Ro-Anne tingled with excitement. Her firm nipples rubbed against her bra. She loved seeing Corky cheered and adored. It meant they were applauding her too. Fame by association.

From an open field of pretty faces Corky had taken his pick. And many a fantasy had been fulfilled when he'd displayed the good taste to have chosen Ro-Anne, the loveliest flower of them all.

She rubbed her ID with affection.

No doubt about it. She was in love.

Guy applauded too and his stomach gurgled. Adrenaline shot every which way. In all his life he'd never seen anyone he'd so instantly admired. For whatever Guy Fowler wasn't, Corky Henderson most assuredly was.

Guy calculated what it would take to be like the amazing fellow now center stage, soaking up all that limelight. Just another twelve inches off the ground; sixty additional pounds of sinewy muscle; the smile, the confidence, the right clothes, the rugged, casual, jocklike air and he'd have it all. Nothing to it.

He wanted to slash his wrists.

Repulsive nonsense, thought Amy as her eyes canvassed the new students idolizing Corky. Look at him up there, King Eagle, bulging out of his letter sweater.

She jotted down the following: *Shame our new students*

don't display the same enthusiastic reception for the Chairman of the Science Fair as for the Captain of the football squad. Even in our atomic age, cavemen still capture the hour.

Amy knew Leonard Hauser would delete the pointed observation with his manic blue pencil, so she wouldn't include it in her piece. Still, she was glad to have noted it.

No doubt about it. She was not in love.

The next part of the assembly found the cheerleaders running onstage. White gloves clap-clapped, tennis sneakers stomp-stomped. Statuesque 34-B cups moved up and down as healthy lungs filled with oxygen. Ro-Anne and her sisters leapt gaily about in spread-eagled flights of fancy. Their prized genitalia became the center of gravity as they performed clean-cut cartwheels and splits, and as white thighs kicked out of red and yellow bloomers, black-and-white composition notebooks dropped to laps, covering up the response of sophomore males to so much school-spirit-raising.

Amy doodled while Ro-Anne demonstrated.

The cheerleaders then ran off, single file, still clapping, still *yea-yea*-ing. An aroused audience cheered its approval.

The program ended after the singing of the alma mater, and students were told to report to second period class.

Disoriented, Guy got lost in the flow of traffic, briefly enjoying the anonymity as he ascended the mobbed Up staircase to the second floor. When he turned the corner, he saw them coming down the hall.

Corky and Ro-Anne.

Freezing, Guy stared. To be blessed with so much happiness . . .

Corky and Ro-Anne strolled down the corridor hand-in-hand. The aura from their cosmic harmony almost glowed as they greeted passing friends.

Guy wished he could run over and join the others greeting Corky. He wanted to be part of their group. To be cool. To be one of the boys, one of the cats. To be special; like Corky.

No doubt about it. He was in love.

16

As Corky and Ro-Anne passed, Guy stood straight and offered his warmest smile, hoping by off-chance one of them might smile back, that a drop of their radiance might fall to him. Hey! Over here! Look this way! *Please*.

But, with eyes only for each other, they passed without noticing. As they wandered off into Paradise, Guy slouched into ████ ██████.

The women in the living room looked up from their canasta tournament and four voices spoke, at once: "Amy, you're home!" "How was school?" "How nice she looks!" "Try a sandwich!"

Amy greeted her mother and "the girls," then excused herself. She had homework.

"First day of school and already she has homework?" Mrs. Kessler, apartment 3-F, thought it odd.

"That's a bright cookie, that one is!" Mrs. Fine from down the hall rearranged her hearts.

"Better not to be so bright a cookie!" Mrs. Abrams, 2-D, laid down her cards. "Better she should find a man and let him be bright for both of them."

Amy's mother picked up a poreclain dish of tiny candies and offered it around the circle. "Mints?"

In her room Amy quickly got her chemistry, French and English assignments out of the way and then whipped together her article on the opening day assembly.

Homework was easy. Had always been easy. Even when everything else was not.

Determined to tighten summer softness, Coach Petrillo stretched and strained his athletes. Twice more around

17

the track at a fast jog and into the showers. It was five o'clock.

Corky showered and dressed quickly. His body ached and he looked forward to a big meal. He wasn't interested in the water fight or towel snappings going on between Butch Fowler and some of his junior varsity pals.

No one dared douse or snap at Corky when he wasn't in a playful mood. And to be sure, Corky was not in a playful mood. His concentration was intently, exclusively, focused on football.

Out of the locker room in fifteen minutes, he jogged to his dilapidated thirdhand '52 Chevy convertible. Pulling into his driveway seven minutes later, he parked behind his father's bought-on-time Edsel. Damn! His old man was already home and that meant they'd go through one of their reunion routines. Though exhausted, Corky decided to make a show of it anyway. His father would like that.

By the time Corky slammed the Chevy door, Carl Henderson was well past the screen door, barreling straight toward the gravel driveway.

"There's my boy!" Carl sounded the war cry as he plowed into his son, throwing Corky to the ground.

His mother Dora ran out too, as always. The small woman yelled at them to stop fighting . . . the neighbors might think they were serious.

Carl and Corky wrestled around the front lawn for a few minutes until, bored with the ordeal, Corky decided to let his father pin him.

"Uncle?" Carl pushed his son's face into the grass.

Corky gritted his teeth.

"Uncle!?" Carl shoved the handsome face deeper into the ground.

"Uncle."

"Get off him, Carl!" Dora pleaded from the driveway. "He's turning blue, for God's sake!"

A grin spread across his beet-red face, Carl Henderson relaxed his grip and stood up. Corky spat out a few blades of grass.

His father extended his arm, helped Corky up and the

18

two of them walked into the house. Dora followed close behind, her face turned to the ground, as if she was expecting to pick up missing pieces.

"Didn't hurt ya, did I?" Carl proudly put an arm around his boy.

Corky swallowed. "No, Dad. You didn't hurt me."

"I'm still the toughest, huh? Gotta get up pretty damn early to beat Carl Henderson, ain't that right?"

"Pretty damn early," his son agreed.

"You're just in time," chirped Birdie as Guy walked through the kitchen door. "Where've you been all afternoon? This cherry crumb pie could really be something. I used three eggs instead of one, and two less teaspoons sugar. The idea is to make us appreciate the natural tartness of the canned cherries."

Guy's mother pressed a firm finger on the boy's shoulder and sat him on one of three stools at the kitchen counter. "Just take a small taste, I wouldn't want you ruining whatever appetite you might have for dinner." She placed a piece of pie on a plate and presented it to him with a glass of Coca-Cola. "Don't mince words. Tell me where I've gone wrong."

Guy bit into the red dessert.

"Well?" prompted Birdie anxiously, her fingers crossed.

"Too soggy," said Guy, after due consideration, wiping the glue from his gums. "Take out the extra eggs, put back the sugar." He took a sip of Coke.

"That's what I figured." Birdie moped back to the enormous refrigerator to start all over again.

Guy picked up the remaining portion of his pie and the glass of soda and took them both to the sink, then kissed his mother on the cheek and hurried upstairs.

Careful about how his free time was spent, Guy allocated hours and allowances into three priorities.

The first was the movies—every weekend, a must.

Second was photography. Guy drained his savings and cajoled his parents into helping him purchase the extensive supplies and second-hand equipment that kept him locked up for hours, shooting, processing, enlarging.

Last, not least, came the fish. They were tropical and Guy could sit, his nose inches from the glass of his fifteen-gallon tank, staring for hours.

While the rest of his family was downstairs watching "Bonanza," Guy was upstairs, watching his fish. He was always cleaning the filter or changing the color of the gravel or rearranging the plant life inside his private aquatic world.

Besides some thirty guppies, there lived an angel fish named Gabriel and a kissing gourami named Romeo. There was a snail that diligently sucked up algae, a catfish who worked overtime scrubbing the slimy bottom, and even a slinky salamander which just snuck about, a miniature Loch Ness Monster named Irving. Guy was fond of them all.

He was, in fact, so preoccupied with his films, his fish, his photography there was just no time left to have friends.

Staying young and beautiful was no easy business.

First came the leg raises. Three sets. Then shoulder twists and hip bumps against the wall. After rocking from thigh to thigh, crawling across the floor, there were bosom stretches and tummy tightenings.

It was Monday evening and a pooped Ro-Anne was working out.

She steamed her face, shaved her legs, clipped her toenails and tweezed her eyebrows. She shampooed and conditioned her hair in the sink, then wrapped it all up in a fluffy white towel.

Next, with Albolene greased all over her face, she fell into a bubble bath and polished her fingernails.

Half an hour later Ro-Anne sat at her vanity table, gazing at a freshly laundered image. She had to set her hair in bobby pins and curlers, but not before her nightly one hundred strokes. She picked up her hairbrush. One, two, three—thank God for her beauty. Seven, eight, nine —she'd always have that. Always—'leven, twelve, thirteen —What in the world, she wondered, did less attractive girls do with their lives? Twenty-two, twenty-three, twenty-four . . .

Ro-Anne stroked her hair, and as she did she naturally drifted, allowing past to become present—thirty-six, thirty-seven, thirty-eight. She stared at her reflection, remembering. . . .

Wherever Ro-Anne Sommers looked, bright lights burned her eyes, made her skin itch beneath her white tulle dress. The pressure was on.

Determined not to squint, not to scratch, she smiled.

Several drops of perspiration, tiny beads, popped out on her forehead. No, she thought. Don't. Whatever you do, don't sweat. You'll ruin everything.

She stopped sweating, and continued smiling.

With a stretch of her mouth she let everyone see each of her splendid teeth. She kept her back straight, shoulders high, feet pointed forward. The lights blinded and cooked and the pressure was on. Still, she smiled.

The emcee moved slowly to the microphone, center stage.

Ro-Anne and the other contestants stiffened.

"Ladies and glentlemen!" announced the emcee. "I have in my hand the names of the five finalists!"

Drum roll.

Ro-Anne steadied herself and remembered her rules of poise, grace, position and stance. What to do when she became a finalist. Where to walk. How to freeze a smile and show excitement for others if she didn't make it.

Didn't make it?

How could she not? Those round blue sparkling eyes. That patrician nose, stolen from a museum. Those sensuous lips, shining in the glimmer of raspberry-ruby lipstick. Those teeth, whiter than winter. That skin, soft alabaster, rouged just enough on high cheekbones to suggest innocent blush. Her golden hair, not a strand astray, shimmering beneath the hot lights.

The perfectly proportioned body. Ro-Anne knew from the judges' smiles how high she'd scored in the swimsuit competition.

And of course the intelligence displayed during her interview: *"I plan to become a nurse; to relieve some of the suffering in the world."*

"Fourth runner-up!" announced the emcee, himself now beginning to sweat. "Linda Miller, Miss Ulbright County!"

Linda Miller's hands flew to her face in great surprise. Who *me?* Walking forward to the winner's circle, she received her bouquet of flowers and stood, toes pointing.

Nine remaining finalists moved, as previously instructed, closer together, filling Linda's gap. Behind them stood the forty other contestants, losers who hadn't made it to the top ten.

"Third runner-up!" barked the emcee, a handkerchief wiping his brow. Breathless, the entire auditorium waited. "Ida Davenport. Miss Tappan County."

Finalists on either side of Ida Davenport screamed with delight. Miss Tappan County forced a smile and moved to the winner's circle. Disappointed, she had expected nothing less than the winner's spot.

Eight girls moved closer together, all smiles. Ro-Anne felt a tightening knot encircle her stomach.

Three to go. She had to be one of them. It was always the winner and two runners-up who got their pictures in the papers. She had to get there. She'd come too far, had won too many preliminaries to lose now.

"Second runner-up!" The emcee sweated. A smiling Ro-Anne braced herself. "Lois Worthington, Miss Sullivan County!"

Touched and thrilled, Lois Worthington accepted hugs, kisses and too honored, broke into streams of tears as she joined the winners' circle.

The seven remaining finalists again inched closer together, eyeing each other, smiles in place.

Ro-Anne worried. What if she didn't get into the top five at all? What if she had to settle for being a dumpy semi-finalist? She'd kill herself, she really would.

"Ladies and gentlemen . . . the first runner-up!" Sweat from the emcee's brow dripped onto the microphone. Butterflies, millions, invaded the auditorium, tickling everyone's insides. "Mary Ligggett, Miss Cisco County!"

Mary Liggett hollered and jumped in the air—a clear loss of poise and control, a clear case of bad taste.

Hugs and kisses, congratulations and tears, and Mary joined the winning beauties.

This was it. Down to the wire. One to go.

The six remaining girls broke formation. No longer tall and stoic, they reached out and held on to each other.

Ro-Anne squeezed the hand of the girl crunched next to her and prayed. Please, God, let me win. Don't make me a semi-finalist. Please. This is only the regional round-up, if I don't win this I can't go on to the nationals next month. . . .

No matter what happened, though, she knew she couldn't cry. Her mascara would run and ruin everything.

Please, God, please. Don't let my mascara run!

"Ladies and gentlemen, I give you the new Little Miss Eastern United States . . ." Not a sound in the hall, not a breath. "From the Long Island town of Waterfield, New York . . . Ladies and gentlemen, *Ro-Anne Sommers, Miss Nassau County!*"

Slapping an open hand to her chest, Ro-Anne rolled her eyes and opened her mouth, stunned.

The five surrounding girls went after her, to touch and hug, to shower her with excited affection.

Ro-Anne could not be bothered. Head high and serene, she breezed forward and humbly accepted the two dozen roses from last year's winner. Her ladies-in-waiting helped her on with her cape, bobby-pinned her crown in place and presented her with the commanding scepter.

Ro-Anne glowed as she floated to the foot of the stage, greeting her loyal subjects in the audience, all of them standing to receive their queen. Marian Sommers was in the audience too, a proud parent, clapping loudest of all.

Ro-Anne took in the warmth of the applause, bathed in the comfort of the lights—somehow no longer hot—and stood there radiating charm, poise and all-American beauty.

Along with her gracious bow, she allowed a modest smile to express her gratitude. She would have liked to cry, just a bit, a few joyful tears to display a rare vulnerability in one so lovely. But dammit, there was the problem of the mascara. . .

Ro-Anne pivoted and walked back upstage to the winners' circle. The orchestra finished playing "Lovely to Look At."

And in this way, sitting on her throne, surrounded by her court of also-rans, Ro-Anne Sommers became Little Miss Eastern United States of 1949.

She was, at the time, eight years old.

3

Guy returned home from school on Tuesday, gathered his camera gear and bicycled to the nearby marshes. It was the height of duck season so he wore his plaid jacket, the better not to be mistaken for lunch by some zealot-on-the-trigger. Though the woods were not too crowded with hunters, Guy still heard a steady stream of distant popping.

His father—Big Nathan—was a hunter. He and two buddies had a shoot planned for Sunday. Guy's brother Butch was going. Guy wasn't. His father said he was still too irresponsible to handle firearms.

Guy wandered about the open fields, his secondhand Pentax poised, stalking subject matter. A family of camera-shy rabbits had obvious difficulty distinguishing shutters snapping from guns cocking and dove for cover.

Looking forward to developing his candid shots, Guy started for home. Half an hour later, as he pedaled onto his block, he saw a large moving van parked outside his house.

No! Guy squeezed the brakes. *They're abandoning me!*

He sped toward the driveway, all set to throw himself at Birdie's feet, to beg her not to let the family move away without him.

Anxious visions of being shipped to an orphangage did not, in fact, subside until he got close enough to realize something was being moved *into* the house, not out. Two men, overweight and fighting for breath, were wheeling an upright Steinway piano past the front steps and into the living room.

"What's this all about?" Guy asked his mother.

"Your father has decided Rose should take piano lessons. She starts tomorrow. Your father feels she's musically inclined."

His father was wrong. Tone deaf and disinterested, Rose cared only to spend her afternoon hours sipping Cokes at Gateway Lanes while watching her boyfriend, Jonathan Leeds, bowl. The very notion of piano lessons made her wince.

Not so Guy. As soon as the moving men drove off, he sat down in front of the new toy and did not get up again for three hours. He fooled around, experimenting with the keys, instinctively discovering chords and, by the end of the day, almost managing a tune.

On Wednesday afternoon Rose sat through the longest hour of her life, having great difficulty locating middle C. When her spinster instructor finally left, she heaved with relief and dashed upstairs to tweeze her eyebrows.

The piano bench was still warm when Guy got to it moments later. Picking up where he'd left off the day before, he continued teaching himself by ear. Rasputin served as Guy's audience. While the eleven-year-old calico snoozed on the window ledge, curled up like a tiny orange puma, Guy practiced.

Two hours later Birdie strolled into the living room with her latest batch of calories. Guy dutifully tasted and rated her baking, then plinked out a surprisingly respectable, almost recognizable version of "The Ballad of Davy Crockett."

Birdie was impressed. "Where'd you learn that?"

"Don't know. It's just easy to find on the keyboard."

Birdie sat next to him and stuffed half a date-nut brownie into his mouth.

Guy swallowed and went back to work.

Ro-Anne hated French. So boring. Useless. There weren't even any French restaurants in Waterfield to show off what she might have learned if she took the trouble to pay attention.

How, she wondered, would she ever make it through an entire term of grammar and parsing sentences if here she was, stifling yawns the first week of classes?

Monday, Tuesday and Wednesday had been an easy enough waste of time; receiving textbooks, filling out Delaney cards, lining up along the walls of the room, being seated alphabetically—you could always count on getting stuck next to the biggest creeps.

Today was different. Work. Bill Rinaldi, up there at the blackboard, conjugating a verb. Ro-Anne looked to the ceiling, wishing the day would end. He can't speak English yet. How's he going to learn French?

Pen in hand, she hastily wrote on three-hole, loose-leaf paper:

I love	*J'aime*
You love	*Tu aimes*
We love	*Nous aimons*
They love	*Ils aiment*

Clouds of romance filtered into the room even as Bill Rinaldi's piercing Long Island French accent faded into the background. Stroking her magic lantern, Corky's ID, the genie of memory soon had her transported far away from French, back to one of her best-loved school-hour preoccupations—reliving the first time they had met. The memory was a favorite among her oldies-but-goodies. . .

It was a year ago, practically to the day. A traveling carnival had come to an open meadow high with weeds. The tall grass of this one-time cow pasture was mowed, a tent was pitched and in just a few hours the area was ablaze with gaudy neon.

Immersing herself totally in the memory, Ro-Anne visualized Corky and four fellow members of the football varsity downing six-packs before arriving at the carnival grounds. In her mind she watched them wandering about, looking for action. When they stumbled upon a Measure-Your-Strength machine, *Sissy* to *Superman,* the biggest of the athletes suggested they have a whack at it. Two shots for ten cents! They were all drunk enough to find the idea amusing.

The boys hee-hawed, slapped at each other, paid their money and took their chances. By the time it was Corky's turn at the mallet there were forty young people watching all this muscle power. None of the boys had connected yet and the highest rating managed so far was *Limp-Wristed*.

Ro-Anne once again saw herself standing in the crowd with her girl friends; once again knew the feeling as she took only one look at Corky Henderson before deciding *that* was for her.

And why not? Her mother had convinced her early-on that she was the prize package who should settle for nothing but the finest. "A girl with *both* beauty and money can take all the time she wants, Ro. They'll be lining up for you, honey, and that's a fact. You just let them wait."

Ro Anne decided she'd waited long enough. Pleased to be wearing her tight maroon sweater, she smiled with confidence and waited for Corky Henderson to notice her, waited for her life to begin.

After more shoving and the mandatory punches-on-the-arms, Corky got down to business. He removed his encumbering football jersey and let it drop to the ground. His long back glistened with sweat. His tensed muscles strained as he wound up and swung the mallet down hard.

The marker slid up to *Not Bad*. The crowd reacted excitedly.

Corky was about to take his second swing when, turning around, he spotted Ro-Anne—a calm picture of loveliness—staring at him. Prettiest thing he'd ever seen.

They gazed at each other a few long moments. Sparks flew like crazy as Ro-Anne calculated her plan of attack.

Inch by inch she would allow him to get closer. Bit by bit. She tingled just thinking about how glorious it would be. First she would invite and taunt, give him

27

just enough but hold him off just enough to sustain his interest. Not until she was good and ready, not until she was confident of his total respect, not until then would she finally bestow upon him full rights to her sacred, long-pursued flower. She had planned forever each and every detail of the momentous event and there was nothing in this world to divert her from them.

Candles. Lots and lots of candles, different sizes and scents, all around the room. Loads of pillows. And music, glorious music, something special. Johnny Mathis singing "The Twelfth of Never" or "Chances Are." Maybe some Kostelanetz or Mantovani for class. Giving up your most valued possession was no ordinary occasion. It had to be arranged with style, forethought and a time of courtship.

Relaxed in the surety of her plan, Ro-Anne smiled.

Corky smiled too. Oh, how he smiled. He smiled at her and the intense message in his eyes was delivered warm and fast. *I'm doing this next one for you, baby!*

He turned, smashed down the mallet and sent the round metal indicator up, up, up, climbing higher and higher until, with a *bong!* that rang throughout the meadow, it struck the bell at the top. *Superman!*

Ro-Anne shivered. A feathery tickle circled the space between her legs. The full thrill of the moment could never be forgotten.

When the noise and whoops had died down some, the concessionaire handed Corky an enormous pink stuffed elephant. He accepted the large animal and without a second thought walked over and handed it to Ro-Anne. She blushed.

He flipped his jersey over his shoulder, took her by the hand and led her silently away from her friends, away from the crowd, over toward the Ferris wheel some five hundred feet away. Their eyes remained fixed upon each other each step of the way.

Finally hidden from view behind the ride, they stopped underneath a tall maple. Corky reached forward and took Ro-Anne in his arms. Then he gave her the kiss for which she had always been waiting. His tongue swept the inside

28

of her mouth as his inquisitive hands investigated the rest of her.

She never objected, her eyes never strayed from his stare.

"You're really beautiful," he told her.

"No. You are," she whispered in their first exchange of words. The Ferris wheel churned and fireworks danced above.

It wasn't until ten minutes later, when a heavily breathing Corky placed an audacious hand on the zipper of her skirt, that the virgin Ro-Anne managed to whimper, "No, no more." Then, summoning all her willpower, she removed his warm hand from the side of her skirt, stood up and rebuttoned her sweater.

Corky stood up too and shook the grass from his jersey.

Ro-Anne hoped he wouldn't be too annoyed, that he would learn to be patient. After all, surrendering her chastity behind a Ferris wheel was most definitely not part of her determined scenario of how it would be. On the grass? Come on, with whom did he think he was dealing . . . some common one-nighter?

She took a deep breath, renewed contact with the pupils of Corky's green eyes, and purred, "Would you buy me an ice cream cone?"

Corky kissed her again. When their lips parted he answered, "Only if you tell me your name."

It was, she decided, going just fine.

Everyone watched the model couple strolling around the fairgrounds that evening. They held hands and traded seductive licks of ice cream cones. The stuffed pink elephant became striped with chocolate and strawberry drippings. The back of Ro-Anne's skirt bore grass stains. The front of her maroon sweater was covered with—*ClangClangClangClang,* the eight-period bell sounded, bringing to an abrupt halt the school day, the French lesson and the hallowed daydream.

Rats! Ro-Anne slap-closed her notebook. Just when things were finally getting interesting. Oh, well. No matter. She didn't really much care to relive the rest of the memory anyway. . . . Particularly the part in which her well-plotted schedule disintegrated two hours later when, out of control and caught off guard, an impassioned Ro-Anne gave up her prized cherry in the most clichéd manner of all—right in the back seat of Corky's beat-up Chevrolet.

4

Friday evening ushered in the new social season. The town buzzed.

Ponytailed and a-twitter, Rose Fowler scurried off to her sorority meeting. A tight woolen sweater made her large breasts stand out, and a wide red elastic cinch belt pulled in her flabby midsection. Her sisterhood, Middle Beta, rated third best in the pecking order because its membership consisted of the third-best-looking girls in school. There was no other criterion.

Her brother Butch, freshly scrubbed, with tiny patches of toilet paper clotting nicks across his chin from his weekly stab at shaving, strutted out of the house. The young peacock burned rubber on his father's borrowed Oldsmobile as he zoomed off to his fraternity meeting. Kappa Phi was his house and it was number one. Waterfield's top jocks belonged. Including Corky Henderson.

Finally, as clandestine Greek gatherings came to an end, the teen-aged citizenry gravitated toward Poste Avenue— pilgrims to Mecca. To see and be seen. To hang out. There was Darcy's for sodas. Gateway Lanes for bowling, the whole of Poste Avenue for cruising.

This Friday was no different for Guy. As always, he went to the movies.

Arriving at the Avalon just as the show was starting, he handed his seventy-five cents to a sixteen-year-old couple, asking them to purchase his ticket so that he would be accompanied by an adult. Once inside, he flopped down in his favorite third row center seat, cemented his front teeth to a caramel Sugar Daddy and, submitting himself to technicolor, got lost in the John Wayne feature.

The audience was spirited—booing and whistling; throwing popcorn, firing spitballs from the balcony, hurling insults at the screen.

Guy's favorite actor was John Wayne. After all, Wayne was . . . Wayne. Tall and tough, nobody could push him around. Surely you couldn't ask more from a man than that.

The last to return home, just before midnight, Guy tiptoed up the stairs of the darkened house until he stumbled over Rasputin, catnapping on the landing between floors. The calico screeched and clung to the flowered curtains by its claws. Guy picked up the fat fur ball and took it downstairs to the kitchen. He opened the refrigerator and prepared a peace offering of cream and crackers. A true Fowler, the cat practically drowned himself in his frantic search for the last saltine.

A thunder of hoofs pounded the stairs. Attracted by the enticing sound of the rattling refrigerator door, Rose entered the kitchen. Her hair in rollers and her face obliterated by thick complexion cream, she darted, straight as a homing pigeon, for the fragile Aunt Jemima cookie jar on the counter.

"There I was," she told Guy vivaciously, "upstairs, reading what Troy Donahue loves about Suzanne Pleshette's cooking, when I heard all this commotion down here and figured why not investigate . . .?" She lifted the dark lady's ancient porcelain head and peered down at the vast selection. "Oh dear!" She sniffed into the open cookie jar the way other teenagers sniffed glue. "Oatmeal! Butter-raisin! And chocolate-chip drop! Which do I want, and how many of each?"

Guy looked to the ceiling and stretched wide his hands, seeking God's wisdom. "Who am I to tell the undefeated winner of the Camp Echo Lark pie-eating contest five years in a row how many cookies she should eat?"

"I know! *Two* of each. For variety. Start my diet tomorrow, anyway." She opened the refrigerator. "And a glass of warm milk to send me off to beddy-bye." As she poured the milk into a pan she asked, "What's Butch up to?"

Guy shrugged. "Probably upstairs. I just got home."

Rose looked at the electric clock above the door. "Midnight!" She frowned. "The dumb movies again?"

Guy said nothing.

"My sorority meeting was fabs. We laughed and sang a lot and . . . *mmmm,* I'll say these are heavensville. Mother sure knows her cookies, doesn't she?"

"I haven't tasted them yet."

"No"—Rose chewed heartily—"I don't suppose you would have. Ecstasy! I wonder if Butchie knows about them. You don't suppose he's still hungry?"

"I can promise you, he's still hungry."

Rose surreptitiously laced her warming milk with an impressive dollop of honey. "Guy, darling, be a good little brother and take some cookies to Butchie."

"I'm going to bed. Why don't you?"

Rose indicated the mug and all her cookies. "I'm so loaded down—"

"Then why not drop some excess baggage?"

Rose turned on him. "How come you're never hungry?"

"Wish I knew." Guy stayed calm. "How come you're letting your milk boil?"

Rose looked down at her bubbling beverage. "My God!" she yelled, quick to extinguish the flame. "Look what you made me do!"

"Me?"

"It's all your fault." Irritated, she poured her scorched milk into the mug. After plopping a couple of marshmallows onto her steaming nightcap, she lifted her mug and piled the batch of baked goods onto her hand, a precarious balance. "I'll tell Butch you're bringing him some cookies."

"I am not bringing Butch some cookies."

"He'll be expecting them."

"He'll be disappointed."

"Butch doesn't like to be disappointed."

"Who cares?"

"He'll punch you and make you cry," said Rose in precious baby talk.

"And maybe I'll tell dad—"

"No you won't. Because if you do he'll punch you again, harder."

Guy couldn't argue with such logic. "I'll bring him some cookies."

With a smile, Rose pushed open the swinging kitchen door. "And have a few yourself, Guy. Put on a few pounds. Live! Stop walking through life a concentration camp victim. Eat and be merry for tomorrow we diet. I'm going to curl my eyelashes." And she was gone.

Butch was stretching a set of coiled springs, expanding his chest, as Guy entered his room.

"What you want, shorty?" he grunted.

"I come bearing milk and cookies," Guy answered with restrained impatience.

"What kind?" huffed Butch, dropping to the floor to knock off a dozen push-ups.

"The cookies are assorted and the milk is white."

". . . White? . . . two . . . three . . . four . . . why *white*? . . . Six . . . seven . . . put 'em on the desk . . . ten . . . 'leven . . . twelve. . . . Whew!"

Guy delivered the platter as the Butcher flexed his way to a chinning bar strapped between the doorposts of his closet.

"One . . . two . . . three . . . four . . ."

Guy turned to leave.

". . . five . . . just a second . . . seven . . . eight . . ."

Guy stood still. "Yes?"

"You know I prefer chocolate milk."

Guy sighed heavily. "Don't you read the papers, Butch? The chocolate cows are on strike."

Both of Butch's chins hung over the bar. His beady eyes peered down, disapprovingly. "Rose and I were talking about you today."

"Oh?"

"We were trying to figure out why you're such a sissy."

That hurt. Guy made light of it. "What did you decide?"

"She says it's genes."

"And what did you say?"

"I said I didn't think it mattered what kind of pants you wore, nothing could help."

"I'll remember that, Butch."

"You were listening in this afternoon, after school, weren't you? Listening at the door?"

"Not me." Guy lied.

"Yes you were. I didn't hear the piano, so I knew you were outside. It was while we were talking about jerking off. Must've made you jealous as hell."

Guy scratched his arm. "Why would I ever be jealous of you or your friends?"

"You can't beat your meat, is why."

"Can too!"

"Liar! You don't even have hair on your pecker. Just like a eunuch, a freak!"

Guy really hated Butch.

"Next year at this time . . . I'm gonna be first string. *First string!* Eagle senior varsity. Did you know *that?*"

"Yes, Butch. You told me two days ago."

"You know, for a shrimp, you got a lot of balls."

"Shrimps don't have balls. They have tentacles. Did you know *that?*"

Butch advanced menacingly. "You are a first-class crud!"

"Thanks." Guy took a few steps back.

"A real fruit bar."

Guy bowed mockingly. "Whatever you say, Mighty Mouse."

"You don't know first thing about football."

"By choice, thank you."

"You wouldn't know a punt from a flying tackle."

"I'll kill myself."

"And that voice!"

Guy's insides tightened. Butch had touched his most tender spot.

"Where do you find the nerve to speak?"

Guy switched on his standard defense tactic. "All right, Butch." He smirked. "Enough brotherly love. If you really want to get to me, why not try some insults?"

"Kiss my ass!"

"Butch, please. I'm still digesting dinner."

That did it. The bull was riled. Godzilla unchained.

"Put 'em up!" barked Butch, lunging forward and slapping Guy lightly across the face.

"Stop it, Butch."

"Make me!" The young Rocky Graziano danced back and forth.

If only I could, thought Guy. If only . . .

"Just a couple-a-rounds. Let's go." Butch weaved, crouched low.

"No."

"Look!" He playfully slapped Guy across the face again. "I'll keep one hand behind my back. You can definitely take me with one hand."

"Butch, I don't want to fight—"

"I can't make it any easier for you than one hand. Jesus, even a chicken-shit like you can take on one hand."

"No."

"I promise not to fight dirty."

"Big deal."

"Put 'em up!"

Butch swung, Guy ducked.

"Aha," Butch glowed with satisfaction. "Two for flinching." He delivered a pair of hard knuckle-knocks to Guy's upper arm.

Guy rubbed the soon-to-be-black-and-blue spot. "I want to thank you for a terrific time, Butch. And any time I can be of service, just whistle. Now, if you don't mind, I'll just pack up my rickshaw and get on to my room."

"Not so fast. One round, just one. My hand tied behind my back *and* I'll hop on one leg. This is my final offer."

"Fine," Guy acknowledged, "and this is my final refusal. Good night."

Guy made a smart about-face and was greatly surprised

when his legs buckled forward, driven by a perfect flying tackle from his brother, the future senior Eagle first stringer.

Once on the floor, Butch flipped Guy over on his back. Enormous knees pinned thin shoulders to the rug.

"Don't hurt me . . . ," Guy pleaded, stalling for time. "I'll make it worth your while. . . ."

"How?" asked Butch a fist hovering above his head.

Guy thought fast. "Take three of my guppies?"

Butch was enticed. The fist unraveled. "Ten!" bargained a greedy Butcher.

"Five!" Guy countered, more confident than he had any right to be, considering their bargaining positions.

"Ten!" repeated Butch, raising a fat fist back up into the air.

"Sold," Guy submitted, suddenly finding it difficult to breathe.

With a gracious smile, Butch helped Guy up and brushed him off.

"I'd like to go to my room now, O great white ruler."

"Sure." Butch assumed his sit-ups position on the floor. "And thanks for the milk and cookies. Appreciate it."

Hoping the milk had curdled and the cookies would crumble, Guy went to his room and sat glumly in front of his well-kept aquarium, counting tails.

Why, he asked a passing neon tetra, did other boys his age have the good fortune to be experiencing not just fluttery buzzings, but legitimate erections? Why not him? Was there something wrong? Maybe he *was* destined to spend his adult life working in a harem, as Butch had intimated. Guy wondered if they'd let him have his own camel.

Searching out those guppies to which he'd grown least attached, a melancholy Guy sorted with his net those leaving from those staying. Ten emigrants soon circled a small fishbowl.

Saddened and bewildered at the state of things, he vowed to each of his finned companions that somehow, some way, he'd find a way to get them home again.

5

Guy delivered a stoic farewell address to the troops late Saturday morning, then lowered his guppies into the long neglected primordial ooze that was Butch's ten-gallon swamp. No doubt wondering who had turned out the lights, the tiny fish scattered into the inky darkness.

With his brunch of three cookies and a glass of Coca-Cola in hand, Guy strolled into the living room and sat down at the piano.

A warm aroma wafted through the house.

Jonathan Leeds, a senior like Rose, sat in the dining room between his bowling bag and his girl friend.

Birdie stood over him, administering baked goods. "Be tough, Jonathan. If it's not right for you, it won't please the judges either."

"Let her know what you really think," Rose encouraged him.

"Delicious," Jonathan decided, his mouth full of banana bread.

Guy hadn't been plunking the piano ten minutes when the ringing of the telephone in the hall interrupted him.

"Deliver the guppies?" grumbled Butch across the wires.

"Unfortunately," Guy assured him. "You'll probably find them floating on top, gasping for air."

"How'd you like 'em back?" asked Butch, strangely conciliatory.

Guy was guarded. "What do I have to do?"

"Well, you see . . . it's like this. Left my cleats at home, dammit. On the closet floor, right next to my sweat pants. Petrillo won't let me practice without 'em."

"So?"

"You got to bring them to me, Guy."

"Forget it."

"Please. Here, to the football field."

Football field? *Ding.* A bell went off in Guy's head. "Can't do it, Butch." *What's on the football field?*

"But I'll give you back your guppies."

"Sorry." The bell rang again, an oddly persistent alarm. "Why not?"

"I'm up to here with things to do." *Football. Football. Pin it down, Guy. Pin it down.*

"Oh, come on. You can bicycle over."

"Sorry, Butch. I'll be playing the piano and developing film all afternoon." *Ding.*

"Please!"

"No can do." *Ding-Ding-Ding.*

"You've got to, Guy. There's no one else."

"Butch, I'd love to help but . . ." *GONG!—of course.*

"But what?"

". . . uhm . . . It's too much trouble." *Corky.*

"But what about the guppies?"

Corky, Corky! The clock struck twelve. The alarm stopped ringing. Guy made his move. "All right, Butch. Talked me into it. I'll take back the guppies."

"Fine. They're yours. Just come."

Bull's-eye. Now for the kill. "Wait. I'm not finished. My guppies, plus"—Guy swallowed nervously—"when I bicycle over, you let me watch practice from the sidelines."

"Are you nuts?" Butch screamed into the receiver. "Seniors are out here today, practicing. I'd be the laughingstock—"

Well aware the seniors were out there, Guy yawned. "All right, Butch. Suit yourself. Have a nice practice."

"Wait!" Butch yelled. "All right, crud-head."

"If you insist on calling me names, pig-face, I won't bring your fungused cleats over for anything—"

Butch threw in the towel. "I was just kidding, you can stay and watch practice. I'll probably have to *kill* myself when this is over."

"If you only would, Butch. I'll be leaving in two minutes."

"Well, goddammit—*hurry*."

The sweet scent of conquest in his nostrils, overpowering the banana bread, Guy rushed to Butch's room and told his guppies to start packing.

He tossed his brother's cleats into a gym bag and dashed to the garage. Astride his rusted three-speeder, exhilarated, filled with trepidation, and grinning like gangbusters, he began the adventurous journey.

He was riding to Corky.

6

The football field was crowded with color. The green and blue J.V. football jerseys on one side offered marked contrast to the red and yellow tops of the senior varsity down at the other end.

A glum Butch stood with fellow players, thoroughly embarrassed to be in *sneakers* instead of genuine flesh rippers.

Pedaling over, Guy jovially jingled his bell, hoping to irk his brother. It worked.

"Quit that goddamn bell!" barked Butch, slamming a hand over the tinny noisemaker.

"Just trying to get your attention, Butch. Don't have a hernia."

"Gimmee cleats!" Butch fumbled into the wire basket and pulled out his gym bag. Now that Guy had arrived, big brother's earlier tone of subservient desperation had vanished.

"Sure nice of you to let me sit in on practice, Butch."

Butch looked Guy square in the face and his small eyes squinted as he said emphatically, "If you do *anything* to embarrass me, Guy, you will regret it for the rest of your life, understand?"

"Trust me."

"If only I could, you little creep!"

And with this understated kindness passing from his chapped lips, Butch galloped, cleats in hand, over to the warm-up bench, preparing to do battle.

Guy watched athletes in green and blue crashing into one another, and was gratified to see Butch demolishing everything that dared cross his enormous path. It was some comfort knowing there were others who felt no end to his insatiable hostility.

Soon weary of muscle-tuggings and discordant grunts, Guy pedaled over to the other side.

Red and yellow shirts broke boisterously from their huddle, lining up against second-string counterparts. The ball was hiked to the senior varsity quarterback, number 33, who made a long run for it.

The quarterback scrambled down the left side of the field, far across from Guy, weaving past Eagle linemen. A graceful jaguar outdistancing everyone, he dashed fifty yards into the end zone. Triumphant, Corky removed his helmet and tossed the ball high into the air. Teammates patted him all over.

On the sideline, leaning against his bike, Guy perked up.

The squad regrouped at the center of the field and huddled. From the side, Coach Petrillo yelled something about stamina, conviction and balls.

Again the hike to Corky and again he ran. This time he traveled to the right, down Guy's side. His knees danced up and down like a prancing horse as he circled potential interference.

Guy was so busy concentrating on the play he paid no attention to the fact that Corky was heading straight toward him. By the time he woke up to the possibility of impending disaster, however, he was so stunned he couldn't move. Though his mind was blank from fright, he was greatly relieved when Corky noticed him. The quarterback immediately altered his course.

Too late. Three bruisers were advancing to Corky's left. His only opening was to continue toward Guy. Thirty yards away and Guy could see Corky's eyes, wide and rolling, a penned Brahma bull. Twenty-five yards and Guy was still confident Corky would somehow manage to zigzag past him. Fifteen yards and he wasn't so sure. Five yards and Guy realized he should have moved out of the way thirty yards ago.

Locked and frozen, he stood his ground as —*pow!*— Corky collided into him.

Eagles rushed from every part of the field.

As this sea of red, yellow, green and blue approached, someone yelled, "Corky! Corky's hurt!"

How? thought Guy, his eyes shut tight. How did this happen?

Together they lay there on the cold ground, Corky and Guy, their entangled bodies interwoven among spokes and handlebars.

The bruisers formerly hot in Corky's pursuit helped him up. Not caring for assistance, he abruptly pushed them away. Breathing heavily, with a crimson face, Corky removed his helmet. He looked down at Guy and yelled, "You crazy kid, what the hell's that bike doing here?"

"I . . . I . . ." There was nothing to be said. How could he explain that no matter what vengeance Corky might crave, Guy wished himself more?

As it turned out, he was spared the trouble as someone on the J.V. completed his day, announcing, "Hey! That's Butch Fowler's kid brother!"

That did it. The end was finally in sight. The only question remaining was, did he want the blindfold?

Corky whirled around and searched for Butch, suddenly lost in back of the crowd looking around like everyone else, for himself. Finally spotted, Corky raised a fist at Butch and shouted pointedly, "Keep your damn family out of my way!"

Then he strutted back onto the field. Players followed hastily, dusting off his shoulders, back, thighs and can.

Butch and Guy stood alone on the windy sidelines.

Braced for whatever was coming, Guy didn't back up as the Butcher advanced.

Snorting like an asthmatic gorilla, Butch grabbed both of Guy's jacket lapels and lifted him off the ground. His eyes registered "Out of Control." Incapable of verbal communication, he gritted his teeth, shook Guy back and forth like a rag doll, then flung him to the ground as one might discard a used tissue.

Guy crawled over to his bicycle, ignoring the blood seeping from his split lip. Mounting the seat, he pedaled off. But bent and twisted, the bicycle was almost in as bad shape as he. It now veered only to the extreme left; so the faster he pedaled, the sooner he'd come full circle and —surprise!—once again found himself face-to-face with Butch.

With the added feature of very hot, very bad breath, Butch seethed, "You better not be home when I get there. I'll destroy you."

Guy's sense of timing told him this was no moment for an injection of comic relief. So once more he tried pedaling off, this time compensating for his veering left factor, pointing his bicycle to the extreme right.

And in this misshapen manner, injured and humiliated, rejected and depressed, Guy slowly maneuvered his way home.

7

After dumping his mangled two-wheeler on the front lawn, Guy limped into the house. Jonathan Leeds, his après-bowling tasting session ended, was swaggering out.

"Wait'll you taste the banana bread"—Jonathan pointed to his bloated belly—"that third batch with the walnuts turned out best."

Guy didn't answer Jonathan as he quickly headed up the stairs. Passing Butch's room, he thought fondly of his guppies. Poor devils, he'd not be seeing them again.

Bare essentials, he decided, pulling the backpack from his closet. Toothbrush, a change of underwear, camera, sleeping bag, his Hellman's mayonnaise jar containing $32.48 in loose change, and he was set.

One-forty-five. Butch could be home in fifteen minutes. Guy hurried.

"Can I see you a minute, Guy?" Birdie called from downstairs.

"I'm busy, Ma," Guy hollered back, strapping himself into the backpack.

A final look around the room and a closing statement for the diary in his head: Saturday, the seventeenth of September, *So long, youth!*—and he dashed downstairs, stopping only to trip over Rasputin, asleep in his favorite spot on the landing.

"Leave that cat alone!" Birdie stood at the foot of the stairs. "I want you to try a piece of banana bread. This last batch with the walnuts cries out for comment." Birdie walked into the kitchen.

"I don't have much time, Ma," said Guy, following close behind. "Wrap some up. I'll take it with me."

"Where ya going?" Birdie asked, now at the stove.

"I'm running away from home."

Birdie looked at him cautiously. Then she caught on. Winking, she elbowed his side. "Always there with the jokes."

Guy ripped a sheet of wax paper from a carton. "Here. Just slap a piece on there."

"It should be eaten from a plate."

"I know, Mother. But I haven't the time."

Birdie cut off a thick slice of bread and placed it on the wax paper.

Guy bit off a corner.

"Well?" Birdie licked her lips.

"Better." Guy nodded mid-munch. "Walnuts a nice touch, but a bit overpowering. Distracts from the banana."

Birdie frowned. "Less walnuts?"

43

"That should do it."

With resignation Birdie beelined for the refrigerator.

Guy looked at her and was momentarily overwhelmed with sadness. He hated good-bys. "I'll write soon as I'm settled, Ma. That's a promise."

"Fine," Birdie responded, pulling ingredients off cold shelves. "And try to be back in two hours to taste the next loaf."

The wrapped banana bread tucked safely inside his backpack, Guy walked out the kitchen door, into the garage.

No sense taking his crippled bicycle. He'd be going in circles. Rose's red one was an alternative, only Guy's sense of insecurity deterred him from riding into the sunset, seeking his life's fortune, on a girl's bike.

The only remaining option was to steal Butch's streamlined beauty. The lemon-colored Schwinn. Butch always swore he'd kill Guy if the shrimp so much as rubbed against his prized baby buggy. It was ironic that Guy had to steal it now in his desperation to get out of town. The necessity of the theft increased his sweeping commitment to never setting foot in Waterfield again.

While pedaling rapidly against the wind in second gear, Guy opted for the circuitous back road to town rather than risk the chance of passing Butch, now probably on his way home.

After Coach Petrillo told both squads how shitty they were, how they played football like old ladies, he sent them to the showers.

Cleaned, dressed and out of the lockers, Corky hurried to his Chevy and drove to town, where he was meeting Ro-Anne at the Sugar Bowl.

Parched and tired, Guy bicycled onto Poste Avenue. One fast Coke before hitting the Southern State Parkway. He parked Butch's bike against a lamppost and hurried across the street.

Like Corky, he was headed for Darcy's.

44

8

Guy drained the last of his soda and placed a dime on the counter. Looking out the window, he saw Corky leave his car, heading straight for the soda shop at a brisk clip.

Omigod! What now? Run? Hide? Stand and fight like a man? Sit and be kicked like a coward? Something, quick!

Guy raced to the magazine rack, plucked a periodical, and buried his face in it.

The jingling of the bells over the entrance meant Corky had just walked in. Guy dug his face deeper into the current issue of *Modern Bride*.

Corky glanced around and saw that Ro-Anne hadn't yet arrived. He made his way to a booth in the rear.

Guy stuffed the magazine into the rack. Turning casually to walk out, his back to the door, he bumped instead into a brick wall, which turned out to be Corky.

"Excuse me," Guy mumbled in someone else's voice. Then, head bent low, eyes at the floor, he walked around the quarterback in his fervent haste to leave.

To Guy's horror a voice from behind demanded, "Just a minute!"

Christ! This could be worse than facing Butch!

Guy spun around in a semi-circle. "Yes?" He gulped.

"You dropped this," said Corky, holding a wax-paper package of banana bread.

Shuffling over, face still to the linoleum, Guy snatched the parcel from Corky's hand—a chipmunk grabbing chestnuts. "Thanks," he muttered as he turned away.

Once again Guy attempted the miracle mile to the door. He hadn't gone two steps before Corky remembered. "Hey, aren't you that kid on the field today?"

—Uh-oh—

Corky advanced. Guy held his breath.

Corky extended his left hand. "Sorry I yelled like that. I don't lose my temper much. When it happens, I just rip into whoever's closest."

Had Guy heard right? "Hey," he squeaked, shaking Corky's hand, looking up for the first time. *"I'm* the one should do any apologizing. I never should have been there. I don't know first thing about football. But it was so exciting watching you play, I just wasn't thinking."

Corky studied the fellow shaking below him. "Who're you?"

"Guy. Guy Fowler," came the gravelly, grunted answer in an attempted deep register.

"Look at your fingers," said Corky.

Guy shoved quivering hands into his pockets and shrugged apologetically. "Just a little out of control." *Come on, stupid! Think of something to say. Something clever. If you're funny, maybe he'll like you. It's your only shot!* Guy rocked back and forth on his heels.

"You always this fidgety?"

"Not always," said Guy, trying to steady his knees. "Sometimes at dinner I'm allowed to cut my own meat."

Corky missed the sarcasm. "Why don't you just relax?"

"I can't." Guy grimaced.

"How come?" Corky glanced at the door, looking for Ro-Anne.

"Don't know. Maybe I'm a little excited about leaving town."

"Leaving town?" Corky repeated half-interested.

"Yeah. I'm calling it quits on Waterfield."

"Where you going?"

"Who knows?" Guy spread his arms wide open. "Wherever romance and high adventure beckon."

Corky looked at the kid. "Why's that?"

"I'm trying to avoid death. Aha-ha-ha." Guy launched another unsuccessful stab at humor.

"What do you mean?" asked Corky.

He suddenly seemed so genuinely interested, Guy felt

obliged to tell. "Well, you know my brother, Butch Fowler?"

Corky stared down at the small fry in front of him, trying to figure out how those two could emerge from the same family. "Oh, right. Big Butch. He's in my fraternity."

"That's the one. He's promised extensive torture when next we meet. He thinks he was as embarrassed at practice today by our collision as me. If he only knew!"

Corky got the picture. "Why don't I speak with Butch?"

Would you do that? Guy's voice rose two octaves too many. "Hey, that would be great, really great if you would. I'd be more than forever grateful to you. Honest."

"No problem. Just relax."

Relax? How could Guy relax?

"This is the best thing's ever happened to me, Corky. Really! If you'd just call him. He'll listen to you. He will. Christ, Butch thinks you're the greatest thing going."

Corky seemed embarrassed by the compliment, dismissing it with a wave of his hand.

"I've got a dime." Guy removed the heavy mayonnaise jar from his backpack. Dipping in, he took out a ten-cent piece.

Corky looked at the jar of coins. *What a strange little boy!*

Guy shook the jar fiercely. "One should never be without loose change."

That one worked. Corky laughed and took the dime.

The two of them looked an unlikely pair, walking together to the telephone booth—Corky nearly six-three, Guy nearly five-zero.

Guy put the dime down the slot and dialed his number. Rose and Butch raced for the phone.

Butch got it. "Hello?"

"Hi, Butchie," greeted Guy as if nothing had happened.

"You son of a bitch! . . ." Butch screamed.

"Yes. Well, Butch, how nice you've had some time to cool off."

"You've never known the meaning of misery before, you shit-ass. What I've got planned for you will . . ."

As Butch continued yelling, Guy fought to say, "Yeah,

sure. Sure, Butch. Listen. Uhm, me and Corky Henderson are down here at Darcy's having a Coke. Just wondered if maybe you'd like to join us."

Butch's rampage stopped cold. ". . . Wha—?"

"Hold on, Butch. Speak to him yourself."

Corky took the receiver. "Hey, Butch. What's the word?"

"That you, Corky?"

"Yeah. Listen. Your brother and I talked it out. He knows he shouldn't've been so close to the sidelines today. I'm not mad at him, so no reason for you to be, agreed?"

Butch was stumped. "Oh, sure. Of course. Whatever you say. Hey, if you guys gonna hang out there a while, I'll come right over."

"Don't bother. I'm meeting Ro-Anne. And give your brother a break, will ya? He's a good kid."

Without waiting for a reply Corky hung up. "Well, kid, that's that. You owe me a thousand dollars."

Guy held out his mayonnaise jar. "Would you settle for thirty-two forty-eight?"

Corky smiled. "I was just kidding."

Guy returned the money to his backpack.

The bell above the door rang. Ro-Anne making a late entrance.

"I gotta go,'" Corky told Guy as he waved to his girl friend.

"Thanks again. Thanks a million. I'll make it up to you, Corky. I will."

"Right, kid," said Corky over his shoulder. "That'll be the day."

Guy bicycled home at full speed, the better to return the yellow Schwinn before Butch might discover it missing. Along the way he reopened his diary to record how strong he felt, being fueled by the idyllic vision of Corky and Ro-Anne kissing hello.

9

That night at dinner, fried chicken leg in hand, Rose announced, "Guy and Corky spent the afternoon together at Darcy's."

Silence.

Birdie stopped passing the broccoli.

Butch discontinued buttering a hot muffin.

Nathan stopped gumming his mashed potatoes. "Guy and Corky *Henderson?*" he asked, suddenly interested in his younger son's life now that the town celebrity's name had been dropped.

"That's right," said Rose. "Can you believe it?"

Nathan looked to Butch for corroboration.

"Yeah," said Butch, drowning his dinner in hollandaise. "Corky Henderson. So what?"

Nathan stared at Guy, calmly stabbing peas and carrots with a fork.

"What's he like?" asked Birdie.

"I'll tell you what he's like," barked Butch, ignoring the tiny ball of white sauce dribbling down the side of his mouth. "He's *my* fraternity brother!"

"I want to hear what Guy thinks," Birdie insisted.

Eight eyes went to Guy, who, sighing, milked it for all it was worth. "Oh, I don't know, he seems nice enough, I guess. . . ."

Butch growled and ripped into the flesh of a chicken thigh.

Nathan studied Guy for the rest of the meal. He'd never seen his son so in control, so much a young man.

Birdie brought in the ice cream-topped banana bread and placed one slice in front of each member of the family.

Nathan tapped his beer glass with a spoon. "I have an announcement."

Everyone looked to the head of the household.

"I've decided to have Guy join tomorrow's duck hunt."

Guy was stunned.

"Him?" sneered Butch. "He can't even hold a gun!"

"You think he's ready?" asked a doubtful Birdie.

"The time has come," said Nathan, a high priest offering his child to the sun god. Looking over at Guy he asked, "What can you shoot with?"

"My camera."

"Don't joke when I'm serious, mister. You can take Butch's twenty-two. He'll be on my shotgun anyway."

"Yes, sir!" Guy smiled. "Thanks a million, Dad. I hope you'll be proud of me."

Nathan looked to the ceiling and exhaled. "Me too, son, me too."

At four in the morning on Sunday, Nathan flipped on the overhead light in Guy's room. Outside it was dark, chilly and pouring rain.

"Rise and shine! Rise and shine!" sang Nathan, walking to the window. He lifted the shade and revealed what looked like the end of the world. "A perfect day to shoot ducks. Up and at 'em, Guy."

A little over an hour and a half later and up to his ass in slimy mud, shoulder-high reeds, gale-force winds and a driving rain, Guy was shivering so hard he could barely keep his twenty-two steady.

Black skies finally gave way to an overcast, gray morning.

Two of Nathan's floor managers, Harry and Ed, were out there too, silently laying low. Shotguns poised, they stood ready to fire at the first flurry of feathers.

Harry's two golden retrievers sniffed about.

Ed tapped Guy and offered him a can of Pabst's. *At five-thirty in the morning?* Guy looked around and saw all four of the other soldiers slugging down the brew, Butch draining his with unspeakable gluttony. Although beer was unappetizing at any hour, there he was in Marlboro country, so what the hell.

"Thanks," Guy mouthed, accepting the can. He then proceeded to gulp it down with what he hoped came off as manly gusto.

They stood around like that, in silence; pointing, eyeing, sniffling, guzzling for more than an hour as the mini-hurricane raged about them.

Suddenly the dogs tensed and froze in place, noses to the clouds, as if someone had plugged their tails into an electric socket.

A lone brown and white duck traversed the sky. A lovely vision, the ideal opening for a documentary on wildlife preservation. *Ka-boom!*

Guy's four hunting companions opened up on the gracefully gliding creature. Strewn with buckshot, its brown and white body splattered across the bleak sky.

In the next moment hundreds of birds blackened the skies. The troops opened their full assault. Shotgun blasts boomed awake the countryside. Squawking and flapping, the ducks scrambled for their lives.

By the time Guy raised his gun, preparing to fire, the birds had flown out of range; off to a nearby moor where other hunters stalked in other beer-guzzling vigils.

Just to get the damn thing out of his system, Guy closed his eyes and pulled the trigger. His weapon fired into an empty, dark sky.

The dogs set out, soon returning from the battle zone gently carrying in their jaws half a dozen dead ducks.

Nathan placed a strong, fatherly hand on Guy's shoulder. "Now that's what I call a duck shoot!"

"Me, too!" Guy assured him with vigor.

"Get anything?"

"Double pneumonia." Guy sneezed as he pointed to his smoking rifle barrel. "Shot the tail off one of those goners!"

Nathan was impressed. "Good for you, son! Hey, fellas! Guy snagged one-a-these mothers!"

Harry and Ed offered congratulations.

"Hot shit!" muttered Butch, reloading his shotgun.

51

"I think we've had enough for one morning," Nathan said. "What say we get the flock outta here?'"

Ed and Harry cheerfully agreed.

Butch wasn't so sure. "You go on. I wanna stake out some more. I'll hitch back."

"Suit yourself," said Nathan.

Their ducks strung together, the woodsmen waded through the downpour, leaving behind in a birdbath of blood, beer and urine, Barry the Butcher, content in his home away from home, the neighborhood mudhole.

Guy had gone a-hunting. He hadn't flubbed it up, hadn't failed his old man. Hell, he hadn't even been shot!

If this was the sort of dividend reaped from hanging around Corky, Guy wanted more. Nothing had ever seemed more important.

He spent the entire ride home staring out the window, watching the rain. Thinking.

Nathan pulled into the driveway and Guy was struck with inspiration. His plan was so simple, he had to smile.

10

Classes ended Monday afternoon and Guy rushed to the football field with his shoulder bag of photo equipment.

Standing away from the sidelines, careful to avoid any repetition of the bicycle fiasco, he observed the afternoon senior varsity practice, then took out his Pentax and attached his longest lens. He brought Corky into close-up focus and began to shoot. He took action shots and candid portraits. The dark, fast-moving clouds were a fine background for black-and-white photography.

He went rapidly through four rolls of film, a month's supply right there.

As devoutly hoped, the pictures processed in the upstairs bathroom, which served as Guy's darkroom, turned out just fine. The tonal contrasts, the excitement of the brutal action and the cool displayed by Corky, who turned out to be exceedingly photogenic, made this series the best Guy'd ever taken.

School on Tuesday was long and tedious. When biology finally ended at three o'clock, Guy strolled outside to the playing field.

He sat in the bleachers, all nerves, and watched for an hour until Coach Petrillo called a time-out. The team dispersed.

This was the moment. Now or never. Corky was chatting with a couple of other red-and-yellows. Guy walked over, opened his briefcase, removed three contact sheets and handed them to Corky. "Excuse me. Sorry to interrupt. Would you mind looking at something?"

Corky fast-scanned the columns, sheet after sheet. "Who took these?"

"Me," said a tiny voice.

"No shit? When?"

"Yesterday."

"They're damn good!"

So much for that. The storm in Guy's stomach settled.

"Here." Guy gave Corky a blue grease pencil. "Check the ones you like and I'll make prints for you."

Corky was delighted. "You mean it?"

"Sure. I figure it's the least I can do after what happened."

"Everything go okay at home?"

Guy nodded. "Better than okay."

Corky started checking off shots.

"And don't worry about any expenses. I've got my own enlarger at home, so it's no big deal."

Coach blew his loud whistle.

"Back to work?" asked Guy.

"Yep." Corky handed the contacts over to Guy, and, in a gesture straight out of an old Ronald Reagan film, vigorously touseled the small boy's hair with his hand and, smiling, trotted back out onto the field.

By Friday, the day before the opening game of the season, Guy had printed and blown up eight-by-ten prints of the five shots Corky had chosen. He placed them in a large envelope which he deposited in the senior president's mailbox in the Student Council office.

Then he waited.

11

Heavy sweaters, reeking of mothballs, were pulled from shelves.

Plaid woolen blankets tumbled out of linen closets.

Cocoa, soup, coffee and gin flowed into thermoses.

Mayonnaise and mustard, ketchup, butter, relish and jelly got slapped onto bread.

The leaves of Waterfield were turning to rust. Colorful branches shook in the blustery wind. Football weather.

At noon, Nathan piled the family into the Oldsmobile and drove off to the game. Assuming he wasn't interested, no one asked Guy to go. So twenty minutes later, when he came out of his darkroom, it was too late to express his sudden attraction to the sport.

Guy spent the afternoon at the movies.

After studying, Amy went to the Teahouse of the August Moon, the local Bohemian coffeehouse, to meet a friend.

Marge Flynn was a complex, soft-spoken girl with a lot of drive who probably would have fitted in fine with the Waterfield sorority set had she not stood six feet in stockings.

Amy and Marge sipped cappuccino, munched on marzipan cookies and chatted.

They talked about the freedom buses heading for Alabama. They discussed their forthcoming unauthorized newsletter, the *Gadfly*. They talked men and mores, Communism and Catholicism, cabbages and kings.

They never mentioned football.

The Fowlers returned home from the football field loud with enthusiasm. They danced about, celebrating the Eagles' 27-6 trounce of Wantagh.

Exhausted, Corky came home, the conquering hero, and fell asleep for two hours.

While he dozed, Dora tiptoed into his room and covered him with a spare blanket.

She stroked the back of his head lightly, trying to remember where along the years her little boy had become the strapping fellow now stretching from the top to the bottom of his bed. When did he grow and how many yesterdays had it taken?

She thought back to a Christmas morning when a far smaller Corky sat beneath a glittering tree, surrounded by presents. . . .

Outside it was snowing. Vanilla cupcake frosting covered Waterfield. A storybook Christmas.

One by one gifts were handed over, ransom for love, to the magical three-year-old. Tiny ice skates and a long hockey stick. A red catcher's mitt of sponge with a yellow baseball of soap. Cowboy guns, boxing gloves, and that was just a warm-up.

She and Carl had skimped on themselves so they could be extravagant with the boy.

The living room became a colorful haven for runaway ribbons.

Carl reached forward and extracted a bright blue box. The most lavishly wrapped, it had the biggest bow. "This one's from Daddy." He placed the prized package in his son's lap. "It's a very special present, Corky."

Small fingers ripped frantically at the wrapping. Corky lifted the top of the pretty box, peered inside and anxiously inspected the contents.

"Well?" said his father.

Corky looked up at his father. His lower lip curled downward. "Not racing car."

" 'Course not." Carl beamed. "It's a football!"

"Feu-baw," Corky quietly repeated.

"Football!" Carl insisted. "You're a big boy. Let me hear you say it."

"Football!" echoed the three-year-old, on cue.

Carl wrapped his arm around Dora, drawing her close. He smiled as his son removed the elliptical pigskin from its colorful package.

Corky twirled it around on one of its points, wondering where the batteries were stored.

"What do you say to your father!" Dora wanted to know.

"I love you, Daddy," said Corky to the football.

Dora went to the kitchen and returned with a batch of gingermen, newly sighted with raisin eyes. She handed Corky a warm cookie and he gobbled it down with a sip of cold milk.

After that, two last gifts. A sturdy lilliputian football helmet, burnt orange with a Georgia Tech decal, and outrageous shoulder pads, hardly suitable for a toddler.

It was Christmas and Corky sported a dairy moustache. His angelic face was lost in the helmet covering shaggy curls. Shoulder pads loomed over his pajamas. He squeezed his new football. Then he started to cry.

He cried because it was all over. Nothing left to unwrap. No more ribbons. No racing car.

Corky kicked the blue box. "Santa forget my racing car!"

Carl knelt beside him. "Hey, calm down. Don't cry. You don't need any racing car. That's for greasers. You're no cheap mechanic. Waste of time. If my father had given me a tenth, just a tenth of what I'm gonna give you, son, I wouldn't be selling dishwashers today and that's a fact. You're gonna be an athlete, son—the best athlete—the damndest football player this town's ever seen."

Corky rubbed his right eye.

Carl patted him on the head. "You have all these presents. Now stand up straight and thank me, man to man."

Corky didn't want to shake hands. He wanted his racing car.

"You're not going to disappoint me, are you, son?" The question rang stern and rhetorical. "Not on Christmas!"

Corky shook his head. No, he wasn't going to disappoint his father. Not on Christmas. Not ever. Corky looked up at the tall man, lifted padded shoulders high and offered a timid hand.

His father shook it vigorously. "That's my brave soldier! Last thing you need is some dumb racing car. Let the others have 'em. You're better than that. You're *special*. I'm gonna take care of you, so for God's sake, don't worry."

"Not worried," sniffed the young soldier.

"You're the best thing ever happened to me, Corky. My whole life. We'll be tossing that football 'round soon as the snow melts. You'll love it!"

"What do you say to your father now?" Dora smiled.

Corky's green eyes never strayed from the bright blue empty box under the tree as he whispered, "Feu-baw."

After a fitting steak dinner with an ebullient father and a proud mother, Corky picked up Ro-Anne.

They drove to their favorite dark spot near the reservoir and rapidly made love, as prescribed, in the back seat.

Corky was keeping his promise to Coach Petrillo.

No sex during training . . . except as release after a victory, and then only once . . . and then home and to bed by ten-thirty.

"*That* was ridiculous," protested Ro-Anne, climbing over to the front of the Chevy.

"Why?" Corky tucked in his shirt.

"You finished before I started."

"You know the rules, lady." Corky got behind the wheel.

"Oh, come off it. When did you become Mister Goody-Goody Cub Scout?"

"Don't bug me, okay? I hardly slept last night."

Ro-Anne placed a soft, well-manicured hand on his shoulder. "Those nightmares?"

57

Corky rested his forehead against the steering column. "No sweat."

Ro-Anne stroked his hair. "I'm sorry, sweetie. It's because you don't relax. We don't even have music when we park—"

"Battery's low."

"It's also freezing. You could keep the heat on."

"Listen!" Corky raised his head from the steering wheel. "When *you're* paying twenty-three cents a gallon for gas, you can let the engine idle all you want. But not on my allowance."

Ro-Anne removed a five-dollar bill from her purse. "Here, sport. This is so we can be warm next time."

Corky stared at her. "Men don't accept money from women."

"Ridiculous." Ro-Anne winked. "Don't think of it as money. Think of it as fuel."

Corky pocketed the five dollars.

"Anything to please you, my fair beauty."

Then he kissed Ro-Anne's nose and drove off.

Guy's week was miserable. He didn't hear a thing from Corky about the photos. Not one word. Not that he really believed he would. After all, Corky had never asked him to take any pictures in the first place. Still, a simple thank you, maybe a short note, a casual offer to become best friends. Something. Nothing.

Guy told himself he had no cause to feel slighted. But inside, where fantasies flourished . . .

He channeled his energies elsewhere—the piano.

Rose soon got fed up and told him to leave the damn thing alone. His growing skill with the instrument merely underlined her inadequacy.

Nathan reminded Rose for the third time that the piano had come leased from Montgomery-Ward at a costly ten bucks a month. Since not too many people were buying Oldsmobiles in this recession, his dealership was hurting. . . . So if she didn't start practicing right away, back the damn thing would go. . . .

On Thursday, Guy found a note pinned to his locker:

Would you come to the *Eagler* office this afternoon at half past three? We're in the basement, next to the cafeteria.

Leonard Hauser
Editor-in-Chief

Curious about the mysterious message, Guy entered the busy newspaper office fifteen minutes early and asked one of the girls at a typewriter where he could find the editor-in-chief. She nodded vaguely that-a-way, while her fingers pounded noisy keys. Guy walked to where the typist had indicated and stopped again at a desk stacked high with old newspapers, yellow pads and crumpled pages. Behind this disorder, chewing on an unlit pipe, sat a butterball of a fellow with enormous glasses. A small sign on his desk read: DON'T KID YOURSELF. IGNORANCE IS BLISS.

"Leonard Hauser?" Guy asked of him.

The fellow glanced up from a page on which he was scribbling and nibbled his pipe. "Who're you?"

"I'm looking for Leonard Hauser."

"How come?" the fellow inquired, striking a long blue line down an entire page of would-be copy. "Marge!" he called out. "Come here and see this!" He looked at Guy. "Do you realize that in the hands of the wrong person a simple typewriter can be a dangerous weapon?"

"Marge's interviewing the principal," came a girl's voice from the other side of the crowded room.

"Well, soon as she returns from the Perils of Potter, tell her to see me," he said with deadpan authority, chomping on his unlit pipe.

"Tell her yourself, creep," came the instant reply.

Taking the pipe from his mouth, he looked at Guy. "Savages. Have you any idea what it's like to work with savages? It's no picnic."

"Could you tell me where I could find Leonard Hauser?"

"What's it for?" asked the pipe non-smoker. He picked up another piece of paper and immediately disfigured it with his blue pencil. " 'Guess which football team can't be beat?' " He quoted the opening line at the same time he crossed it out. Then he pointed his smokeless pipe at Guy, instructing, "Never open a story with a rhetorical question. It's a waste of column space, is sloppy syntax and what'd you say your name was?"

"Didn't. It's Guy. Guy Fowler. Found this note in my locker."

The fellow with the pipe grabbed the note and looked at him suspiciously. *"You?"*

"What?" asked Guy, feeling accused.

"You took those photos of Corky?"

"That's right."

"You're Guy Fowler?"

"Correct."

"Amazing!" he said, dumbstruck.

"What's that?"

"Nothing. I just thought you'd be much more . . . I don't know . . . *different.*"

"Yeah? In what way?"

"I don't know. *Bigger,* for one thing."

"Oh," said Guy, slighted.

"Don't get the wrong idea. I mean . . . Corky . . . and . . . you know . . ."

"No. I don't know."

"Well . . ." —a search for words —"it's just that Corky praised your work and was so insistent I have you cover tomorrow's game against Mineola rather than have old standby Tom Dilliard do it. I just thought, hell I don't know what I thought . . . I guess that you'd be more like *them.*"

"Them *who?*"

"You know . . . those Kappa Phi mentalities. That bunch of gorilla jocks."

"Oh . . . *them!*"

"Yeah. But you're fine. I mean I think it's terrific getting a short photographer. Gives the staff a touch of character. So . . . are you interested?"

"Interested in what?"

"In covering the Mineola game tomorrow. What the hell have we been talking about?"

"Who could tell?"

"Well now you know. You buy the film. Don't take more than two rolls. Submit a receipt; we'll reimburse. Corky says you do your own printing.'"

"True."

"Terrific. We'll pay costs. Can we see contacts by Tuesday?"

"I'll have them Monday."

"Even better!" He handed Guy a small blue card. "Here's a pass to get you onto the field. Our hall patrol gets rather Fascistic if your papers aren't in order."

"Thanks a lot."

"Don't thank me. Tom Dillard's been drinking since he was twelve. His pictures are always blurry. We've been looking for a decent photographer for a year. You just may be the one."

"I'll do my best!" Guy got enthusiastic, and squeaky. "Really I will. I'll give it everything I've got!"

"Please. Don't get dramatic on me, kid. I puke easy. Just do the job."

"I will! I will!"

"Okay. Okay. Now, if you don't mind . . . I've got a paper to put out. They don't call me the young Hearst for nix!"

"Sure thing. Thanks again!"

As Guy turned to leave, the young Hearst called out, "By the way, Fowler . . ."

"Yes?"

Putting out his hand to shake Guy's, he said, almost warmly, "*I'm* Leonard Hauser."

"I had a hunch." Guy smiled.

Guy wandered down the hall and through the cafeteria in a daze of euphoria. He'd finally gotten a response from Corky—a humdinger—and couldn't have been more excited.

Sneers and snide remarks directed his way over the past fifteen years became at once meaningless trifles. Now that his photography had been recognized, what matter the height of the cameraman? What difference the squeal of the voice? Who cared if he looked twelve?

Guy was going to be *there* tomorrow—*Guy Fowler*—the Waterfield midget, smack in the thick of it. There—with the Senior Varsity Eagles, the school big shots. There—amid all the color and pageantry, the power, the glory, the yellow and the red.

And Butch, Guy gloated. Poor Butch, that asshole, will have to sit way up back in the bleachers along with everyone else.

Everyone but him, for he was going to be right down on the field. Right there!

In the space of an afternoon, the ugly duckling emerging a swan, Guy had suddenly become a star. Even if only a tiny one.

October

12

Saturday arrived, chilly and gray.

Not knowing how much time he would need to prepare, Guy got to the field hours early. He was the first one there.

By two o'clock the area had come alive with activity. Rose and Jonathan Leeds joined the spirited booster section. Birdie and Nathan sat beneath them. Butch stood in a cluster of fraternity brothers at the top of the bleachers. A full house.

A loudspeaker announced the players as they ran out, one by one. Corky's name, announced last, blared forth, and Waterfield roared.

All business, Corky trotted straight to the middle of the field.

Carl Henderson placed a proud and weighty arm around Dora's frail shoulder.

Guy stood with the Eagles, on the forty-yard line as everyone rose for the singing of "The Star-Spangled Banner."

Moments later, the Mineola Mustangs kicked the ball to the good guys. An Eagle wide receiver caught it and ran. Everyone cheered.

Plays, downs and touchdowns passed. Guy clicked his camera in the brisk afternoon.

The half-time gun went off and the scoreboard told the story: *Eagles 20—Mineola 6.*

Guy thought about drifting up into the bleacher's during the recess, say hello to the folks, chat with the fans, find out if Butch could see all right. But the air down there with the action was far too intoxicating to leave.

Half-time entertainment consisted of the school band

forming the loyal letter *W* on the field while marching in step to "The Eyes of Texas Are Upon You."

Ro-Anne and her sister cheerleaders kicked high in time to the music, a chorus line of future Rockettes.

Minutes later, both teams reentered; Eagles' red and yellow to the left, Mustangs' maroon and gray to the right. The fans were stirred anew.

As the gun ushered in the second half, it began to rain. Heavily.

Guy packed his gear, preparing to leave, until the assistant equipment manager informed him that nothing short of a major earthquake could cancel Waterfield competition.

So Guy put the hood up on his poncho and stood there in the downpour, teeth chattering like a typewriter.

Most of the spectators called it quits. Guy saw that Rose and Jonathan, Birdie and Nathan had left. Butch and his buddies, the rocks of Gibraltar, hadn't budged.

The playing field waxed muddy and slippery. Players sloshed about like Keystone Cops in a mud-pie fight.

Both sides lost their color to the clinging mud. Where all was red, yellow, maroon and gray, there soon appeared a blur of browns.

Corky scored another running touchdown in the glop and kicked an additional point before the last gun went off, ending the mud-fest.

The final score: *Eagles 27—Mineola 13*

Leonard Hauser wasn't in the busy *Eagler* office Monday afternoon, so Guy left the contact sheets he'd developed over the weekend on the editor's messy desk and left.

That night at the dinner table, Rose interrupted a silence of communal chewing to reiterate how very much she hated the piano, great big bore that it was. She asked her father if she could finally stop taking those awful lessons.

Guy looked up from his half-eaten meal.

"If that's what you want, young lady," Nathan allowed, glad to be rid of the costly nuisance. "Birdie, call the piano people and tell them to pick it up at the end of the week."

"Wait, Dad!" said Guy. "I play the piano too, you know."

"You've got too many hobbies as it is," Nathan stated. "One this week, one the next. You're a little too expensive for me, young fella. You've got enough to do now with the camera. Finally got you to a football game. So if Rose is finished with the piano, back it goes. You don't need it. Birdie, what's for dessert?"

"But, Daddy . . !" Guy squeezed his fingers and bit his lower lip, fighting back a sudden threat of tears.

"Dad!" Nathan corrected him. Only sissies call their father *Daddy* and Nathan hated nothing as much as he hated sissies.

So this was no time to cry. Guy took a deep breath and feigned a cool sobriety. "Please, *Dad*. Don't send back the piano."

To no avail. Nathan noticed the tears mounting in his younger boy's eyes and that did it. His face flushed red as he pounded the table. "Now you listen to me, young man! You've been spending too much time with that damn thing, anyway. It's unhealthy. Look at you, the color of marble. Outdoors is where boys should be, playing ball, clean and good. Not cooped up like some sick prisoner. A piano? Christ, Guy . . . that's for girls!"

The subject was closed.

Guy pushed his plate toward the middle of the table, folded his arms.

Butch concealed his joy by beating his meat loaf to death with a fork.

Guy was about to ask to be excused when the telephone rang.

Rose abandoned her appetite for the moment and dashed to the receiver.

"Tell whoever it is to call back!" Nathan demanded. "We're not finished eating!"

After forced coquettish chatter, Rose cupped the receiver and told the entire table, "It's *Corky Henderson* for heaven's sake! He wants to talk to Guy."

That did it, all right.

"He'll take it!" Nathan snapped his fingers.

Guy's spirits lifted as he walked into the hallway and took the phone. All action at the dinner table ceased as everyone stared.

Unable to control his nervousness, Guy delivered a high-pitched "Hello?" The old squeakbox revealed all.

"Hiya, kid. Busy?" came Corky's voice over the telephone.

"Not really," Guy replied in falsetto, staring into the living room at the piano.

Nathan made a gesture with his hands, signaling Guy to lower his voice, talk slower, calm down.

How? thought Guy.

"I stopped in at the *Eagler* this afternoon," said Corky. "Leonard showed me your pictures of the game."

"And?" Guy responded cautiously.

"They're super, Guy! Just super!"

"Pssst! Pssst!" Butch interjected from the dining room.

"Uhm, Corky. Can you hold on a minute?" His hand over the receiver, Guy snapped, "What the hell is it?"

"Ask him over!" said Butch, excitedly. "Ask him to come watch television with us."

"Good idea!" added Rose.

"Tell him I've just finished a cheesecake," Birdie chimed in.

Guy rolled his eyes skyward and signaled them to simmer down. "Sorry, Corky," he said, back on the line. "What were you saying?"

"Ro-Anne and I are down here at Darcy's. Would you like to join us for a soda or something?"

Would he?! "Sounds terrific." Guy tried remaining in control. "Hold on a second."

Again cupping the receiver, Guy repeated Corky's invitation.

"Tell him YES!" Nathan was emphatic. "I'll drop you off on way to my poker game."

"Fine, Corky. My Dad's going to a friend's, so he can drop me off."

"Swell," Corky answered. "We'll drive you home later."

"Thanks. Thanks about a million. Be there in a little while."

Guy hung up and turned to see his family staring at him with new eyes, breathing in unison and wondering what was going on.

"Well," he shrugged, "guess I'll get my coat."

As Guy walked into Darcy's, the jing-a-ling bells announced his entrance. Corky, down at the last booth with Ro-Anne, waved him over.

Ro-Anne was vacuuming up the remains of a tall and noisy buttermilk. Corky nursed a glass of milk.

"Have a seat," said Corky, taking a small sip.

Guy plopped down across from them.

Corky's arm hung around Ro-Anne's shoulders and her hand rested securely on his near thigh. "You know Ro-Anne, don't you?"

Guy waved. "I've seen you perform. I mean cheerleading."

"Hi." Ro-Anne winked at him, never removing her clenched teeth from the straw.

A waitress came to the table.

"What'll you have, Guy?" asked Corky.

"Oh, I don't know. Coke I guess."

"*Coke?*" Corky made a sour face. "Bring me another glass of milk."

"You?" the waitress asked Ro-Anne.

Ro-Anne held the grip on her straw and shook her head, *no*. Her freshly shampooed blonde pony tail swayed with her response.

"Tell you why we asked you here," said Corky, squeezing Ro-Anne and her straw closer. "We found out the big news tonight. It's still hush-hush. Ro-Anne's been elected this year's Queen of the Hawaiian Moon Ball!"

"Congratulations! That's great!" said Guy, having little idea what that meant.

Lock-jawed, Ro-Anne mumbled, "Thanks."

"So she gets to preside over the dance after the big game against Sewanhaka on Saturday."

The waitress returned and dropped off the drinks.

Corky continued. "That means she'll need really good pictures for the *Venture*."

"What's that?" asked Guy.

"Yearbook," muttered Ro-Anne, matter-of-fact.

"Oh." Guy pinched himself for not knowing such rudimentary information.

Corky clapped his hands together. "You say yes and I'll see to it you become the official *Venture* photographer. Think about it."

Guy thought about it. "Yes!" he said, too loud.

"But first you gotta agree to something."

"Anything."

"You gotta take more pictures of me and Ro-Anne than anyone else."

"I will. I will."

"I want to be all over that yearbook, kid. Cover to cover! I want my kids to look through it someday and see what a hot shot their old man was."

Ro-Anne coughed into her buttermilk.

"And what a beauty Ro-Anne was," Corky was quick to add.

"You got it!" Guy gushed.

"Terrific," said Corky. "I know you won't let us down."

"Oh, no. . . ." Guy promised. "I won't let you down."

"Swell!" said Corky.

"Neat-o!" said Ro-Anne.

"I'll drink to that!" said Guy.

And the three of them lifted glasses, toasting their pact. Ro-Anne finally parted with her straw.

A jing-a-ling above the door. Corky and Ro-Anne both strained past Guy to see who'd entered the hangout. Ro-Anne nudged Corky and giggled. Guy turned to see who was there.

Amy.

"That's *her!*" Ro-Anne whispered to Guy.

"Who is she?" Guy whispered back.

"Oh, just the weirdest zombie you can imagine. Amy Silverstein. She has the hall locker next to mine. Always stuffing the strangest books into it."

"Yeah?" Guy asked. "Like what?"

"Oh, I don't know. Things you never heard of. *Atlas Shrugged*. You can hardly ever get a word from her. Jewish *and* ugly. Can you think of a worse combo?"

"Ro-Anne!" Corky scolded.

Ro-Anne brought an innocent hand to her mouth. "Did *I* say that?"

Amy stood at the magazine rack, aware she was being made fun of. God how she hated Darcy's; hated the shallow, anti-intellectual crowd that gathered there. All those cattle, she thought. Dressing, looking, sounding alike. Fraternity-sorority bullshit. Love-me-let-me-in-love-me! *No Thank You!*

She'd never have entered the place, but it was the only store in town that carried *Atlantic Monthly*.

She was careful to avoid eye contact with the patrons as she lifted the magazine from the rack.

Guy watched the tall girl with the long nose, the odd hair, the bad skin and poor posture purchase a magazine.

Shoulders hunched forward, eyes cast down to the floor, she walked from the shop.

As the jing-a-ling signaled her exit, Guy couldn't help feeling sorry for her.

"Seems to me," reasoned Ro-Anne with a dimpled smile, "every town's got to have its share of creeps, no?"

At first no one answered. Then Corky laughed and said, "Long as we're not one of them, right?"

Guy laughed too, his pang of empathy short-circuited. He'd fought too long and alone and was finally too near the inner circle to fend for anyone else.

Amy stood on the corner of Poste Avenue, thumbing her way through *The Atlantic Monthly*. An article on the Lost Generation. Enticing. A piece on Sputnik, the Russian satellite. Fine. Poetry by Allen Ginsberg. Her evening was set. She could now hurry home and get lost in the magazine. Now she could erase the awful moments just spent in Darcy's. Most likely, she wouldn't be able to. She never had. Even way back when . . .

Amy had loathed Rose Cliff. She had little in common with the other girls, many of them delicate WASP snobs, future cotillion Debs hailing from Grosse Point, Oyster

70

Bay and Wellesley Hills; most of them labeled with cutesy-poo nicknames—Mimsy, Pipsi, Muffy, Woozy.

It was 1951 and ten-year-old Amy already stood an ungainly five-feet-six. The tallest in her class, she towered over everyone. Ten years old!

Other girls at Rose Cliff had the smallest of noses, the silkiest heads of hair, the loveliest of petite bodies, little or no trouble heading into the awkward years. All the good genes old money could buy.

Morning hours at Rose Cliff were devoted to academic studies. For Amy, a breeze. Afternoons covered the domestic arts. Sewing. Cooking. Charm. How to stand, sit and walk; how to dance the fox trot, the rhumba; how to speak softly, ladylike, with just the right finishing school accent; how to tell the fish knife from the butter knife. Torture.

Amy's mother had given up her annual Miami Beach vacation and Dr. Silverstein drilled overtime so they could send their daughter to so fine a training ground as Rose Cliff. They sacrificed so Amy would be best prepared for the one accomplishment expected from her in their lifetime: *The Right Man!* . . .

One night Amy finished reading *Little Women,* and wept.

She didn't cry because Meg had married a nice young chap—they deserved each other. It didn't upset her that Jo was off to New York, writing her way to fame and fortune—best of luck! She wasn't even especially thrown by Beth's death at such a tender age—she'd been expecting that.

What brought her to tears was that it was Amy—Amy, her own namesake—the true beauty of all the sisters, who got to marry Laurie, the adorable boy next door, the best catch in the book.

Amy wept because it was all so typically unfair. Ever since she'd escaped into the world of literature, it kept happening, one book after the next, from author to author.

The beautiful girl caught Prince Charming at the end and got to live happily ever after. Always the beautiful girl.

And what about *us?* thought Amy. What about those of us not blessed with the physical graces of a Bronte heroine or a Colette ingenue? What happens to us?

With a deep sigh, she wiped her eyes and sat up straight. Dorm lights had to be out in half an hour, at precisely nine-thirty, and Amy had put on her pajamas hours earlier so she could read until then.

Amy's roommate, Bobo Weeks, a pipsqueak of a child, strawberry blonde, brazen, befreckled and just about the right peanut size for a ten-year-old, hurried into the room.

"Hi, Amesy! Reading again?" Bobo bounced onto her bed.

"My name is Amy."

" 'Scuse me for living!" protested Bobo, jumping up again. Hopping to the bureau, she picked up one of the dolls from her international collection. "What'd you read tonight?" Bobo pretended to be interested as she got lost in the mantilla of her stuffed Spanish señora.

"My love letters from Tony Curtis," answered Amy, slamming shut her book of poetry.

Bobo undressed her Dutch doll. "I was down in Missy's room earlier. Her oldest sister married a cousin of one of the DuPonts and her parents threw a giant tent wedding. There's a picture of it in this month's *Town and Country.*"

"So what?" said Amy. "I'm planning to marry a DuPont some day, myself."

"Mmmm," hummed Bobo dreamily to her Scottish lassie. "Wouldn't that be nifty?"

Amy put on her bathrobe and went to the door. "I'm going to brush my teeth."

"Aren't you going to take a book with you?" Bobo called after her, sharing a hearty laugh with her French can-can dancer.

The bathroom window was open and the chill autumn night gave Amy a shiver. After shutting out the cold air, she went to the sink. She turned on the faucets, reached for the soap with one hand, untied her bathrobe with the other and that's when she first saw it.

72

Blood. All over her pajama bottoms, right there in front.

Horrified, she ran from the room. Water still poured from the faucets.

Flying down the stairs, Amy hurried to the pay phone in the lobby. To call Evelyn. She'd know what to do. That's what mothers were for.

Her near-hysteria began to subside even as Amy neared the phone. Then she ran into Miss Houghton.

"Amy?" asked the puzzled gray-haired English teacher in her monotone-nasal New England accent. "Down here in the lobby like this?"

"I have to use the phone!" said Amy, trying to conceal her anxiety.

"It's five minutes to Lights Out. Telephone privileges ended at seven-thirty."

"I know, Miss Houghton. But it's real important!"

"An emergency?" asked Miss Houghton, not changing her critical tone.

"I think so." Amy pulled the sides of her robe together, praying nothing obvious was showing.

"Tell me what it is," insisted Miss Houghton, peering through wire-rimmed glasses.

"I can't!" Amy declared. "It's personal!"

"Well it certainly can't be too personal if it's a genuine emergency, can it now, Amy? You tell me what it is and I'll decide if it's any kind of emergency."

Tell Miss Houghton what it was? Was she crazy? How could Amy tell *anyone* about something so embarrassing, so private? Well, you see, Miss Houghton, it's like this. There's this blood oozing out of my honeypot and I'm a little concerned, is all. It would never do. *Primary social grace: a young lady never mentions anything connected with human plumbing.*

"Well, Amy . . ." Miss Houghton folded her arms in her favored *Goodbye Mr. Chips* manner. "I'm waiting for an answer!"

"I don't want to talk about it, Miss Houghton. Please let me use the phone. Please!"

73

"Why don't we discuss this in the morning, Amy? I'm going to ring the Lights Out bell now, so I suggest you take your problem to bed with you. If you wish to call home, you may do so tomorrow evening at six-thirty. You know the rules."

"Miss Houghton, *please!*"

"And next time you come to the lobby, I suggest you appear in appropriate attire. In case you haven't noticed, we're doing our best to turn all of you into *proper* young ladies. We cannot do our work without your cooperation, now can we? Good night!"

Tears in her eyes, Amy climbed back upstairs.

The Lights Out bell had donged by the time Amy finished washing away her predicament. It was dark in her room when she got there—small blessing, as she could avoid banal banter with Bobo.

Carefully crawling into bed, Amy did her best not to disturb anything crucial. Lying there in the dark, all alone, she was sure something had gone haywire inside; God in heaven, she knew not what—but holy shit, was she scared!

Rose Cliff taught its girls, future wives and mothers, all the social graces. But no one, not even Louisa May Alcott, had ever once suggested what to expect when you got your period.

In fact it wasn't until the following morning, after a sleepless night, when Amy went to sick call, that she learned about this basic fact of life.

That evening at six-thirty, Amy finally got to the telephone.

In a torrent she told Evelyn all the terrible things she'd gone through and how frightened she'd been. She told her mother the traumatic story and at first Evelyn said nothing. Then she spoke. "My dear! Nothing to be upset about. You've been given a blessed gift. Other girls have to wait three and four more years to become women. And though I wasn't there to help, I'm sure you handled it beautifully, as always. Wait 'til your Aunt Bernice hears about this! We'll be dancing at your wedding before any of us know it."

74

13

A strong wind early Saturday morning changed a murky, hazy sunrise into a crisp fall day. The last of an Indian summer.

The football-crazed town of Floral Park had been Waterfield's biggest rival for decades. The game shaped up to be the toughest of the season. A current of vengeful excitement surged through the crowd, both sides renewing their annual contracts for mutual hatred, both calling for blood.

"I don't give a crap how many balls we have to bust today," Petrillo told his boys in the locker room. "Just as long as we win."

No ordinary contest, this was *war!*

The last Eagle to trot out onto the playing field, Corky made a typically electric entrance, juicing up the volume of school spirit from hundreds certain number 33 would deliver. Hundreds blissfully ignorant of a not-so-unusual scene acted out late the previous night at the Henderson house when, as a quiet town slept, a cry rang out, building to a scream until a light went on and Dora shook Corky gently awake, soothing her son out of his pregame nightmare.

The gun went off, the game began and by the time they were well into the first half Guy was totally confused by the 7-to-13 score.

The confusing part: Floral Park's Sewanhaka High had the thirteen. The Eagles were losing.

Losing! Sewanhaka outsmarted Waterfield with every move. They passed when least expected and ran when a pass was anticipated.

Guy watched carefully, trying to figure out in his naiveté what was going wrong.

Ro-Anne was a pile of nerves. She knew a loss on the field would mean no go in the heated back seat after the dance. "Go, Eagles, go!" she shouted, loudest of the cheerleaders.

Guy paid close attention as he studied the game through his camera. He saw the Sewanhaka quarterback licking his lips in a strange way sometimes, just before the ball was hiked.

The halftime gun went off as Guy realized his close-up lens, seeing what none of the others could, might have broken a code. But what?

Forget it, he told himself. Their quarterback has a stiff case of raw lips. Period.

Halftime on the Eagles' side was not one of hope and happiness, so Guy strolled down to the locker room.

Petrillo, surrounded by disillusioned players, was leaning against a rub-down table, laying it on as Guy silently entered.

"What can I say, boys? I thought this year we might make it. I thought with our offense, our teamwork, with Corky, hell, I don't know what I thought. Maybe I should've known better."

Athletic heads drooped lower. A cloud of gloom permeated the locker area, as thick as the stench of perspiration.

Coach went on. "Doesn't mean much. Not really. I don't need another trophy in my den. Naw. I've had enough in my time. What's the difference, huh? Win some, lose some. Right? Just that . . . hell, I don't know. I thought you guys had that special chemistry that occasionally clicks on the field and makes for memories when coaches like me sit alone in front of fireplaces years from now. But look . . . if you can't, you can't. And all the work, all the slave-driving we've done, simply means diddley-shit. So let's just forget it, okay? Let's go back and throw away the second half too. What's victory to our seniors in their last year, anyway?"

Guy saw tears welling up in some of the players' eyes.

What a luxury, he told his diary, to be able to cry over a game and still not forfeit one's masculinity. . . .

Coach switched his tone. "Those Sewanhaka turds are cocky now. They could blow it. They can be beat. If you assholes would just go out there and act like a team! Get out there, crack a few heads. Haul a little ass!"

Close together on low benches, players coming out of their despair blurted back staccato grunts of agreement. Cautiously, Guy snapped pictures of the dramatic scene. Looking through his lens, he reviewed in his head the first half of the game and suddenly it all made sense.

Full speed ahead, Petrillo eventually shifted this down-and-out wake into an up-and-at-'em rousing cry for blood and victory.

With shouts and whoops, the boys were on their cleats again, trotting from the locker room in single file.

A grim Corky passed before Guy. He was almost out of the locker room when Guy blurted out, "Corky! Can I see you a moment?"

Corky trotted back to Guy. "What's up?" he asked, impatient, like Guy should know better than to detain him.

Guy's voice and fingers shook as one. "Listen, uhm, I know you're going to think this is probably ridiculous . . ."

"Come on, kid. What is it?" Corky implored, still trotting in place, anxious to get out of there.

"Well," Guy said in the screechiest voice he'd ever heard, even from himself, "I've been watching closely and I don't know if it means anything or not, but before Sewanhaka hikes, their quarterback almost always licks his lips in a really weird way, like it might be a signal or something . . . and I could see it clear as day through the long lens in my camera, and I hate to bother you at a time like this, but you see the ridiculous conclusion I've drawn is every time he licks his lips he eventually passes the ball and every time he doesn't, he makes a run for it."

Corky stared at Guy, saying nothing.

"That's all I wanted to say, Corky." Guy waved a friendly hand.

Corky still said nothing. He even stopped jogging in

place and just stood there staring at Guy with a blank expression. The roar from the battlefield swelled. Players were making their second-half entrance.

"Let's go, Henderson!" yelled an insistent Petrillo from the doorway.

Corky shook his head and put on his helmet. "Do me a favor, kid. Just take the pictures. You're good at that. Leave the game to me, okay?"

Before Guy could sink to the ground with embarrassment, Corky ran from the room.

Deflated and upset, Guy slowly made his way back to the field, arriving several plays late. He took pictures only of spectators and paid little attention to what remained of the game.

Enthusiasm on the Eagles' side picked up during the second half when Corky intercepted a long Sewanhaka pass.

The ball recovered, Waterfield's eleven moved closer to the goal, first and ten, until Corky dashed into the end zone.

The touchdown tied the score, 13–13.

Corky kicked in the extra point and suddenly the Eagles were ahead. The Waterfield crowd ripped programs into confetti.

Coach Petrillo's "Let do this one for the Gipper" pep talk had worked after all.

When the final gun went off, Waterfield went into a fit of delirium, Sewanhaka into a valley of despondency, and Guy into a splitting headache edged with remorse.

The locker room was jubilant pandemonium. Players still in uniform threw one another into showers. Others, already cleansed, waged spirited towel fights. Coiled terry-cloth tips snapped into naked skin, bruising, searing, eliciting cries of momentary anguish and pained celebration.

In the middle of all this festive rampaging, Corky sat on the bench in front of his locker, unwinding. Clad only in jockstrap and shoulder pads, knees spread apart, he thanked teammates congratulating him.

Off to the side, leaning against a locker wall, silent and unobtrusive, a fly on the wall, was Guy.

As the party rose in intensity, volume and exuberance, a sports reporter from the *Eagler* made his way through the circle of athletes to get to Corky for a statement.

"What was it?" asked the enthusiastic reporter, pen poised. "How'd you break their offense?"

The noise in the locker room dwindled fast. Everyone wanted to hear.

Corky was about to say that he was not the only hero of the afternoon; that there was a young man named Guy Fowler who also deserved some of the lavish praise.

He was all set to tell them about Guy's halftime discovery, which eventually had him anticipating their offensive moves, but eager eyes and familiar stares of adoration just wouldn't let him share the approval. So he switched stories fast, telling captivated faces, "They confused me most of the first half. But they're not so smart. Sure, they look tough in their uniforms, but padding can be as misleading on guys as girls. Don't print that last part!"

Everyone cheered and whistled. Guy too. The reporter took it all down. Petrillo beamed like a proud papa.

And Corky smiled. He smiled a dazzler for his fans while trying hard to ignore the pangs of guilt thumping in the back of his head.

14

Tissue-paper orchids clung to chicken-wire palm trees. Tropical travel posters covered cracks in the walls. Coconut-shaped balloons filled the baskets. Fish nets everywhere.

Guy entered the pulsating gymnasium that evening, apprehensive, uncomfortable in his itchy woolen suit, and found an exotic South Seas paradise right in the middle of mid-Long Island.

In one corner, an "underwater" lagoon had mobile cardboard sharks swimming from the ceiling. Below these paper maneaters a chair of plastic seashells served as King Neptune's throne. Guy's guess was this Atlantis-near-Flushing was where Ro-Anne would be crowned later in the evening.

He climbed to the top of the bleachers and set up his camera equipment. Focusing, he spotted Amy, the awkward girl he'd seen at the Sugar Bowl the other night. She sat alone, a few rows below him, writing on a small note pad.

The four-piece rock and roll band, seemingly determined to make up in volume that which they lost to talent, segued from their bang-it-out hot stuff into a lazy foxtrot.

No sign of Corky or Ro-Anne.

Intrigued that Amy seemed to be the only unescorted girl there, Guy decided to introduce himself. As he stepped down the few rows, a fidgety finger accidentally triggered his flash attachment. The searing light burst in Amy's face.

"Jeez, I'm sorry." Too late, Guy put his hand over the bulb.

Blinking brown eyes, Amy squinted. "Don't shoot! I give up!"

"I'm Guy Fowler."

"I can't see a thing. Do we know each other?"

Guy stood high above her. "Saw you the other night at Darcy's."

Amy's eyes adjusted to the light. "My favorite haunt!" she said sarcastically, hardly moving her lips.

"May I ask what you're writing?"

"Covering this bash for the *Eagler*."

"No kidding?" Guy was excited. "Me, too!"

"Really?" Amy was unimpressed. "How?"

Guy held up his Pentax.

Amy snapped her fingers. "Leonard mentioned you.

Now if our memories should forget this tasteless bore, we'll have your indelible photos to remind us."

"I sure hope so," said Guy. "This is my first dance."

"No! Your first taste of raw excitement and here's old cynic Amy in her jaded senior year spoiling it for you."

"You're not having fun?"

"I should hope not!"

"How come?"

"Oh, I don't know. Little things. The music. The decorations. Refreshments. Atmosphere. The crowd. Things like that."

"That's all?"

"Not quite. I object to the leering chaperones; spinsters treating us like ten-year-olds. The ass-kissers who dance with them, thinking they'll get better grades with their box step. I don't like any of it."

Guy studied Amy. "Know something? You're unusual," he said.

"Thanks for noticing," she answered icily.

"No, I mean unusual *interesting.*"

"Well, I'm glad one of us thinks so. I find myself fairly un-unusual this evening. All this rush to have a good time exhausts me."

"I sure wish I wasn't having a good time," said Guy.

Amy yawned. "That some kind of clever remark?"

"I don't think so." Guy smiled apologetically. "Just trying to keep up with you."

"You're doing rather well. Most people don't stick around this long. I scare them off."

"They probably don't understand you."

"Or me them."

"Hey, listen!" Guy adjusted his skinny blue tie. "I'm no Fred Astaire or anything, but would you like to dance?"

"Listen, friend. I'm no Ginger Rogers, so it hardly matters."

"Fine."

Like Alice in Wonderland, Amy stood up and up until Guy realized how very tall she was. Now on flamingo feet, she hovered a good head higher than him.

Too late to back out.

The slow song was still playing. Guy placed his arm around Amy's slim waist, and was afforded a lovely view of her neckline. They danced.

Too soon, surrounding couples snickered.

Guy wondered if she was finding this embarrassment as excruciating as he, and looked up at Amy.

Stoic and composed.

He cupped a hand over his mouth and quietly called far into the distance, a mountaineer: *"Hell-o up there!"*

She stopped dancing. "Listen. There are no rules. Nothing is sacred. Give me irreverence or give me death. *But* . . . I will not tolerate any cracks about my height. I'm self-conscious in that area. Got it?"

"Well . . ." Guy defended himself. "Don't you think I'm self-conscious about my shortness?"

They resumed dancing. "Then we understand each other. You have my word, I'll never mention it."

"Fine, Amy. You've heard the last from me on that subject, too."

"Thank you, Guy."

"You're welcome, Stretch."

Amy peered down, trying to look offended, but also stifling a grin. He looked up at her cross-eyed, and that did it. She burst into an honest giggle and then a full laugh.

Along with this wide-angle smile came her overwhelming display of hardware. Guy now understood why she spoke most of the time through tight lips.

Dancing couples continued to stare and sneer.

Guy glanced up at his lanky partner and asked, "Does it bother you people are laughing?"

"No," Amy replied, flat and fast.

"How come?"

"They don't matter."

"No?"

"No. People who find joy in cruelty to others are themselves insecure. I get the impression they laugh mainly because they're grateful not to be the object of ridicule."

"You're a pretty sophisticated person," Guy told her.

"True," Amy agreed.

With a flourish, the band concluded its strange rendition of "Earth Angel."

Amy and Guy walked to the bleachers to retrieve his camera and her pad.

Rose, a vision in pink fluff and baby-orchid wristlet corsage, descended upon him with great urgency.

"Oh Guy, may I see you a moment?"

"Hi, Rose. Do you know Amy?"

"I don't think so," Rose insisted, never taking her eyes off her brother.

"We had English together last year," Amy told Rose.

"Did we?" Rose asked indifferently, giving Amy the benefit of eye contact for part of a second.

"Yes," Amy went on, undaunted. "Mr. Einlach, the penguin. Remember?"

"Of course!" Rose responded frostily, looking only at Guy. "Can we talk? Need your advice about something."

Before Guy could answer, Rose walked off.

"Of course!" he called after her before turning to Amy. "Will you watch my camera?"

"Maybe you should take it with you," Amy suggested, mouth clenched once again. "You may not choose to return."

"I'll be back!" he said, turning to catch up with his sister.

Rose waited impatiently in the nearly empty hallway outside the gymnasium. Pink fingernails tapped nervously against her folded arms.

"What is it?" asked Guy.

" 'What it is?'! What the hell are you trying to do to me?"

"I don't unders—"

"Anything, just anything for a laugh, huh? Are you that desperate?"

"What are you talking about?"

"As if you don't know!"

"Amy?"

"You're goddamn right, Amy."

"What's the problem?"

"The problem, Guy, is I'll be the laughingstock of the entire school."

"How?"

"Trust me, okay. You're new here. Chalk it up to bad judgment. Just take my word for it. Stay away from her."

"Why?"

"Why do you think? Look at her. She's a giant!"

"So what?"

"So that's the point, brat. She's about a mile high. You know how ridiculous you look together?"

Rose's lashing tongue stung. "Why?" Guy managed to ask.

"Why? Why the hell do you think? She towers over you like an Amazon!"

"So? Jonathan Leeds is a lot taller than you!"

"In case you haven't notice, Guy . . . Jonathan just happens to be a *boy!*"

"So?"

"So . . . *boys* are supposed to be taller than *girls!*"

"Says *who?*"

"Says *everybody!*"

"Oh, really? Well, just where is that rule written?"

"It doesn't have to be written anywhere, dumbbell! It's a rule of life!"

"Well, maybe it's a stupid rule!"

"Do me a favor, Guy. If you want to change the world, don't do it on my time, okay?"

"Rose . . . all I did was dance with her."

"If you must dance, Guy . . . pick on someone your own size. Amy is one of the school freaks. I will not suffer indignities because of your rebellious shenanigans. Didn't you see everyone laughing?"

"Of course."

"Well?"

Trying hard to remember Amy's words, Guy paraphrased, "Insecure people need someone else to laugh at."

"I don't know what that means, Guy Fowler, but I will not stand for any of your psychological horse manure!"

A loud fanfare inside interrupted their family get-together. The few people in the hall filed into the gym.

"They're probably going to bring Ro-Anne in. I've got to get some pictures. Can we fight about this later?"

"Please, Guy. Please." Rose switched gears. "Don't embarrass me. I don't want them laughing at you."

Guy looked straight into his sister's cherubic face. "Jesus Christ, Rose. Neither do I. Don't you know that? Neither do I."

Straightening his tie, he hurried back into the gymnasium.

15

The Pentax was there. Amy wasn't.

"Ladies and gentlemen . . ." the drummer announced into the microphone, "will you please welcome this year's Queen of the Hawaiian Moon Ball, Ro-Anne Sommers . . . her royal court . . . and her escort, our favorite quarterback, Corky Henderson!"

Through a crepe-papered canopy ready to topple at the slightest touch, Ro-Anne, lovely in blue, made her entrance. In one hand she held a bouquet of flowers, in the other, Corky. He looked terrific in dark suit and snappy tie.

Three attractive attendants-to-the-queen followed.

The entourage arrived at the lagoon. Ken Crawley, student body prexy, told six humorless jokes in a row.

Guy snapped pictures as Ro-Anne got crowned, caped, throned, catered to and adored.

The ceremony completed, all eyes upon them, Corky led Miss Moon to the dance floor.

The band played "Love Me Tender." Lights were lowered. Corky and Ro-Anne circled in the glow of a follow spot.

A spinning mirrored ball splintered the light, creating

a dreamlike effect. Ten thousand stars whirled around the room.

In their minds, the others floated with them. No longer smirking at Guy and Amy, the least likely couple, they now concentrated on Ro-Anne and Corky, their most ideal.

Focusing on the model pair, Guy clicked off a roll of film.

Immersed within each other, Corky and Ro-Anne hardly reacted to the distracting flashes.

Other couples soon joined the Queen and her handsome escort.

Guy was still feeling guilty about his dumb halftime suggestion to Corky, so rather than get in the way again, he slipped out of the gymnasium. His departure went unnoticed.

On Monday, after classes, Guy went directly to the *Eagler* office.

Leonard Hauser was mid-tantrum. "Wait 'til I'm running the *New York Times*," he yelled across the room. "I'll hire and fire so fast, no one's going to walk over me! Now . . ." He turned to Guy. "What's your problem?"

Guy waved the contact sheets of the Sewanhaka game and the Hawaiian Moon Ball before his editor.

"Oh, right. Brownie snapshots of Waterfield royalty. Hold still." Leonard took them from him.

"Did Amy turn in her story on the dance yet?"

" 'Course not," Leonard huffed. "What do you think I'm running here, a newspaper? . . . These are pretty good, Fowler."

"Thanks. How would it be if Amy and I picked out an appropriate picture to go with whatever angle she's using?"

"Sounds good. Come up with something our comic book readers might understand." Leonard looked up from the photos. "Why couldn't I have been born rich as well as brilliant? Don't answer that. I should be in some expensive prep school, paving my way to Harvard and the Pulitzer prize. Families move from Brooklyn to Queens and finally to Waterfield, thinking they've made it. At last, an all-white neighborhood—the American dream! Christ! I'm drowning in a sea of mediocrity."

"A pearl before swine, huh?"

"Thank you." Leonard placed an affectionate hand on Guy's shoulder. "At last someone understands me."

Guy looked around and spotted Amy seated behind a typewriter. As he walked over she stated, "No damn *E!* What kind of a story can I write with no *E* on the lousy typewriter?"

"Avoid words like *cemetery*."

"Good advice."

"What happened to you Saturday night?"

"When?" Amy erased part of her story on the type-writer.

"I came back and you were gone."

"What can I say? I'll lie. Had a splitting headache."

"You missed the crowning of the prom queen."

"You don't say."

"I do."

"Quick!" cried Amy, attracting everyone's attention. "Find me a razor! I'm going to slash my wrists!"

"How 'bout a letter opener instead?" Leonard hollered from across the room.

"You'd like that, wouldn't you, Leonard? Blood all over the office. Anything for a headline! Well, forget it. I've decided to live and make your life miserable!"

Leonard raised a fist in the air. "I'm not taking you with me to the *Times,* Amy!"

Horrified, Amy pretended a faint over her typewriter. Leonard was pleased with himself and went back to work.

Guy looked around. "Are all of you always so brittle?"

"Always." Amy sat up straight.

"That's too bad."

"Too bad?! Please! What else keeps us going? The day this viper's tongue dulls, I turn in my typewriter ribbon!"

"But it all seems so nasty," Guy protested.

"That's just on the surface," Amy explained, batting

little girl eyelashes. "Beneath these hardened exteriors there lies unabashed, open hostility."

"Doesn't make you sound like happy people."

"Happiness is for others!" Amy stated, pounding the desk for emphasis.

"That a quote or something?"

"Something. Listen. It's still new to you. Hang around a few weeks. You'll grow as neurotic as the rest of us."

"God, I hope so!" Guy was enthusiastic. "Now. Can we discuss business?"

"Only if it has sexual overtones!" Amy answered with a toss of her shoulder.

"Okay. Leonard wants us to pick out a photo that best suits your story."

"Fine. Got any shots of Ro-Anne doing the hula with Jungle Jim?"

"See for yourself." Guy handed over his work.

Amy skimmed the columns. "What can I say? Each picture is worth a thousand words. You've done my job for me. Tell Leonard I've quit."

"Come on."

"You snap a wicked photo."

"Thanks."

"Don't thank me. I'm just being honest." Amy almost smiled. "Let's use this one." She pointed to a candid of Ro-Anne and Corky dancing. "That'll quicken heartbeats, punch up circulation."

"That's one of my favorites too." Guy peered over Amy's shoulder and observed, "They look good together, no?"

Amy sighed. "Like white bread and processed cheese!"

"Huh?"

"It's a metaphor."

"What's it mean?"

"It means sentiment is dead. Conventional beauty comes easy. To be a true aesthete, one must appreciate the offbeat."

"Like you?" Guy asked sheepishly.

Amy imitated Leonard, singing, "At last someone understands me!"

"Nothing around here makes sense." Guy started to leave. "You're all crazy."

"Now you're learning!" Amy called after him.

Guy left the office and hurried down the corridor. He turned the corner, and ran smack into Corky, coming the other way.

"Watch it!" warned the quarterback, placing his cleats behind him.

"Sorry," Guy squeaked. "Didn't see you coming."

"You always seem to be bumping into me."

"At least this time I wasn't on my bike."

"I'll count my blessings." Corky continued down the hall.

"We were just talking about you." Guy caught up with him. Corky stopped walking. "We who?"

"Me and the news staff," Guy boasted. "Just gave them your latest. I hope you'll be pleased."

"Me too."

"Off to practice?"

"No, kid, I always roam the halls with my cleats."

"And why not?" Guy grinned. "If I were you, not only would I take them everyplace, I'd have 'em dipped in bronze."

Corky smiled. "Listen, smart aleck. Don't cheer me up before scrimmage."

"Why not?"

"I play better grumpy. Brings out El Animal."

"Sorry, Tiger." Guy saluted. "What can I say between here and the locker to get you vicious again?"

"Nothing. You can walk me there," Corky allowed.

"Gladly." Guy joined the quarterback in long strides down the corridor, fighting to say something of interest. "Hey! How 'bout us beating Sewanhaka on Saturday?"

Corky quickened his pace.

Owning up, Guy decided it was time to apologize, adding, "And how 'bout my *clever* interference at halftime?"

"That really upset me, kid."

"Listen, Corky, don't you think it upset me too?"

"I'm sure. And I didn't mean to take all the credit afterwards. It just sort of happened."

Guy was confused. "Huh?"

"I'm talking about the bit with the lips."

"Wait a second. You mean I was right about that?" Guy's mouth dropped open.

Corky reached forward and closed it.

Dazed, Guy shook his head. "I had no idea. *I* was apologizing to *you!*"

"Me? You mean you didn't know?"

" 'Course not."

Corky looked around. "Hey . . . you told anyone about this?"

"How could I?" Guy squeaked. "I didn't find out 'til just now."

Corky pointed an admonishing finger. "Okay, then. It's private information between you and me, understand?"

"Fine. I'd never tell." Guy was emphatic. "They could torture me, pull out my nails, break my arm and still I'd say nothing. Swear to God!"

"Don't overdo it, kid. Just don't blab, okay?"

"Absolutely!"

"I've got a reputation, you know. It's a lot of fucking pressure, believe me."

"I can imagine," Guy assured him.

"Last thing I need is some new soph cutting through my field."

"I wouldn't."

"Don't get me wrong. I'd never trade places with anyone for all the happiness in the world!"

"Can I tell you something?"

"Go ahead."

"Well"—Guy lowered his voice—"happiness is for others."

Corky thought about it. "What the hell's that mean?"

"Who knows?" Guy shrugged. "It didn't make much sense when someone else said it a few minutes ago, either."

"Do me a favor, kid. Leave the brain waves at home."

"Will do."

"I gotta get to practice. You be sure about this now. I don't want what we talked about getting back to me. There'll be hell to pay."

"Don't worry about me. I was glad to help. Honest!" Guy held up two scout fingers.

Corky looked down at his loyal fan. "You're okay, you know that?"

"Thanks!"

"A little weird, but a sweet kid."

Guy jiggled his eyebrows, a junior Groucho Marx.

"Someday I'll do something for you, return the favor . . ."

"Oh, you don't have to—"

Corky snapped his fingers. "Maybe the fraternity. Sure. Why not? How'd you like to go to the Kappa Phi smoker a week from Friday?"

Guy looked up, overwhelmed.

"That's what I'll do, kid. Put your name on the invitation list." And with that, Corky tossed his cleats over his shoulder and bounded into the locker room. He felt bad knowing the kid didn't stand a chance of making it as a pledge, but at least he'd know the honor of having been considered.

Guy stared at the swinging locker room door. Kappa Phi. The jock house. The best frat in Waterfield. In the world. He and Corky were going to be fraternity brothers!

Bursting with excitement, Guy went straight home and read the sports section of *Newsday,* word for word.

16

The J.V. was scrimmaging early Saturday morning, so Butch, in training, chose not to attend his fraternity meeting the night before. Since he went to bed early, he had no way of knowing Corky had added Guy's name to the list of candidates asked to their smoker.

When the invitation arrived in Wednesday's mail, Guy had a hunch Butch still wasn't aware of it, else the beast would surely have registered some complaint. Fearful of his brother's probable overreaction, Guy put off mentioning anything about it.

Butch would find out soon enough.

Front page articles in Thursday's *Eagler* covered both the football win over Floral Park's Sewanhaka and the Hawaiian Moon Ball. Accompanying pictures gave due credit—*Photos: Guy Fowler*.

A spirited Guy gallivanted into the office and went directly to Amy. Atop a desk, knees pressed to her chest, she sipped a Coke.

"Hi!" He waved. "How'd you like being on the front page?"

"Eh."

"No great shakes?"

"Naw. How 'bout you?"

"Loved it. What a charge!"

"Calm down. Your enthusiasm's bursting my soda bubbles."

Clapping for attention, Leonard entered the office. "All right! This isn't the Fourth of July! Someone declare a legal holiday? Let's not rest on laurels, kiddies. We've got a next edition to get out. What goes?"

No one spoke. No one moved. All eyes on Leonard while he kicked a desk, pulled at his hair and yelled, *"I said I want to hear the happy sound of typewriters clicking and I mean now!!"*

Groaning and giggling, everyone settled at desks.

Guy turned to Amy. "You got an assignment?"

"Natch. I'm covering rehearsals for the fall play. *Arsenic and Old Lace*. Real avant-garde!"

"Going to work on it now?"

"What? And give Leonard the satisfaction of getting something in on schedule? Never!" Amy rested her elbows on her knees. "I'm weary of this day, anyway."

"What'll you do?"

"Don't know. Go home, I guess. Wanna come?"

Unaccustomed as he was to invitations from older women, Guy was intrigued. "What for?"

92

"Who knows? I can brew some tea. We'll sit cross-legged and compose haikus. Very beatnik."

"Sounds fine. What are hi-cooz?"

"Little Japanese poems. But let's get out of here before Leonard cracks his whip again."

The Silversteins lived upstairs in six rooms of a three-story garden apartment complex built just after the war. On permanent display, the place was immaculately clean. Except Amy's room.

Stacks of books and magazines. Articles ripped from newspapers. A bulletin board crowded with notes and memos. The bed sloppily made; Sheets hanging down beyond the mattress.

"Here we are!" Amy announced, walking in. "Welcome to the city dump."

Guy studied a pile of books. *The Prophet, Catch-22, Mein Kampf, The Catcher in the Rye* . . .

"Interesting collection." He tried sounding knowledgeable while tapping a copy of *Tropic of Cancer*.

Amy raised an instructive finger in the air, postulating, "Only if we listen to what others have to say can we then best make up our own minds as to how to run our lives!"

Guy wasn't sure what she meant, but he was impressed. "We're reading *Silas Marner* in English."

Amy smiled fondly at her guest.

Guy clicked his teeth. "And not only that . . . I'm a Democrat!"

"Big deal. I once knew a bigamist. Now then, would you like some tea?"

Guy slanted his eyes with his fingers and bowed, a humble Oriental.

"I'm glad no one's home yet. My mother'd drive us crazy."

Guy studied the tall girl, trying to figure her out.

"How 'bout Lapsang Souchong?" she asked.

Guy was stumped. "He some famous Chinese Communist?"

Amy didn't answer.

"I know!" Guy hit his head. "It's a breed of dog!"

"Not quite. It's the name of a tea."

"Oh. You mean there are others besides Lipton?"

"Hundreds. And warmed pumpkin bread with kumquat marmalade?"

Guy stuck a finger down his mouth, pretending to get sick at the suggestion.

"I'll be right back. Why don't you read a few books while I'm gone?"

As Guy thumbed rapidly through *Das Kapital,* none of it making sense, he heard the front door open. A woman's voice called out, "Yoo-hoo!"

"In the kitchen!" yelled Amy.

There followed a series of jumbled words. Both parties raised voices until someone said, "I'll see for myself!"

Insistent footsteps approached and a handsome brunette entered the room.

"Oh!" The woman stopped short, releasing a breath of air. "Excuse me. Amy said she was entertaining a *man* in her room."

Guy looked around for possible candidates. "Who'd you think *I* was?"

"Well"—she grinned—"you're obviously a very *young* man."

"True," Guy confessed.

"I never know what to expect from Amy."

"I guess that makes two of us."

"I'm Evelyn Silverstein. Amy's mother."

"Guy Fowler."

Evelyn slowly surveyed the room. "Can you believe this mess? You could eat off my living room floor, it's so clean. I'm forever hoping Amy might entertain her friends in there. But no, she drags them into this den of bacteria."

"I think it has character," Guy volunteered.

"Want some sage advice, young man?"

"Sure."

"Don't have children. Raise puppies. You won't be disappointed."

"I'll remember that."

Balancing a crowded tray, Amy now joined the party. "How was the beauty parlor, Evelyn?"

"News under the dryer practically singed my hair. Jeanne Wright's pregnant *again* and Martha Ames is having an affair with her dry cleaner. Lucky stiff, she's had all her curtains cleaned free." Evelyn fingered her hair. "But just look at this comb-out. Barton's losing his touch. You know how much that fruit gets to make me think I look like the youngest mother on the block?"

"How do you know he's a fruit?" Amy said wearily.

"Don't go liberal on me, dear. *All* hairdressers are. Same as men ballerinas and Jesuit priests. Save the propaganda for your readers."

"It's not propaganda!"

"Good thing my friends haven't seen some of your book collection. We'd all be under investigation.

"No doubt!" Amy agreed.

Evelyn turned to Guy. "Tell me, young man. You part of that group, too?"

"What group?"

"He's not, Mother."

"Well, that's a relief. I'll start dinner." Evelyn raised an eyebrow and looked at Amy. "*He* eating with us?"

"No, Mother. Why subject him?"

Evelyn looked at Guy appraisingly. "Seems a rather nice young man. Not like the others."

"Thanks." Amy pretended to be flattered.

Mrs. Silverstein turned to leave. "Can I get you two anything?"

"No." Amy's impatience was about to show. "We *were* doing fine."

Evelyn looked to Guy. "Get her to clean up this room, Guy. Tidiness is such a virtue."

"I'll do what I can, Mrs. Silverstein."

"Who wants to marry a sloppy woman? Okay, children. Have fun. And Amy . . ." Evelyn smiled cheerfully.

"Yes, Mother?"

"Keep the door open!"

With a crooked grin and a further adjustment of her newly coiffed hair, Amy's mother left the room.

Silence.

Guy looked at Amy. She looked at him, lifted the small ceramic pot into the air and politely asked, "Tea?"

Guy and Amy sat on the floor in a lotus position she'd quickly taught him. With small candles mystically burning about them, and a heavy cloud of incense stinking up the place, they sipped the oddly named tea and nibbled on marmalade toast.

Amy twirled a spoonful of honey and let the sweetener plip-plop into her cup. "My mother goes to the beauty parlor. What's yours do for a living?"

"Bakes."

"Bakes what?"

"You name it. This week she's concocting an upside-down pineapple-apricot something-or-other."

"Sounds dreadful." Amy licked the sticky residue from her spoon.

"Sometimes yes. Sometimes no. She experiments a lot. Every year she enters the Pillsbury Bake-Offs. Even got honorable mention once or twice."

"Sounds like something out of *Good Housekeeping*," said Amy. "My Mother has no interest in baking. Too busy planning my future. Believe me when I say she and my Aunt Bernice have been fighting over the wording of my engagement announcement for twelve years."

"Well, why not? Isn't that what mothers do best?"

"I suppose." Amy sipped her tea. "Can I tell you my favorite Evelyn story?"

"Please."

"Last year, for my Sweet Sixteen, I told my folks in no way did I want a party. I agreed to let them take me in to New York for a show and a fancy meal at a restaurant of my choosing. It was after *West Side Story*, over crepes suzette at 21, that Evelyn handed me a savings book. My birthday present. She'd been putting aside ten dollars a week into a private account, for the past four year.

"Naturally I was thrilled. I mean all that money. My joy was cut short when she explained the accumulated treasure. To finance my overhaul. Bob the nose, unkink the hair, make me a beauty. Well . . . wasn't I excited and grateful?"

"And you weren't?"

"Certainly not! I handed the savings book back, mentioning I'd rather use the money for a trip to Europe. Evelyn—who carries in her wallet photos of movie stars who've had nose jobs—accused me of deliberately sabotaging my chances for happiness, and I displayed what I thought was great restraint by not dumping my dessert into her lap."

"I guess she meant well."

"I guess. Still, who wants to look like everyone else? My dear . . ." Amy pretended to have a headache. "Wait 'til Christmas recess. You return from vacation and twenty girls have new faces. Ba-ba-ba. More tea?"

Guy held out his cup. As Amy filled it with the smoky-flavored brew, he asked, "You know Debbie Wiener?"

"We have gym together."

"Well, she's my sister's friend. Jewish. She had her nose fixed last year and I think she looks pretty good."

"Do you?" Amy placed the white china pot on the floor.

"A lot better than before, anyway."

Amy was casual. "I think they sliced off her face."

"Oh? . . . you really preferred her old nose?"

"I'd *prefer* something natural to one of those piglet jobs. Why do you think they call it *plastic* surgery?"

"I never—"

"Don't misunderstand. I'm not particularly thrilled with the piccolo in the middle of my face. But it is mine and I'll live with it. I only consented to have my mouth barb-wired like this because my father's an orthodontist. It's bad public relations having me walk around like the Wicked Witch of the East."

Guy tilted his head to look at Amy's braces.

"Sometimes when Evelyn's serving one of our more scintillating dinners around the television, a commercial will come on. She'll look at me and then say something like, 'It was always such a *small* nose when you were young.' Does wonders for my confidence." Amy stared at the floor.

Guy snapped his fingers, bringing her back from a momentary drift. "Hey, what'd your mother mean when she asked if I was part of 'that group'?"

"She means the Gadflys."

"Who?"

"Friends of mine. You know some of them from the paper. Maybe you should come to our next get-together."

"Love to!" Guy accepted eagerly, glad to be included in any social gathering, anywhere.

"The school refuses us the editorial freedom we've been demanding, so we're putting out our own newspaper."

"How can they tell you what to print?"

"Because they think they're Big Brother!" Amy said staunchly.

"Who's he?"

Amy sipped her tea. "It's a literary allusion."

"But they can't do that," Guy protested. "It's a free country!"

"You are naive. We're going to shake up a few institutions, I can tell you that. Show these obnoxious fraternity-sorority types there's another world outside the womb of Waterfield."

"Wait a minute!" Guy interjected. "What's wrong with fraternities? I just got brought up for one myself. Going to their smoker tomorrow night."

Amy placed her cup on the floor. "You're not serious."

"But I am!" Guy bragged. "And guess who brought my name up? Corky Henderson himself!"

Amy stared at her grinning guest several seconds, saying nothing. Why, she suddenly wondered, was she wasting time with this juvenile? What was it made her think he had any potential in the first place? Had his photography talent clouded the fact he was probably as dull as the rest of them? "If you think you could ever be happy in a sheepherder's organization like Kappa Phi, I'm afraid we don't really know each other at all."

"But why?" Guy asked, hurt by her switch in tone.

"Because Kappa Phi is composed of rowdy, beer-guzzling, dumb jocks. What the hell have you in common with them?"

"It's the best fraternity in school!" Guy was firm. "And I'm becoming very fond of beer!"

"Sorry, Guy. They're just not for you. You're far more sensitive than any of those—"

"Sensitive?" Guy raised his voice. "I am not sensitive!"

"It was meant as a compliment." Amy tried soothing him.

"And it just so happens Corky Henderson—"

"Corky Henderson is a mindless monkey," Amy stated with a vehemence that surprised even her.

That did it. Guy bit his lower lip to hold back unwelcome emotions, "I have to leave." He stood. "My legs are killing me."

"I understand," Amy said softly, trying to figure out how their mad tea party had suddenly gone so sane. "The lotus position is an acquired discomfort."

Neither of them said anything as Guy picked up his books and walked, Amy trailing, to the front door.

"Thank you," he said softly.

"Sorry if I upset you, Guy. It's the last thing I meant to do. And if things don't happen to turn out the way you hope, I'd be happy to discuss it with you."

Guy opened the door and stepped into the hall. "Everything's gonna be fine!" he assured her. "But thanks for the concern. And for your information, Miss Smarty-Pants . . . Corky Henderson is not just a casual acquaintance. He happens to be my friend. My best friend. My very best friend in the whole goddamn world!"

17

Choosing the right outfit for so important an event as a rush smoker was a difficult challenge. Looking cool and detached, smooth and bon vivant, the casual man of the world was not so easy when your wardrobe revolved around *nothing* that looked good on you.

After trying on and discarding everything he owned, Guy finally opted for his old red alpaca cardigan. Buttoned up, he looked in the mirror. Perry Como before Geritol.

After ten minutes of brushing down his cowlick, he went downstairs, a nervous wreck. Strolling into the kitchen, he found Rose and Birdie awash in dinner dishes, still nibbling leftovers.

"This is it!" he announced. "How do I look?"

"Just fine," said Birdie, his reliable support, rubber-gloved hands deep in suds.

"*Yucch!*" decreed Rose, his reliable non-support, polishing up a plate. "Where'd you get that sweater?"

"Arrived in last month's Care package," he tossed back.

"Looks it," said Rose, placing the dish inside the cupboard.

As Guy kissed his mother good-by, she asked, "Where you off to?"

"Oh"—very casual—"Just the Kappa Phi smoker."

Birdie smiled innocently.

Rose looked at him in disbelief. "You're such a liar!"

Guy swung out the kitchen door.

Nathan was tuned into a boxing match as Guy entered his lion's den.

"Am I interrupting?"

"No, no. Round just started." Nathan downed a sip of beer and bit into a pretzel.

"I'm off to Butch's fraternity smoker, Dad. Wanted to say goodby."

Nathan turned around. "That's a pretty snappy sweater, fella."

"You like it?"

"Sure. You look fine."

Guy relaxed.

"Good luck, son. Just talk slow, act calm and you'll be fine."

In his deepest register, with his tightest grip, Guy shook hands with his father. *"Hi. My-name's-Guy-Fowler."*

"Not bad," Nathan reviewed the performance.

Guy turned to leave.

"Don't fall down, you mother!" Nathan pounded the arm of his chair and screamed at the tube. "I've got fifty fat ones on you, son of a bitch. *Get up!*"

Flat on the mat, the fighter didn't hear Nathan. The referee was counting as Guy left the room.

Dick Lanier's front door was ajar when Guy arrived at the smoker.

Should he be polite and ring the bell or do the manly thing and just push his way in? While he was deciding, the door swung open.

"Hi!" said Guy pleasantly to the eleven-foot basketball monster behind the door.

"Come in!" said the colossus.

"Dis must be de place!" Guy addressed both knees as he passed them.

The living room was empty.

"Everyone's downstairs. Throw your coat in the bedroom."

"Thanks." Guy carefully extended his hand. "My . . . name's . . . Guy." Low and slow. "Guy . . . Fowler."

"Dick Lanier!" returned the square-jawed jock without expression, before walking into the kitchen. So much for friendly chatter.

Guy dropped his parka on the pile in the bedroom and then walked to an open door. A lot of noise was coming up from down there. His heart pounded.

Taking in a deep breath, Guy stuck out what there was of his chest, stood tall as nature would allow and then, ever so slowly, descended the stairs, down, down into the first circle of hell—Dick Lanier's finished basement.

The paneled room was packed. Forty guys surrounded a poker table.

Talk was subdued. Everyone watched the six gamblers.

Corky, one of the players, sported an unseemly cigar from the side of his mouth. Across from him, scooping in winnings from the previous hand, sat Butch. His hair was greased back, overdosed on Vitalis.

Guy reached the bottom of the stairs.

"Hi there!" A handsome, broad-shouldered fellow introduced himself. "Chuck Troendle."

"Guy," came the response, slow and soft. "Guy . . . Fowler."

"Wadda ya know?" asked Chuck, firmly grasping Guy's shoulder. "Don't tell! Let me guess."

A visionary summoning spirits, Chuck closed his eyes. "Swimming!"

Long pause. Chuck looked at Guy for confirmation.

Guy stared back, saying nothing.

"Not swimming?"

Guy shook his head. Not swimming.

Sizing him up, Chuck again pinpointed Guy's specialty. "Skiing!"

Guy couldn't disappoint him. "Yep," congratulating Chuck's perception, "skiing."

"Thought so." Chuck chuckled. "It's you short toads always zoomin' past us. Make the best downhill demons. Something to do with shorter bones being more flexible. Anyway, I'm rush chairman. I greet everyone and it's nice to have you here, Farley."

"Fowler," Guy politely corrected him.

"Right, Fowler. Hey! We've got a Fowler. Big Butch!"

"Yeah. Big Butch is my big brother."

Chuck looked at Guy quizzically, trying to figure out the gimmick. Then he turned to the poker table and yelled, "Hey, Butch! This kid here says he's your brother!"

In unison, brothers and guests alike turned to see to whom Chuck was referring. They stared at Guy. Then, spectators at a tennis tournament, heads turned to Butch.

Stunned by Guy's unexpected appearance in his sanctuary, Butch could think of nothing to say.

Heads went back to the short visitor. Guy lowered his voice, smacked a fist into the palm of his hand very hard, and grunted, "Wadda ya say, Butch?"

All eyes traveled back to the poker table. Up to Butch. Hunched like Fagin over his winnings, wondering if

102

if others had found Guy's locker room greeting as trumped up as he had, Butch ended the match, acknowledging, "Guy! Wadda ya know?" Then he took the deck and announced, "Seven-card stud!"

"I'm out!" said Corky, gathering his small pile of money. Leaving the casino area, he walked to the stairs. "How're you doing, kid?" he asked Guy in passing.

"All butterflies. Can't quiet down."

"You're too delicate. Take deep breaths."

Corky excused himself and left to help set up an interview area upstairs.

Butch kept shoveling it in. Nathan had carefully taught him a wicked poker, a training which gave the big boy a definite edge over other card players in the group.

At Butch's summons, Guy hurried over. "Why didn't you tell me, for Christ's sake?" Butch whispered into his little brother's ear.

"Tell you what?" Guy whispered back.

"That you wanted to join? What'd you do? Ask Corky? I'd've brought your name up."

"I never asked Corky. It was his idea."

"How do ya think it makes me look? My own brother brought up and not even by me?"

"I asked you, Butch. Before school started. You said you'd get me in soon as I made the football team."

"*I* said that?" Butch was all innocence.

"Come on, Butch. Up to you!" a player interrupted their whispered conference. "We playing poker or not?"

"Go stand on the other side," Butch told Guy before picking up a stack of coins. Without even looking at his newly dealt cards, he opened. "Half a buck, wise-ass!"

As instructed, Guy walked halfway around the table, watching without comment.

Neither the high stakes nor the growing animosity toward his long winning streak bothered Butch. Draining weekly allowances, he played on. Three, five and ten dollars a pot.

Guy stood directly behind the hulk of a first-string offensive tackle named Jenkins, who was incurring the heaviest losses.

Butch shuffled cards and named the game. "Five-card draw." Then he dealt.

Jenkins, the offensive tackle, beamed; too happy to be faking it. What he lost to subtlety, he scored in bravado, tossing out two dollars, the maximum bet.

Only Butch and a jock named Calvin stayed.

The offensive tackle took three cards. Calvin took one. Butch three.

The heavy betting began.

The offensive tackle threw in another two bills. Calvin, obviously not having made his straight, cursed and folded. Butch saw the bet and raised it another two. The offensive tackle saw Butch's raise and bumped him another two.

Butch bumped him back, and there was suddenly a green salad of money on the table.

Butch squinted at Jenkins. "Okay, hotshot. Let's see."

Nobody breathed. The offensive tackle laid his cards down. "Two aces!" he gloated.

"Very good," Butch said quietly as he placed his cards on the table. "Jeez, awfully good. But I got three two's."

Everyone took a deep breath at the same time.

"Shit!" seethed Jenkins, pounding the table with a heavy fist.

"Temper, temper!" scolded Butch, wagging a naughty finger at the sore loser.

Guy felt some recognition of family pride might be in order, so excited and even momentarily proud was he of the dramatic way in which Butch had pulled off that last hand. So he encouraged Butch to go on, blurting out in a high-pitched cracked voice, "Keep it up, Butch, you'll soon be driving an Oldsmobile all your own!"

At which point the seething offensive tackle in front of Guy raised his head, turned and asked, in all sincerity, "There a *girl* in here?"

Everyone stopped talking and looked at Guy.

No. Please, no. Guy shut his eyes and looked down, devastated. Damn. Everything had been going so well. He'd been in total control. Now, in one unguarded moment he'd let himself go and out had come the dreaded piercing tone, the sissy Mickey Mouse squeak no one with any cool would ever care to call fraternity brother.

A small, stifled giggle burst from somewhere to Guy's left. Then another.

More humiliated for the genetic association than for Guy, Butch fast shifted the focus. "Pick up your cards!" he snapped gruffly to the other players. "Up to you, Pete!"

The game went on, and Guy, looking only at the floor, waited for this most costly of embarrassments to pass.

Three quarters of an hour later he had still not uttered another word. Cold-eyed, he stared at the poker table until Chuck Troendle trotted down the basement steps and tapped him on the shoulder. "You're next, Farley. Follow me."

Guy followed.

Corky and four other upper classmen were seated around a banquette just off the kitchen. They rattled off to Guy the virtues of fraternity life. The giving the getting the camaraderie. Safety in numbers. The comfort of knowing there were thirty others like you in there pitching behind you a hundred and ten percent all fighting for Kappa Phi.

But being asked to pledge for this select group was no easy affair. Besides needing a unanimous vote of the brotherhood to be polled later that evening, eventual admission would come only after a long and demanding hazing period. Is that clear? Are there any questions?

Guy had no questions.

The lecture concluded, members of the exclusive fraternal order cross-examined their guest.

Guy played the role, catering to their loaded questions, speaking of friendship and trust. Any fraternity brother of his could most assuredly stay the night at his house, borrow his car, share his girl friend.

After the interview Guy was directed back downstairs. Silently, he observed the poker game still being waged.

Another hour passed before Chuck Troendle finally announced, "Any of you already interviewed can leave whenever you're ready."

Guy was ready. He excused himself, found his coat and then, after an attempted smile to Dick Lanier, now serving as gracious doorman, he left the Kappa Phi smoker.

18

Drawn by the lights Guy wandered to town, hating himself for having believed the impossible.

More depressing than all the wasted evening's bullshit, though, was that it was Friday night and he'd just missed the last show at the Avalon.

Hands low in pockets, he walked into the wind.

As soon as all the prospective pledges had left, the brothers gathered downstairs to decide which of them would be honored with invitations to become slaves on trial.

One by one, names were called. Each was discussed before being accepted or rejected. Candidates were running half in, half out when the secretary read aloud, "Fowler, Guy!"

Heads turned to Corky and behind him, to Butch. Fraters fidgeted in their seats.

Corky looked down at the flowered pattern of the linoleum wondering how he had gotten himself into this mess. While he speedily juggled thoughts, preparing to say he knew not what, Butch raised his hand.

A low murmur came to an abrupt halt as the Butcher stood to take the floor.

Corky looked up.

"Listen, guys"—Butch shuffled his feet—"to save any of you from being embarrassed in front of me, I think it'd be better all 'round if I . . . uhm, vote to blackball . . ." Butch's voice trailed as he sat down.

A relieved membership took a few moments to compose themselves.

Butch jumped up again. "And I'm sure I don't have to remind any of you about our honor code. No talking to outsiders about what goes on here in our meetings!"

Twenty-seven heads nodded in unanimous agreement.

After putting a black pencil mark through Guy's name, the secretary called out the next candidate. "Friedman, Mel!" Hands rose in the air and debate began.

Two of Butch's brethren patted him on the back, letting him know they understood what a difficult sacrifice he'd made, axing his own kin and all.

Corky also turned around. Leaning backward, he placed a hand on Butch's knee and whispered sweetly, "Gotta hand it to you, Butch"—the Butcher's face lit up—"you're even more of a prick than I thought." And the light went out.

Much later, standing outside the Avalon, Guy watched the late show audience leaving the theater and studied faces to catch reactions.

Rock Hudson and Doris Day in *Pillow Talk*. The plight of the virgin. In color, no less. You couldn't get a better bill.

When the last of the moviegoers had drifted down the street, he resumed his aimless stroll, kicking at whirling leaves. Without conscious intent, he approached Darcy's then stopped short when he spotted Corky at the entrance with Ro-Anne and some friends.

Corky glanced casually down the block and saw Guy standing silently still. His stomach dropped as if a ball was hiked, and he couldn't imagine why the sight of the kid standing there in that strangely frozen state should so affect him.

He turned to Ro-Anne. "You go on in, I'll be right back." Just then, to Chuck Troendle, "Get a booth."

With a tug of the zipper on his team jacket, Corky left the hangout.

A strong wind severed leaves from branches.

Corky walked up to Guy. "Nice night for a hurricane."

Guy nodded.

The huge Mobil disc at the corner station swayed. Spiraling leaves chased one another around the pavement.

"What'cha doing out so late?"

Guy looked down the street, up at the illuminated clock on the church steeple. Five after eleven. "What am *I* doing?" he asked softly. *"You're* the one in training."

Corky punched Guy's arm. "Playing hooky for an hour or two. Give me a break, kid. It's Friday night."

"Fine with me," said Guy, uncaring.

"Don't tell Petrillo you saw me out late. I'll buy you a malted if you'll promise to keep your trap shut!"

Guy ignored Corky's pleasantries—thinking it important to explain how mortified he was over the evening's travesty. "I hope I didn't embarrass you too much, Corky."

"'What're you talking about?" Corky dismissed the notion. "You want that malted or not? I don't spring for drinks every day, kid. I'll even go you a mug of cocoa, a hot alternative, seeing as how you caught me in a weak moment."

Hands in his pants pockets, Guy said, "I don't feel much like anything." Why was Corky being so damn nice, Guy wondered. Only made him feel worse. It saddened Guy because it seemed so decent a gesture, so damn decent, in fact, he wanted to cry.

Cry? No! Not now! God, not here. Not in front of *him!*

Guy sunk teeth into his lower lip, practically breaking skin. Don't open that reservoir. Don't let him see you cry. Men don't cry, dammit! Guy turned and hurried away.

"Hey!" a surprised Corky called after him. "Where ya going?"

Guy flung his hands in the air, indicating he didn't know. He knew though that he couldn't stop to talk; that if he didn't keep walking rapidly, didn't keep his upper teeth deep into his lip, that he'd burst, for sure.

"Will you slow down?" yelled Corky, catching up.

Guy forged ahead, rapidly passing the red light on the corner. A Pontiac Bonneville screeched to a halt. Guy paid no mind to the young driver who rolled down his window to curse savagely.

Oblivious, he crossed the street, rounded the corner and headed off the main thoroughfare, down Centre Street, Corky still directly behind.

Guy traveled another quarter of a block before Corky caught up with him on the deserted street. Reaching out, he firmly grasped Guy's upper arm.

"Let go of me!" Guy demanded through tightened teeth. His rage surprised them both.

"Make me!" Corky's intense eyes bore into Guy's face.

Guy tried pulling his arm free. It wouldn't budge. *"Leave me alone!"* Guy hollered, tugging to free himself.

Corky held firm . . . and Guy snapped. "It's not fair," he yelled out. "Why did I have to run into *you?* You're about the last person I'd . . ."

And that was it. The words could no longer come out because the tears that had been swelling inside suddenly poured as if out of some dam collapsing.

Corky placed impatient hands on either side of his waist, stared down at the kid and tapped his sides, waiting. When it appeared the worst had passed, Corky instructed, "All right, kid. Can the hysterics, huh?"

Guy's cheeks flushed red. His head pounded. He took a deep sniff, pinched his fingers and whined, *"My Grand-father died!"*

Silence. Corky felt terrible. "Oh, no! So that's what this is all about!"

"Of course!" Guy wiped his nose on his sleeve.

"Hey, kid. I'm real sorry. And here I thought it was that stupid thing tonight. You must feel awful. When did it happen?"

"Oh . . ." Guy blew into his handkerchief. "About ten years ago."

Corky and Guy stared at each other.

Unamused, Corky spun around, huffing his way back up Centre Street.

Guy ran after him. "Wait up!" the little fellow shouted. "Let me explain!"

Corky stopped walking. Furious, he told Guy, "This better be good, kid! Better be damned good!"

Out of breath, Guy offered the truth. "It's like this.

Sometimes I cry, see? Not often, but sometimes it comes and there's nothing I can do. *Pow,* Niagara Falls! I wish it weren't so. I swear to God, but those are the breaks. It's the way I am, and so when it comes, it's best if I'm left alone. I'm fine soon as all the juice is out."

But all the juice wasn't yet out. As a fresh cloud threatened to break, Guy turned away.

Corky reached forward, spun him around and held Guy's arm. "Stop it!" he shouted. "Enough of this crying shit! You're acting like a real sissy!"

Those were the magic words. Guy swung with his free hand, desperately trying to connect; to smash Corky across the jaw, to land one Sunday punch.

Corky caught the clenched fist and held it tight. It was then Guy realized he'd been provoked into venting all this seething hostility and self-hatred. Like a stringless puppet, he sagged and folded.

Corky let go.

"All right. You win." Exhausted, Guy wiped the wet from his face.

"Jeez, kid. You're one tough little customer."

"Yeah." Guy stood up straight. "You ought to catch me sometime when I'm upset."

"But what's the big deal, kid? It's only a lousy fraternity. Not worth crying over, like some dumb schoolgirl."

"Oh yeah? Well, would you mind telling me what is worth crying over?"

"Whenever you gotta," said Corky with finality, crossing his arms. "I cry whenever we lose a game."

"And that's all right, I suppose?" Guy sniffed.

"Of course that's all right. The whole team cries when we lose!"

"Seems awfully sissyish to me!" Guy argued. "A dumb football game!"

"More important than a dumb fraternity bid, I can tell you that!"

"Says who?"

"Says me!"

"Oh yeah? Well I think if someone wants to cry at the weather report, he should fucking well be allowed to!"

110

"Hey, kid. Stop the music! Wipe the snot from your nose and settle down. Lecture your smarter friends. All I did was try to get you into the fraternity. It's my fault, okay? I should've said straight out it was a long shot. Fact is you came really close. Closer than I'd have thought!"

The color in Guy's face improved. "Really?"

"Sure!" Corky lied. "Don't take it so personally. We couldn't take in everyone. The guys naturally went for members of the ball teams. That's what a jock house is all about, get it?"

Guy got it. "And here I've been crying like a schoolgirl over some dumb fraternity bid!"

Corky nodded. "Exactly."

"Well, thanks. I feel a lot better."

"Naturally." Corky snapped his fingers. "All included in the Henderson charm. Okay! For the last time, if you can manage to control yourself, are you coming to Darcy's and letting me buy you a drink or not?"

From somewhere down in his elusive repertoire of deep voices, Guy said, "That'd be great. A Coke is just what the doctor ordered."

"Coke?" Corky frowned. "Not on your life. Forget it. Your days of Coca-Cola done gone. A growing man needs stamina. You're having a glass of milk. Giant size."

"Milk?" Guy contorted a wretched face.

"Bet your ass, Buster!" Corky raised his voice. He headed up the block emphatically adding, "From now on, kid, you're in training!"

November

19

Guy decided to change his life.

Carefully marking the moment for posterity, he worded the final entry in the diary he was now closing for good: *Wednesday, the First of November,* he etched on his mind. *I have resigned as the family dwarf.*

No longer would he show up at gym class, bandy-legged and scrawny-armed, underdeveloped in his baggy uniform.

No longer would he stare enviously at others, piecing together a fantasized composite of all he wanted to be: his rugged face on that athletic neck atop those broad shoulders framing his muscular chest, flexing strong arms and solid legs like the fellow over there and . . . enough was enough.

At last, he would be himself. Only better.

Just as his father was now displaying the new line of '59 Oldsmobiles, so too would Guy soon be coming out with the new, toned-down, fattened up, improved version of himself.

Guy Fowler for 1959. Coming your way. Put your order in now!

Forget the days of coasting into the Avalon on child's fare.

Farewell tears. No more crying. They'd have to bludgeon him senseless before he'd again show raw, girlish emotions.

So long outcasts; hello you cool cats, you smooth sons of bitches who mandate fashionable behavior.

If Brooks Brothers was Beau Brummel, so be it.

If it would take nothing less than a dirtied pair of white bucks to hang out in, then fine. Only chinos with vestigial buckles in the back and shirts with button-down collars would be worn from now on.

Guy rampaged through his closet, throwing out anything that wasn't currently acceptable ivy-league.

He found out the name of Corky's barber and sat through a clipping, instructing Mario to fashion a smaller version of Corky's head. Damned if it didn't suit him, too.

He bought a small bottle of Canoe and splashed it onto his cheeks each morning before school. It was comfortable smelling like all the other with-it boys.

A promise was a promise. Guy had sat down to his last half-eaten meal.

At breakfast he began devouring eggs like candy. He gobbled whole-wheat toast and strips of bacon, always had seconds, and washed everything down with glasses of milk.

Birdie was ecstatic. "It's a miracle. We have another mouth to feed!"

Butch told Guy he was wasting his time, but since no longer paying attention to Butch was one of Guy's new guide rules, it didn't bother him. Both had been staying clear of each other ever since the night of the smoker anyway.

After school, Guy came home and snuck into Butch's room. There he lifted the lesser weights of his brother's dumbbell collection. He surreptitiously purchased several copies of *Strength & Health* at Darcy's. Smuggling them home, he followed routines laid out by beefy giants who promised he too would soon have nineteen-inch arms. Guy's head swam at the very notion of such extensive power.

Day after day, diligently and secretly, he worked and sweated, looking forward to driving girls crazy and boys mad with envy. Mr. America, move over!

The first week of this concentrated physical program passed and Guy looked no different, felt no better.

The second week, still no change.

After the third week he stopped inspecting himself. Resigned that it might be months before he would see any muscles, he just kept at it.

The next two football games of the season were played

away. Guy was assigned to travel with the team to take pictures.

He rode to Rushport and Cold Spring Harbor, sitting in the back of the bus, pretending to be involved with his camera equipment. He wasn't.

He was observing, listening, studying the football players. He noted the harsh way they spoke. Their lazy language patterns: *It don't matter none; I ain't gonna; Wadda ya say?* Their pet expressions: *cruddy-creep, cockteaser, creamin' in my pants.*

He heard them talk about the girls who put out. How much tit they gave. How their pussies smelled; sometimes sweet, sometimes sour. How five of them went over to Barbara Deutsch's and got blow-jobs, one after the other. Two of them even almost came in her mouth.

Man-talk!

He picked up the rules. The uglier the girl, the sooner you had to bang her. If she was a real looker, well then you respected that and didn't lay a finger. Those were the good girls, sorority ladies you took to parties and to Darcy's; virgins you eventually married.

Guy watched the players walk from the bus, their bow-legged, rugged strides; the way they held their hands when trotting.

Most of all, he watched Corky. He noted the way the quarterback smoothed down the back of his short hair; imitated the way he stroked his chin in concentrated thought; observed facial expressions, hand gestures, body movements. All of it.

Guy looked and learned. He didn't say much on those two highly educational bus trips. Almost a third of the team was composed of Kappa Phi's, and he was still too intimidated to talk with any of them.

Corky was engrossed only in the game. Going there, he sat with Petrillo, reviewing plans and plays. When Petrillo left to work on some others players, Corky climbed far inside himself, into some capsule of concentration from which he wouldn't emerge until after the contest.

On the ride home from both battles, each the easy victory anticipated, Corky curled up in the back, across

115

from Guy, and collapsed, so great was his release from tension.

Even asleep, Corky was studied from across the way.

The day after the second away game, Corky passed Guy in the hall, between classes.

"Hey, Guy! You catch that draw play, third and fifteen on their twenty yard line yesterday? I was in top form!"

The new Guy looked up at his mentor and slowly shifted his weight, letting one shoulder alternately dominate the other. With confidence, he calmly answered, "Sure. Already gave them to Leonard."

"Terrific!"

"I'll get a set to you."

Corky was pleased. "You're a real find, you know that, kid?"

Guy avoided the temptation to get gushy and sloughed it off. "We all gotta make a living, no?"

"Yeah, but you always catch my best moments."

Guy wanted to smile but instead shifted in place again as if the weightier muscles on one side of his body needed a rest.

"See ya!" Corky poked Guy on the shoulder, jocklike, on his way down the hall.

"Bet'cha," Guy responded, subdued.

Corky bounded on down the hall and Guy watched, step after step, fixing in his mind the cool rhythm of each movement.

It wasn't until Corky had walked into Spanish, nodding and smiling at his teacher Señora O'Brien, that he began to wonder if there hadn't been something strange about the way the kid had just handled himself.

That night Guy printed the set of pictures he'd promised Corky of the Cold Spring Harbor game.

In the library the following day, during study period, he hid the photos inside the binding of his history notebook, planning to leave them in the senior class president's mailbox after school. He was leafing through them when someone with gentle fingers suddenly put hands over his eyes.

116

A little girl's voice asked, "Guess who?"

Guy felt the fingers.

"Three guesses!" said the little girl's voice.

"Okay. Uhm . . . Amy Silverstein!"

"Drat!" Amy removed her hands. "How'd you know?"

"I'm psychic."

"That's okay. I'm not feeling well, myself. Can I join you?"

"Of course."

Amy sat down. "Studying?"

"History. You?"

"French," said Amy, casually turning Guy's notebook toward her to see the cover. It spun on the table and most of the photos spilled out, onto the floor.

"Now look what you've done!" Flustered, Guy dropped to his knees.

Amy jumped down to help. "I'm sorry. Why didn't you say you were hiding your famed collection of dirty French postcards?"

The librarian at the front of the room was checking out books when she heard chairs shuffling down at the other end. Without looking up, she stamped the inside of a book and in a loud, crisp voice warned, "Quiet, back there! This is the *library!*"

"Shucks!" Amy winked at Guy. "I thought it was the Oval Room of the White House!"

"Very funny!" Guy snatched the photos from her fingers.

"Easy!" Amy raised a hand in surrender. "Relax!"

"I am relaxed!" Guy insisted, banging his head on the underside of the table.

"What are they pictures of?"

"Corky at the Cold Spring Harbor game."

"Can I see?" asked Amy, again in her little girl whisper. Guy handed them back to her.

Amy scanned the photos, quickly placing one behind the other, making a strained point of not appearing too interested in the subject matter. "Nice photography," she allowed.

Without knowing it, the camera in her eye was doing

117

its own focusing and clicking. Sighing sarcastically, she commented, "How 'bout our number one jock? Sure has a nice set of calves, don't you think?"

Guy grabbed the pictures away from her once more and again banged his head on the roof of the table.

"Ouch!" Amy yelped, saving him the trouble of complaining. She sat down again. "Didn't that hurt?"

" 'Course not!" the new he-man sloughed it off as he took his seat.

"Okay. Tell Aunt Amy everything. How's fraternity life?"

"How should I know?" Guy whispered, reassembling his photos.

"Aren't you *pledging?*" she asked in distaste.

"Nope."

Confused, Amy switched tones. "But I thought. . ."

"Trouble with you, *Aunt* Amy . . . is you think too much. Anyone ever tell you that?"

Amy ignored the insult. "But why not?" she asked. "What happened? Change your mind?"

"Something like that," Guy answered under his breath.

"Tell me," Amy said with enough interest and sudden warmth that Guy knew she really cared.

"I never even got to pledge. They didn't accept me."

"But why?" she asked, bewildered.

"Why do you think, egghead? Look at me!"

Amy snapped open her briefcase and removed her eyeglasses. Putting them on the bridge of her nose, spinsterlike, she reviewed Guy up and down as if appraising a statue. "All right. I'm looking. Now tell me what happened with the fraternity." She tapped her fingers on the table.

"Isn't this where I came in?" He sighed.

"Probably. Why don't you stay and see it again?" She grinned.

"You're really quick, you know that?"

"Greased lightning! What happened?"

"Nothing. They didn't want me."

"But what about Corky?"

118

"What about him?" Guy removed Amy's glasses and placed them on the table.

"Well, if the Greek god put you up, wouldn't that practically guarantee your canonization?"

"Apparently not."

"Pourquoi, mon chéri?"

"English, Amy. I'm a simple peasant from central Long Island."

"But why, my dear?"

"Who knows? Let's say I'm not athletic enough."

"Balls!" declared Amy climbing atop her soap box. "That's the trouble with the world. Each man wants bigger balls than the next. You hurl your little leather testicles around baseball diamonds, bigger ones around football fields, basketball courts. Even cannon balls are enormous balls of war!"

"Hold it!" said Guy, before paraphrasing Corky. "Save the political stuff for your smarter friends."

"All right. I do get carried away. But I mean it. If those jerks measure acceptability by your performance on an athletic field, then all I can say is I'm glad I'm a girl!"

"So am I, or else you'd understand how right they are."

"All right, Guy. You asked for it. What are you doing Friday night?"

"This Friday?"

"I do not mince words. *This Friday!*"

"Nothing. Going to the movies."

"Forget it. Plans canceled! You're coming with me. The Gadflys are having a Thanksgiving party at Leonard Hauser's—though I can't imagine what we have to be thankful for—I want you to meet some of *our* people and find out there's more to a man than how well he fills a jockstrap."

"Wanna feel my muscle?" Guy popped his arm up in front of Amy.

She looked at him, puzzled. "Sure. Want to feel my pulse?"

Guy stood, collected his books and photos and slapped Amy on the back. The husky-voiced caveman then growled, "Se ya Friday night, kid. We've got a date."

That night, alone in the dark of her bedroom, Amy developed the photos she had fast zipped through in the library that afternoon. Reviewing them in the privacy of her head, she could now take the time to linger over each shot.

Her subconscious soon had the pictures moving in her mind and she saw Corky coming to life in slow, graceful motion. Eventually, the static film dropped its celluloid limitations and found a life of its own.

As Amy floated into an ungoverned sleep, she hardly realized her hand had drifted down between her legs. It was another Amy who directed her fingers to comb their way through the curled hairs to the sensitive membranes inside.

When next the football player in her head raced through a sunny field of flowers, he wore not a stitch of clothing.

Across her mind he ran, a naked animal.

No doubt about it. She was in love.

20

When Evelyn Silverstein heard the front doorbell, she ran to the hall mirror, fluffed her hair and straightened her dress. She opened the door excitedly, and promptly tried masking the letdown she felt when her daughter's escort for the evening turned out to be not a Robert Taylor, but a Mickey Rooney.

"Guy!" She half-smiled. "Nice to see you. Here—give me that ridiculous coat. Must weigh more than you! Amy's not quite ready; you know women, ha-ha, so you'll just have to put up with me for a while."

"My pleasure," said Guy, following her into the living room.

"Well?" Evelyn stretched her arms in presentation. "Don't you just adore French furniture? Every piece a genuine copy of Louis the Fourteenth. Such an elegant style, no?"

To make certain Evelyn understood interior decorating was not his field, Guy shrugged his disinterest.

The tour continued. Evelyn pointed out her precious porcelain collection—dainty cups and delicate vases; pointed out her impressive display of crystal ware—wine glasses and water goblets; and then pointed out her husband, meek and prematurely gray, sitting in a corner, hidden behind the current *TV Guide*.

"And this is Amy's Daddy!"

"Hello, Dr. Silverstein." Guy extended his hand.

Dr. Silverstein sat up straight and shook hands. "Amy's mentioned you."

"Nothing she can't print, I hope."

The Silversteins chuckled politely.

"Have a seat. I'll tell Amy you're here." Evelyn left the room.

Guy sat on a pastel blue pristine couch. He and Dr. Silverstein smiled at one another until at last the doctor spoke. "Been reading about Ed Sullivan."

"Oh?"

"Imagine putting that show together every week?"

"Hmm," Guy agreed.

"One thing I don't like."

"What's that?"

"Animal acts. Dogs dressed up like people. Bears on trampolines. There's no dignity, the Royal Ballet following tumbling penguins."

"Are you boring this poor boy, Howard?" Evelyn returned.

"We were talking about 'The Ed Sullivan Show.'"

"Leave it to Howard to go on about most any topic in the world. You never met anyone who likes to talk so much."

Guy searched for something to say.

"So!" Evelyn patted her knees as she sat next to Guy.

"You two kids just running off into the night like a pair of gypsies?"

"No. We're going to a party. Didn't Amy tell you?"

"Amy-tells-me-nothing!" Evelyn hit the side of the couch with an open hand.

Guy hoped he hadn't divulged classified information.

"You'll know what it's like someday, Guy, when you're a parent."

"No kids for me." Guy shook his head. "I'm raising puppies."

Evelyn smiled wryly. "It's easy to see why you and Amy are friends."

Amy saved the day, rushing in with her loden parka. *"Sorry* to keep you waiting!" she said, and Guy knew she really meant it.

"No need to worry." Evelyn was calm. "Your father and I have been very entertaining."

"Well, good night." Dr. Silverstein got up from his chair.

"Howard?" Evelyn questioned in a surprised tone.

"Seven-thirty." Howard pointed to his watch. " 'Wagon Train.' " He looked at Guy and Amy. "Have a good time," he said, and left the room.

"Nice meeting you!" Guy called after him.

"Guess we'll be off," said Amy.

"Just where is it you're going, darling?" Evelyn inquired.

"To a friend's."

"What if we should have to reach you?"

"Why should you have to reach me, Mother?"

"Who knows? A million reasons. An emergency."

"Like what?"

"A fire in the apartment."

"If there's a fire in the apartment, Mother, don't take the time to call me. Run!"

"Who was it always said children would be a comfort in my old age?"

"I don't know, Mother. Who said that?"

"Amy, if I could remember, I swear I'd take them to court!"

"I wouldn't blame you. Good night."

Amy led Guy through a light snow flurry, down Vesper Street, into an old Victorian house alive with noise and activity.

They stumbled through the crowded living room, over to a corner where Leonard Hauser, their host, was holding court. Leonard brought the newcomers into the conversation telling them, "I was just saying how our quagmire of social amenities weighs us down and retards our progress."

"And?" Amy asked.

"And that perhaps even obviously secondary graces couldn't withstand the test of time."

Amy exhaled impatiently. "How about an East Coast translation for us non-polylinguals?"

"Sure." Leonard puffed his unlit pipe. "I'm suggesting that we all take our clothes off right now, break down these walls and see which of you girls has the best tits!"

"Trust Leonard to bring any discussion down to basics," said Marge.

"Trust basics to bring themselves down," answered Leonard, very smug.

"This is supposed to be a Thanksgiving party, Leonard. Let's be a little more festive."

"What shall I do, Amy? Fart 'The Lord's Prayer'?"

Amy would not be intimidated. "Don't bother. With your rhythm you'd be flat and off-key."

As this attempted battle of wits went on, Guy looked around, taken with the lack of good looks in the room. He knew these kids. Knew them well. Outcasts.

With few exceptions, these were the students everyone else made fun of as they walked to school, these brainy types who were always dashing to violin lessons or spending hours studying. These oddballs with thick eyeglasses and acne who never went to football games or Darcy's; never joined sororities or fraternities, these valedictorians and merit scholarship winners.

In one circle someone was reading aloud a poem and in another a heavy political argument raged. Occupants of a third circle were locked in some Zen yoga trance.

Guests drank spicy cider and munched on home-baked cookies. Had Guy but known, he could have had Birdie cater the entire affair.

"Attention, everyone. Please!" A squat girl with a loud voice clapped her hands until the room grew quiet. "Welcome to another Gadfly gathering. Tonight, in celebration of Thanksgiving, some of us have put together a little entertainment."

Polite applause.

"Thank you. You're very kind. Now if you'll just shift around this way, you'll be able to see the Gadfly players on parade!"

More applause. A lanky fellow carrying oak tag posters entered the room. He held up the first sign and displayed it to the seated group:

THE GADFLYS PRESENT—
UNCENSORED NEWS OF THE YEAR

Applause. A second sign was placed over the first.

ACT I. INTERNATIONAL NEWS

Two boys walked out. One wore a white rubber bathing cap. A pillow stuffed under his shirt made him very fat. The other boy had a long paper cone attached to his nose and his beard was darkened with burnt cork.

Khrushchev and Nixon. People applauded as they caught on.

The politicians acted out the famous Moscow "kitchen debate," except Khrushchev exchanged ideologies in perfect English while Nixon enunciated only in Russian.

The skit ended. Everyone applauded and Guy gave Amy a short jab, letting her know what a good time he was having. She jabbed him back.

A new sign appeared.

ACT II. NATIONAL NEWS

The boy who'd just played Khrushchev now came out in a floppy golf hat, carrying a golf bag. Eisenhower.

He was followed by a boy in blackface. The squat girl who'd introduced the show joined the act in silly, dark bangs which drooped to her nose. Mamie Eisenhower. She carried an oversized bottle of gin in both hands and wobbled about, drunk.

The skit involved the black fellow trying to convince Eisenhower to do something about integration. But Ike, with a golf ball to hit and a wife to sober, had no time.

Howls of delight.

The skit ended with Mamie collapsing on top of Ike's golf ball.

Another sign.

ACT III. LOCAL NEWS

The applause didn't stop as the squat girl now entered in a blonde wig. She displayed, under the tightest of woolen sweaters, enormous falsies. Sticking these balloon breasts high in the air, she bent forward, assuming a Marilyn Monroe-type kissing gesture.

The audience loved it, yelling, whistling, laughing.

A football player barreled in. He wore an oversized helmet, outlandish shoulder pads and carried a deflated football.

People cheered as the athlete drooled on the floor. And on the front of the drooling football player's jersey the numbers, though sloppily sewn on, were nonetheless unmistakable. 33. Corky.

The fellow was Corky and the girl Ro-Anne. It hit Guy like a slap in the face.

The football player walked up to "Ro-Anne" placed a hand on one of her exaggerated breasts and stuttered, "Duh, someone flattened my f-f-football, Ro-Anne. I-I-I can't go on wit-out it. What do I dooz?"

"Ro-Anne" responded by removing one of her breasts, which turned out to be a real football. Offering it to him she breathed heavily, à la Monroe, "Here, Corky. Take one of mine."

That really broke everyone up. As the audience stomped and whistled, Guy looked at Amy. Unable to meet his gaze, she lowered her eyes and reached over, squeezing his hand, her way of apologizing for what was going on. He squeezed back, hard, his way of letting her know how livid he was.

The painful skit ended and everyone cheered.

Amy leaned over. "I don't want you to get the wrong idea."

Guy jumped up and ran out of the crowded room, into a bedroom.

Amy followed.

"Can we go?" he said, turning to face her. His face had flushed red.

"Go?"

"Leave! Get the hell out of here. I hate it."

"I think you're overreacting."

"You can think any damn thing you like. Coming with me?"

"Hey, settle down." Amy took a step toward him.

"I am settled down!" He backed away. "I just don't like it here. Don't like these people. You coming with me or not?"

"What's gotten you so stirred up?"

"What the hell do you think?"

"It wasn't meant to be taken seriously."

"I might've expected something like this from them. The others. Your so-called jocks. They're supposed to be the cold, vicious ones, aren't they?"

"I suppose."

"They're the ones always making fun of you and me, right?"

"Right."

"So here we are and everyone pretends to be on some different plane of communication; some damn aloof awareness. Terrific. Well, I don't care if Leonard Hauser can fart 'The Lord's Prayer.' You're all no better than the rest of them. They laugh at your ugliness and you laugh at their weaknesses and it all stinks!"

Amy and Guy stared at each other, while he tried to catch his breath. Finally he sighed. "I think I'm starting to calm down."

"Good. Good for you. I admire your loyalty and your passion for something you believe in."

"I don't need a review of my performance."

"It comes free with the rest of the evening's entertainment."

"I might've guessed."

Amy walked over to Guy and took his hand. "Come on, Slugger. Let's go back to the party. Give us another chance."

Guy quietly agreed. "But not for long. I've got an important football game to cover tomorrow."

"Football?" Amy pondered with fake naïveté. "That anything like a casaba melon with an appendix scar?"

Guy chased her out of the room.

Across town, Corky was getting ready for bed.

"Leave the door open, son!" his father instructed from downstairs.

"Don't worry, Dad!" Corky yelled back. "I won't have trouble tonight."

"Let's not take chances. Leave it open so I can hear!"

No sense arguing with the old man. Corky left the door open.

In his bathroom, clad in pajama bottoms, Corky took the small plastic bottle from the medicine cabinet. Coach Petrillo had given it to him that afernoon.

This season the nights before a game had become hell. Once asleep, Corky would bolt awake from a horrifying dream. Afterward, his anxiety compounded, the fear of another nightmare returning kept him awake, turning in his bed until it became light outside his window.

As the season progressed, his bad dreams had gotten more and more frightening. When he'd finally told Petrillo about it, the coach had said he'd take care of it.

Friday afternoon Petrillo had called Corky into his small office adjacent to the locker room. Closing the door behind his star player, the coach handed him the small container. "You mention this to no one, understand?"

Corky nodded.

"Listen carefully. Take a pink pill tonight, before bed. You'll sleep real soundly, so be sure to set the alarm."

Corky looked at the plastic bottle.

127

"When you get up in the morning," Petrillo went on, "take a red one. Understand?"

"What are they?"

"The pinks will help you relax, let you sleep, and the reds are called amphetamines. Nothing to 'em. Just like a few cups of coffee, only more energy. Okay?"

"Okay."

"Now put it some place safe, hide them and get your butt outta here!"

"Thanks, I . . ."

Petrillo patted his ass and sent him on his way.

Corky stared at the pink pill in his hand. *Oh, well, Coach must know what he's doing.* He popped it into his mouth, slurped some water from the faucet and then looked in the mirror. The image on the other side smiled back. Messing his hair, he growled his menacing quarterback sneer.

Corky brushed his hair back into place and smiled again. Once more, the face of a movie star.

He flexed a bicep at his reflection and kneaded the round hardness.

Stiffening, he punched himself in the stomach. Tight as ever.

Having passed evening's inspection, he sprinkled athlete's-foot powder between his toes, went to bed and was soon asleep.

The nightmare wouldn't start for another two hours.

21

Amy sat cross-legged in a corner, arguing about modern poets.

Guy was on the other side of the room, listening to an oddly shaped girl strumming a guitar.

Bored, he waved to Amy, signaling that it was time to leave. The party was breaking up anyway.

After fetching their coats, Guy and Amy said good night. Leonard said he sure hoped they'd had a shitty time and they assured him they had.

It was snowing harder as they walked home. A windless snow with large flakes that stuck to everything.

Amy wrapped her arm in Guy's. "Well?"

"They're kind of a strange bunch," he told her.

"I suppose. Still, a lot more interesting than your snap-crackle-and-pop crowd at Darcy's."

"I'm not so sure."

"Don't be asinine. *Their* idea of a stimulating evening is sitting around watching the ice cream melt."

"And your friends would rather sit around trading insults."

"Please! Once you realize most of that abrasiveness is only to sell you on how bright they are, you can relax, because they're only trying, odd as it seems, to get you to like them."

"You're a great analyzer, Amy."

"So why am I so confused?"

"Beats me."

He kicked at the rising snow.

Like a demon let loose, Corky's dream crept out of his subconscious and played on his brain. . . .

Carefree, he sees himself running with a football toward some faraway rainbow.

Looking down, he sees the ground suddenly covered with snakes. Hissing, they coil around him, tongues spitting, fangs snapping for his legs. The faster he runs, the thicker they grow.

Suffocating in his dream, falling through the air, he screams. No noise comes out. . . .

Next thing Corky knew, he was sitting up in bed, awake, shaking and clammy with sweat.

At least this time he hadn't cried out, waking his parents and a sleeping neighborhood. Too drugged.

Groggy and confused, he soon fell asleep again. Fully at work, the Seconal sealed off his terror. For now.

Ro-Anne wondered if the steaks would ever arrive.

She'd been stuck with Lester and her mother in the red plastic leather booth of the Cattle Car restaurant all evening, watching them wade through several extra-dry Beefeater martinis.

Lester was her mother's boyfriend of seven months. Big, surly and divorced, Ro-Anne assumed from his gruff manner and extravagant style that he was Mafia-affiliated. In truth, he owned an air conditioning factory outside town.

Draped over her gentleman friend, Marian opened the top two buttons of his shirt, slipped her hand inside and massaged his hairy chest, telling him what a *hunk* he was. Ro-Anne was repelled by it all.

"Don't look so unhappy!" Marian slurred. "She's a football widow is what she is! Sixteen in a few months and already in mourning."

"Cut it out!" Ro-Anne pouted.

"Here." Marian eased a martini glass toward her daughter. "Have some of this. It'll cheer you up."

"Muth-thur!" Ro-Anne pushed the gin away. "Can't we eat?"

"Sure. Soon as we finish drinking." Marian held a hand to her chest, stifling a hiccup. Then she gazed into Lester's bloodshot eyes and twirled a lock of his thin hair. "Okay, handsome?"

"Whatever you girls say. Sky's the limit!" This from the Diamond Jim Brady of Waterfield.

In time Marian and Lester downed their third "tinis" and the steaks were served. Ro-Anne concentrated on eating rather than watching her mother playfully cutting Lester's meat and feeding him like a baby.

These were the times she wondered if Corky was worth all this celibacy. Girls had always meant competition to Ro-Anne. Since she had never sought their full trust, her girl friends were no more than telephone companions.

With no one special to play with this long football season, she'd been spending time with Marian and Lester. And Lester, dammit, was so revolting she didn't even care to flirt with him.

Marian, a tall, youthfully attractive, overly done, blonde, with an ample figure and full smile, seemed too good for him.

She had grown up in Philadelphia and had been twice married before she met Allan Sommers. He was a workaholic twice her age, short, stout, and Marian would never have looked twice but for the fact he owned a chain of supermarkets around the central Long Island area.

Marian often said, "Good girls go to heaven. The rest of us settle for Palm Beach and mink."

She and Allan got married after a five-week whirlwind courtship. They settled in Waterfield on his family's estate there, and Ro-Anne was born a year and a half later.

Soon bored with domesticity, Marian was even more bored with the half-hearted affair she was having with a too-young, too-dumb—if gorgeous—check-out clerk from one of Allan's supermarkets.

She was about to ask for a divorce when Allan suddenly checked-out himself. Collapsing from exhaustion at work, he knocked over an enormous Campbell's soup display in aisle 5. As bargain hunters fled, Allan lay there, sprawled between rolling cans of green pea and chicken noodle.

After three days' rest in the hospital, he was told he could go home. He was being escorted down the corridor, toward the elevator, when he died in his wheelchair. Marian and Ro-Anne were fixed for life. . . .

Finally! Ro-Anne thought as Marian and Lester downed the last of their after-dinner drinks.

Lester proceeded to drive them home in his new Cadillac Eldorado, proudly demonstrating as he steered, the power windows, brakes, antennae and cigarette lighter. Ro-Anne could hardly wait to get home.

Marian invited them both into her Las Vegas palatial living room for a nightcap. Ro-Anne could imagine nothing more boring and declined. She went to bed with the latest *Glamour,* to find out what shades of lipstick were the coming rage.

After another hour of brandies and cigars, Marian and Lester climbed into bed.

Ro-Anne heard their door close and put down her magazine. Curious to know just what was going on, she waited a few minutes and then tiptoed down the hall, putting her ear to the door.

There seemed to be a great deal of sloshing about, a lot of heavy breathing, heaving and ho-ing. A verbal romantic, Marian was moaning, "Oh . . . baby . . . beautiful . . . too much . . .!"

Sufficiently repulsed, Ro-Anne tiptoed back, plopped onto her frilly four-poster bed, and cried herself to sleep.

Down the hall, Marian moaned, still trying to stiffen the soft love-muscle of her boyfriend. But numbed by too much alcohol, it simply would not rise to the occasion.

Marian coaxed and stimulated, lubricated and rubbed. Lester started to snore.

Time to quit. Marian rolled over next to him and slurred, almost coherently, "A hard man is good to find . . ."

Then she too went to sleep.

As Amy and Guy arrived at her garden apartment, Guy climbed the steps of the outside stoop. Amy remained on the ground and suddenly they were the same height.

"Did you know this is how Alan Ladd makes movies?" Guy asked.

"Standing in the snow?"

"No. Standing on a crate. Most people don't know it, but he is, in reality, only three feet tall."

"Amazing."

"Yeah. They have to surround him with little trees and tiny horses. Undersized sets. Everything."

"Sounds like *Gulliver's Travels.*"

"Sort of."

"Well, Guy. Good night."

"Good night, Amy. And thanks for a most . . . informative evening."

"Most informative evenings should be a way of life."

"I'll write that down."

"Good. You may kiss me good night. For Thanksgiving."

Guy took advantage of their rare equal height status and placing a hand on Amy's shoulder, brushed a white flake from her hair and then kissed her on the cheek.

Amy smiled sweetly, and it occurred to Guy that for an ugly girl she was surprisingly beautiful.

December

22

Corky played as never before.

Valley Stream's Central High wasn't much competition, still the quarterback could do no wrong. His feet had never exerted such strength. His endurance stretched to new peaks as he orchestrated touchdowns, one seemingly easier than the next. The day was his.

Coach Petrillo sat on the sideline bench, calm and confident.

Guy was so charged up by Corky's extraordinary performance, he disregarded his budget and clicked off five rolls of film.

Ro-Anne shivered in her skimpy cheerleader's costume and screamed at the top of her lungs. The bigger the win, the more passionate the romance that evening.

Thirteen seconds remaining and Corky intercepted still another pass. As he raced down the field, without interference, an entire stadium followed with their voices. Cork-ee! . . . Cork-ee! . . . Cork-ee! they chanted.

He crossed into the end zone, the gun went off, the crowd went wild,

A walk-over: Eagles on top, 43–6!

Hoisting Corky aloft, teammates carried him to the lockers. Jubilant spectators left the bleachers, mobbing the field.

As the stands emptied, Carl Henderson remained rigid, staring ahead.

Dora studied his silence before placing a concerned hand on his lap.

He turned to her. "I don't understand it, Dora. I always knew how I wanted him to grow up. Always. I planned it that way forever. But he's so much more than even I dreamed . . . so much more, it confuses me."

Her small hand patted his tight fist.

Carl gazed ahead at nothing. "He makes me feel small, dammit. Small and unimportant. My own son! I don't like it, Dora and I hate myself for not liking it. . . ."

She squeezed his fist. "You want to go to the locker room?"

"No, Dora"—he shook his head slowly—"let's just go home."

Guy was taking pictures all around the locker room. Though no film remained in his camera, he hardly cared. He knew how much everyone enjoyed having their picture taken and had finally found the ticket to ingratiating himself with the jocks. He also had a knack for catching them at their beastly best.

Chuck Troendle, stripped to the waist, shoving Calvin, in full uniform, into the steaming shower.

"Hold it!"—*click-flash!*

Jenkins, dripping wet, a towel around his middle, proving in an argument he could bend a locker door.

"Don't move!"—*click-flash!*

Two others in a playful face-slapping exchange. *Click-flash!*

In no time, Guy had snapped a full roll of no-film.

Amy had dinner with her mother, her father and Jackie Gleason.

She finished her fruit salad and excused herself.

"Should we call you for 'Your Hit Parade'?" Dr. Silverstein asked, unable to imagine anyone anyplace but in front of their Sylvania when Dorothy Collins was singing.

The slamming of the bedroom door prevented her hearing him.

Amy went over the pile of work she'd created for herself that evening, then stared at the black telephone on her desk.

Saturday night. Thanksgiving weekend. College boys home from school, calling girl friends.

There was energy out there, vibrating. Something going on. Something she'd never been a part of. Never . . . not really.

As Amy sat at her desk, a cold and familiar loneliness returned. . . .

It was the Boy Scouts' Halloween party. Amy and her eighth-grade girl friends had arrived a little after seven-thirty.

Slinky paper skeletons and fuzzy jack-o'-lanterns covered the walls. Orange and black crepe paper streamers crisscrossed below the ceiling.

Thirteen-year-old Amy, wearing a new woolen skirt and checkered cotton blouse, stooped low, trying her best to look shorter than five-nine.

She and the other girls were introduced around the room to all the scouts. As feared, most were tiny. At the end of a row of little men, however, was Michael Kutscher.

God, he's gorgeous, thought Amy, fixing her eyes on the dark-haired, pockmarked string bean.

The party was a boring affair, spent in foolish games of the holiday—dunking for apples, pin-the-tail-on-the-donkey, telling ghost stories.

Once the parent chaperones had left the room, someone suggested they play post office. A few giggles, a twitter here and there, no real protests and suddenly everyone was deciding who should get whose mail.

Amy was the fourth girl's name listed, and when it came up, her heart pounded nervously. The boys' hat was passed and the name drawn to be her mailman was . . . Michael Kutscher.

What luck, thought Amy. Hey, maybe there really was a happily-ever-after for Cinderella's ugly stepsister too.

Another hat was handed to Michael to determine how much postage Amy's letter would carry. He dipped in and pulled out the answer.

Air mail. Six cents! Six kisses on the lips! Amy couldn't conceal her excitement. Where was Charlotte Brontë when she needed her?

Michael Kutscher signaled for her to follow. She glided into the supply closet, directly behind him.

137

Once inside, he closed the door. Never saying a word, he reached up and pulled the metal beaded string, switching off the naked bulb in the tight space.

From the outer room came whistles, laughter and cat-calls,

Alone in the darkness, the two of them together, Amy braced for the romance to come. An extended moment in paradise.

Michael stood right next to her, breathing nervously. He took her hand, and, holding it tight, inquired softly, "Amy?"

"Yes, Michael? . . ."

"Listen. Okay if I just kiss your hand six times! That way they'll hear it in the other room and think we're really kissing. That okay with you?"

"Sure, Michael." Amy wished she was dead. "Who wants to kiss for real, anyway?"

"Who, indeed?" Amy asked, snapping back from her recollection. The memory was painful and she wished she knew why she chose to relive it so often. She bit the eraser off the end of her pencil and stared at the telephone again. Wasn't it ever going to ring? She studied late into the night.

Dressed, radiant, perfumed and fuming, Ro-Anne couldn't imagine what had gone wrong. Nine-thirty and still no sign of Corky.

Was it possible she was being stood up? Out of the question. Five minutes. She'd give him the next five minutes to phone or show and that was it.

Fifteen minutes later, Ro-Anne vowed that at ten o'clock, no matter what, she'd step out of her clothes and into a tub of cold cream. If he arrived, Marian would simply have to explain her unavailability. Miss Hawaiian Moon Ball was pissed.

Where was he?

Maybe she should call. No. What if he's out with someone else? Someone prettier? He's tired of me . . . wants out . . . I can't give him enough . . . don't be ridiculous. Ro-Anne caught herself in time to stop the tantrum. Who's prettier than me?

She rushed to the mirror. Thank God. Still the fairest of them all. She picked up her hairbrush and started counting off her nightly strokes. Two, three, four—Oh, well—seven, eight, nine— You can't have everything—thirteen, fourteen—And why not, dammit? She slammed the brush onto the glass-topped vanity table. To hell with Corky. I'll find my own amusement.

She wandered downstairs into the living room and spent the evening playing gin rummy with Lester. To her surprise, she had a far better time than she would have imagined. While her mother sat in front of the television, thumbing through *Town and Country,* Ro-Anne sat across from Lester, playing an off-and-on, hesitant game of footsies with him under the table.

So by twelve-thirty, when she decided to cash in her chips, not only had she gotten him aroused, she was also in debt for a little over thirty-eight thousand dollars.

Ro-Anne crawled into bed and cried into her lace hankie. She cried because she'd been stood up. She—the holder of more beauty trophies than anyone this side of the Long Island Sound.

Sniffling, she struggled to think of better moments, happier times . . . like the carnival night she and Corky first met. She let the memory sweep her away, back to the hurdy-gurdy music, the twirling colored lights, Corky's powerful strength, the intensity in his smile and . . . No! No! No!

Ro-Anne opened her eyes. She would not give him the satisfaction. Let him suffer!

Instead, she closed her eyes once more and fought to remember back to still earlier days, still happier times. The handkerchief dropped to the floor as she brought her hand to the tuft of hair between her legs. Although she knew masturbation was reserved for sad and lonely ladies, she didn't mind being just a little playful with herself while she smiled through an old rerun of that last night of her two summers' ago—let's see, it was 1956—summer vacation. . . .

Ro-Anne stood before the full length mirror, naked and

beautiful. Turning slowly, she examined herself from all angles. Each was better than the last.

She brushed her warm hands along her ribs, down her curving hips, into the darkened crevasses of her sacred privates, then back up to the flatness of her stomach and the roundness of her exquisite breasts.

She pinched each nipple hard and watched in the mirror as they sprang to life, saluting in response to her touch.

Quite a gift she was. Quite a package.

And what a summer it had been. For openers she'd excited the handsome, twenty-two-year-old tennis pro. He couldn't believe she was only thirteen—"Wadda ya mean, *only!*" Then there was the bright seventeen-year-old bus-boy on his way to Amherst who put down *War and Peace* so he could pick her up. And of course the owner's son who at nineteen still had pimples, but made up for them by showering her with cuddly stuffed animals. And she'd certainly never forget what'shisname, the shy cashier who worked at the front desk and one night allowed her to play with the cash register while she sat on his lap.

A summer of enticement to be sure, and after that night's Labor Day celebration, she and her mother would be going home, back to Waterfield.

It was Marian who had first suggested the two of them spend the summer at Blueridge, a particularly fashionable resort in the Connecticut Berkshires. "Good hunting!" Marian had assured her thirteen-year-old daughter. And she ought to know. After all, as Ro-Anne had grown, she and Marian had become less and less like mother and daughter. More like sisters. And since Marian wanted to look younger and Ro-Anne older, it was a perfect pairing. Fittingly, they'd gone off—as a team—to Blueridge for a summer's scouting.

Marian worked the long, crowded cocktail lounge while Ro-Anne cruised the Teen Club. Both drove the male population of the place crazy.

Under Marian's guidance, Ro-Anne flirted coquettishly. But she never gave a thing.

"The uglies have to put out to keep their men," Marian coached. "Not us. We're far too in demand to give to any

140

but the best. You gotta save it, Ro. Save it for the one man good enough. You're worth it."

Ro-Anne saved it through the whole summer.

Now, on this last night, she dressed for the Teen Ball.

After fastening the snaps on her dark-green full-skirted crinoline dress, she stepped into her two-inch pumps, fluffed her blonde hair in place and once again stood before the mirror.

She had to admit it. She was a knockout.

The Teen Ball was already crowded when she made her belated entrance at ten o'clock—keep 'em waiting—and the seventeen-year-old busboy and the owner's son and a dozen others were pleased as the fruit punch to see the well-tanned, stunning vision in dark green that had finally wandered in.

One by one they came to her, all evening. Ro-Anne agreed to dance with the better-looking boys, feigning exhaustion whenever one of the outcasts dared ask.

She went outside with the owner's son for a few minutes, shared a swig from his bourbon flask—hated it—and insisted they get back to the ballroom as soon as he started fingering his way through her golden hair.

She danced. She smiled. She spoke only in soft, seductive tones. She allowed her eyes to weave their hypnotic spell, hinting of untold pleasures within. She charmed them all for two hours until the final stroke of midnight when the three-piece band played "Good Night Ladies."

Everyone began drifting out of the Blue Note Ballroom, away from the main house, back to cottages, bungalows and suites.

Adolescent couples walked arm in arm to the white arch at the top of the hill. There, as an early September wind whistled about, hinting at the death of summer, they embraced. All the boys kissed the girls with whom they'd paired off during the course of the summer, the week, the evening.

And Ro-Anne, a young and beautiful princess, walked past the arch, past couples kissing beneath the stars in a meadow of pines, past all the sad good-bys and fond farewells and went back to her room, by herself. Not a white knight in sight.

She lay naked on her bed, the green crinoline dress spread out next to her. Her blue eyes wandered over to the full length mirror, locking as she discovered her reflected loveliness.

As she lay there gazing at herself, she thought of the dance and all those boys she'd excited. Massaging a breast with one hand and her sacred locked vault with the other, she couldn't understand why, with so many attentive suitors, she felt so saddened, so very much alone, so . . .

No!—dammit, no! Again Ro-Anne snapped open her eyes. Hell, what's the good of living in the past if when you get there it isn't pleasurable?

The thought of fantasizing about playing with herself while she actually played with herself so upset her, she quickly completed the act, rolled over onto her stomach and let a few new tears send her off to dreamland.

Of course she had no way of knowing Corky's red pill had spent its magic; that, having arrived home depleted, he'd laid down for what he thought would be ten minutes and slept until six the following morning.

23

A private meeting was held early Monday before first period in Coach Petrillo's tiny office. Corky and his coach agreed that relaxing at night and then being stimulated the following morning was just what he needed.

Saturday's game at Rockville Centre's Southside High would be the last of the season. A Waterfield victory would make them division champs, allowing the Eagles to compete for the league trophy. Petrillo told Corky to repeat the medication.

Guy awoke Saturday to find a snowstorm raging in his backyard. The ancient steam pipes against the wall coughed and complained.

Rasputin had crept into the room during the cold night, curling into a fur muff at the end of Guy's blanket, displaying rare sociability.

As Guy got out of bed, the cat stretched grandly, a fat ballerina on tipitoes.

Shivering, Guy dropped to the floor for his morning exercises. He noticed it mid-sit-up.

The bottom of his pajamas seemed unusually far from his ankles.

Guy jumped up, found his yardstick and marked off five feet on the wall. Tall and erect, he then scratched a pencil mark directly across the peak of his head. It registered a solid three inches above the five-foot mark.

Guy's eyes popped open. Had those little workers inside his body been stretching the kid these past months while he wasn't looking?

Five-three. *Five foot three!*

Further observation revealed other signs of sudden growth. Above the lip, mingling casually with peach-fuzz, two, no three darkening hairs, practically whiskers.

Guy flung off his pajama pants, frantic to get to the next inspection. Sure enough, south of the border, a light density of fragile blond curls had tentatively begun a clandestine gathering.

If things were finally blossoming, Guy reasoned, could the greatly anticipated, widely discussed joys of masturbation be far behind?

It was Guy Fowler the late-but-finally-growing man-boy who boarded the bus bound for Rockville Centre that snowy morning.

The ride was endless, every inch a milestone. The driver couldn't distinguish sky from expressway.

The half hour trip took two and the battered bus limped into a snow-covered parking lot just before kickoff.

The white sprinkle covering the playing field before

143

the starting gun went off was soon churned to freezing mud by determined cleats.

The wind picked up. Snow beat hard against faces. Red-cheeked players wiped running noses with muddied sleeves. Frozen toes lost feeling. Ice caked around cleats and exposed calves cramped in the bitter chill. Pain was pleasure.

Charged by Coach Petrillo's catalyst, Corky played as if it were an afternoon in May.

Guy was too cold to take pictures. It was snowing so heavily anyway, they'd have only come out looking like poor television reception.

It was a game played in frozen slow motion on a glass surface. When it was over, most of the triumphant Eagles were sneezing.

Petrillo had his best season as his last. For the first time in years, he'd be getting a crack at the regional trophy, which he had been pursuing his entire career.

He made a point of interrupting the celebration in the locker room, standing on a bench and promising—in booming stentorian tones—to drive each of them well past exhaustion, to the brink of cracking; straining and readying his gladiators for the most important contest of all.

The athletes cheered, agreeing they were girded for anything Coach could dole out.

Petrillo was good for his word. During the next two weeks he pushed his boys as never before, keeping them on the field late into the afternoon and sometimes past sunset, into the cold darkness of night. He would have kept them longer—perhaps till dawn—if the field had been equipped with adequate lighting.

Corky poured total energy into the title game against Hempstead High. If Petrillo told him to put in two laps before quitting, he ran three. If Coach ordered fifty push-ups, Corky gave him sixty. Whenever Petrillo whistled a rare ten-minute break, Corky insisted upon having the team back on the field, scrimmaging, in five.

They worked well together. Committed only to winning, Corky and Petrillo made a solemn pact: no second best.

The Friday before Christmas vacation was not a day for education. Festive parties were held in decorated homerooms and students exchanged useless grab-bag gifts purchased for under a dollar.

There were special assembly programs.

An angelic choir of carolers, too flat, was followed by a weary Santa Claus, too thin.

Dr. Potter, too melodramatic, read passages from *A Christmas Carol,* after which the numbed audience had their drooping eyelids further challenged by three girls in purple crepe paper sacks twirling to a recording of "The Dance of the Sugar Plum Fairy."

Ken Crawley, big man on campus, snapped everyone back by reading a letter from Sim Lu, the school's adopted Korean orphan.

The correspondence thanked all the wonderful American students for providing her with money for rice and education. Her one dream in life was to be able to travel to America someday to visit each of them personally and say thank you for Uncle Sam's charity.

Sim Lu's hundreds of parents applauded.

Amy and Guy were assigned to cover the annual Homecoming Dance for fifth-year alumni that evening.

The gym was crowded when they arrived, filled with the class of '54. A scream of recognition occasionally broke through a low murmur as once-familiar faces renewed contact.

The reporters climbed to the top of the bleachers and observed; she with her pad and pen, he with his camera.

"How'd everyone get so old, so fast?" asked Amy.

Guy looked around, mystified. "You realize these people are already out of college!"

College. That far-off place where you went to grow up. An eternity away.

145

Guy looked at Amy. "How many of these girls do you suppose are already married?"

"Most." Amy finished a note in her pad. "Unless they became teachers, nurses or secretaries. Bless the joy of alternatives!"

"Tough darts, Silverstein!" Guy snapped a photo. "It's a man's world!"

"Don't remind me. My nineteen-year-old cousin Jane got engaged last night. My Aunt Bernice phoned in details this morning. You'd think the Japanese had attacked Pearl Harbor again the way Evelyn took the news."

"Wasn't she pleased?"

" 'You know what this means, don't you, Amy dear?' " Amy imitated her mother. " 'Now all the girls in the family are spoken for. All married, pinned or engaged. Now we just have to find you a fella so your father can die a happy man!' "

"May I have your attention, please?!" announced the student body president from behind the microphone.

The noise died down.

"Hi, kids! I'm Ken Crawley!" Big smile. "Well! Here we are at the class of fifty-four's homecoming reunion. Boy, it's been a long five years, huh? Must feel great being back in the ole Eagle gym. What say we all join in the singing of the alma mater?"

The returnees resumed talking.

Corky couldn't sleep.

He tried on his stomach. On his back. His side. Nothing.

The pink ticket to unconsciousness had been in his system an hour and a half, yet here he was, at eleven-thirty, pent-up and anxious, staring at the ceiling. This won't do, he decided, getting out of bed.

In the bathroom, he swallowed another pink pill from Petrillo's bottle.

Back in bed, he was asleep in twenty minutes.

The dream didn't start for another five hours. Scrambling abstract thoughts and dormant fears, it gnawed at his brain. Lucky for him, he slept through it.

He barely heard the alarm in the morning. Groggy and exhausted, he stumbled into the bathroom.

If one pink pill couldn't get him to sleep, it followed one red one wouldn't wake him up. So Corky took two.

In the locker room, getting ready for the game, Corky did not stop talking. Jazzed and overflowing, he bounded from one bench to the next, patting teammates on the back, interrupting conversations with gibberish, telling half-finished stories and disconnected snatches of trivia.

It scared the hell out of Petrillo.

The stands were jammed, not a vacant seat. Kids carried signs and waved pom-poms. The roar of anticipation around the sunny field was deafening.

In the bleachers, Carl and Dora waved to friends.

Chuck Troendle's father pushed his way through their row, commenting, "Well, folks. This is the day we've been waiting for all our lives!"

Carl and Dora smiled.

Just before kickoff, a man presented himself to Guy.

"Hi. Rollings. Ned Rollings of *Newsday*. Your quarterback says I should see you if I want the best pictures of the game."

"He did?"

"We don't usually cover high school sports, but this being a championship game and all, you know. . . "

The reporter handed Guy his card. "If you'll drop off your film, we'll develop. Maybe run a couple shots if they're any good. Five bucks per. Wadda ya say?"

"Will do, mister!" Guy studied the card. "Thanks a million!"

The whistling noise from the stands followed the opening kickoff until the ball was high in the air.

The first half was played tough and scoreless.

Five yards forward. Two back. Six forward. Three back. Nothing exceptional on either side. A tug-of-war at stalemate, both teams evenly matched.

Petrillo's halftime speech was more than his usual rouser. He poured everything into this, his swan song.

When he looked over at his prized quarterback and saw Corky's eyes dancing in their sockets, he started to cry.

These were not his ordinary crocodile tears, used to stimulate guilt and provoke the will to win. This time he meant it.

The Eagles began a second half push, gaining ground until they were first-and-ten, twelve yards from the end zone.

Corky called the play. Ace-in-the-hole runaround.

The ball was hiked. Half the line moved forward to confuse, half dropped back to protect.

Now was the time. The right end was clear, home free in the end zone; Corky was well-protected.

He brought a hesitating arm back to throw the ball, and his head began to swim. Colors reeled within and suddenly nothing made sense. Two of Hempstead's linemen were almost on him, so Corky threw the ball, a perfect bullet, to the end, still in the clear.

Everyone was on their feet screaming and Corky relaxed as the receiver caught the ball and started to run.

Run?! Where was he running?

Corky took a second look, this time in focus, and saw that he hadn't thrown the ball to his right end at all, but directly to Hempstead's defensive halfback ten yards away who, surprised at the gift, was now busting his ass, heading in the opposite direction.

The Hempstead back made it past two Eagles, both still stunned as the crowd, staring in disbelief at the confusion. He rammed his way over a third lineman and then there was only Corky between him and eighty-five yards of open field.

Corky saw him coming, knew what he had to do.

He dove, a miscalculated leap, barely catching the side of a sleeve.

The Hempstead side roared. A hush fell over the Eagles.

Alone, the Hempstead halfback crossed into the end zone. Touchdown!

While one side of the field rose in celebration, the other was plunged into mortification.

Ro-Anne held white-gloved hands over her mouth.

Guy lowered his camera.

Carl stared at the wooden floorboards.

Petrillo couldn't catch his breath.

As the Eagles' defense ran out to try to block the extra point, Coach stood his ground, forcing himself not to lose control.

A defeated Corky wandered past him, onto the bench. He flopped down, disoriented, burying his head in his hands.

Petrillo crouched angrily before his quarterback. "What the hell was that all about?"

Corky looked up, trying to stop the foggy visions spinning everywhere. Squinting, he took a deep breath and then grabbed Petrillo by the lapels, pulling the coach's face smack against his, *"What have you done to me?"* he seethed. *"What the fuck have you done to me, you son of a bitch?"*

Petrillo tried pushing his face away; but it wouldn't budge.

"Do something for me," Corky pleaded. "Help me!"

The noise of the crowd swelled and Corky's attention immediately shifted to see Hempstead miss kicking the extra point.

A natural response from years of training made him automatically jump up and run onto the field. Now he understood the problem. He would not let it beat him. If his muscles still worked when ready to give out, so could his mind.

Incorporating all his intensity, Corky went back and played football.

The ball was kicked off to the Eagles. A scatback receiver caught it and ran to the fifty yard line, where he was stopped by two powerful Hempstead tacklers.

The team huddled, down and disillusioned. Corky tried snapping them out of it, insisting vehemently, *"Listen to me carefully. We're going to win this game!"*

A lineman to his left muttered something about it being a little late for that.

"Hey, shit-face! Goddammit, I'm talking to you!" Corky flared. "We are going to win this game, and anybody doesn't

149

believe me had better damn well get the fuck off this field right now, is that clear?"

Corky's eyes darted face to face around the circle, making ten momentary contacts. Once again, they were all with him.

"Okay. Reverse split. On two. Let's move!"

And they did. With seven minutes left, the squad ignited. Surrounded by blockers, Corky carried the ball into enemy territory. Nothing could stop him. Padded players toppled like toy soldiers.

Touchdown. The Eagles kicked the extra point and moved ahead, 7–6.

Ro-Anne cheered and did her split. Guy clicked his camera. Carl stopped holding his breath. And Petrillo finally caught his.

All was forgiven.

With three minutes to play, Corky flew in from nowhere, Captain Marvel intercepting a Hempstead pass, before dashing forty graceful yards for another touchdown.

The gun went off and the crowd went berserk. The Eagles had their trophy.

24

The locker room was filled with hugs and whoops.

Corky wanted none of it. While winners partied, he sulked.

Petrillo and he avoided eye contact, one more embarrassed than the other.

Corky washed, dressed and pushed his way past happy hordes invading the area. Alone outside, he sucked in a deep breath of cold air. His knees felt weak, as though about to buckle. He clenched his fists as he hurried to his car. It was the only way to keep them from trembling.

When he got home Carl and Dora were in the living room, waiting.

His mother put her slender arms around his waist, expressing her understanding of his pain by holding him tight. Corky kissed her forehead.

"Close one, huh?" Carl came over to place a solid open hand on Corky's shoulder. "For a while I didn't think you'd make it."

"Me neither," Corky agreed.

"Guess we all make mistakes." Carl smiled.

An hour later Ro-Anne and Corky were driving around the back roads in his Chevy. She sat pressed next to him.

"God, you're tense!" She swatted the Styrofoam dice dangling from the windshield.

He floored the gas pedal.

"I love driving fast with you. Reminds me of the Indy five hundred."

The tires screeched as Corky went around a sharp turn, assaulting the brakes.

Ro-Anne suggested going for pizzas. Corky said he wasn't hungry. Besides, he didn't feel like seeing anyone. Just wanted to drive around a while. Not talking. Not thinking. Unwinding.

They sped through the darkening night. Half an hour later, Corky pulled off the road and killed the engine.

Turning, he put his hand behind Ro-Anne's head, drew her to him, and kissed her with such force it startled her.

Pleased, she wrapped her arms around his neck and kissed back.

He warmed his hands under her sweater, wrestling with the ribs of her bra until he found the soft downy flesh of her breasts. When he pinched one of her extended nipples, she moaned with such pleasure he sprang to life against his pants. He lifted the tight sweater up, above her breasts and brought an open mouth to the smoothness of her skin.

While his tongue washed over her breasts, she closed her eyes and scratched his back hard with her long nails.

He took her hand and placed it on top of his crotch. She obligingly stroked it once and, ever the lady, removed it. He took hold of her hand as custom dictated, and brought it back down assuredly, this time orchestrating her fingers to engulf the outline of his erection. She stroked it gently.

While his tongue rolled over her gums, she placed both hands inside his open shirt, squeezing his muscular chest.

As he unzipped his fly with one hand, he used the other to coax her fingers inside his pants, between the metal zipper teeth.

She massaged his Jockey shorts while he chewed on her ear. Now very aroused, he opened his trousers wider. A fast shift around and he had separated her legs. Carefully, he brought a knee to the crotch area of her wrinkled woolen skirt.

She wiggled her way onto his kneecap.

He took her hand and showed how he wanted her to masturbate him. Hesitant at first, she tried pulling away. But he was calm and affirmative as always. His eyes looked down at her, telling of his need and she melted and placed her hand around the fat head of his stiff cock.

Breathing excitedly, he fought to get out of his team jacket and then his shirt. She struggled out of her sweater and bra, then shifted so he could lower the zipper on the side of her skirt.

The warm-up was over. Time to climb into the back seat.

He stroked her hair, kissed her hard and when their lips parted she looked into his dark-green eyes and asked, "How come you tossed the ball to the wrong guy this afternoon?"

Zap! Corky wilted as his spirits took a nose dive. He sat up.

Ro-Anne brought an innocent finger to his lips. "I said the wrong thing."

"No. 'Course not," he groaned.

She sat up quickly and threw her hands around his neck, kissing him, coaxing his tongue back into her mouth.

He pulled back and removed her hands.

"What's wrong?"

"Nothing." Corky positioned himself behind the wheel.

"What are you doing?"

"Nothing. I'm all right."

"I didn't mean anything. . . ."

"Not your fault." He zippered his fly and put his shirt back on.

"You're mad at me!"

"I'm not."

"You are!"

"I'm not." He started the engine.

"Where we going?"

"Let's get a pizza. I'm hungry." He drove off.

"I don't want any pizza. You hate me!"

"I do not."

"Me and my big mouth."

"Forget it."

"You're mad at me. Go on. Admit it."

"Will you stop saying that? Get it straight. *I am not mad at you!*"

"No?"

"*No!*" Corky stared into the night, burned rubber and screeched around a bend in the road. "I'm mad at *me!*"

25

The telephone rang and Ro-Anne filed her nails. It rang again.

Let him wait.

Three rings and she yawned.

After the fourth ring she picked it up and offered a casual "Hello?"

"Hi, sweets!" said Corky.

Long pause. "Who is this?"

"It's *me!* Who'd you think?"

"I wasn't sure. I get so many calls."

Oops! One of *those* moods. "Sorry I was so creepy last night. Wasn't like I planned it that way."

Hard at work on a stubborn cuticle, Ro-Anne dismissed the apology. "Perfectly all right."

"I'll make it up tonight. Honest."

"Tonight?"

"Yeah. We'll do whatever you want. Wherever you want to go."

"Sounds wonderful. Shame I'm busy."

"Busy?"

"Didn't I mention it last night?"

"Mention what?"

"That I'd made other plans."

"Other plans?!" He raised his voice. "What kind of other plans?"

"Just *other* plans."

"What's his name?"

"None of your beeswax!" Ro-Anne filed and smiled. "Besides, it's almost six. A little late to be first asking me out, don't you think?"

"What are you talking about?"

"I'd love to see you, Corky. If only I were free."

"Did I dial the wrong number? Since when do I have to ask you out in advance?"

That was the one she was waiting for. "Since you started treating me like a doormat!"

Oh, Christ. "What doormat?"

"I wouldn't mind so much if it was another woman. That I could compete with. Easy. But obviously I'm no match for a football fetish. So take your sleeping sickness, your lousy tantrums and your teasing games and when you decide it's time to treat me with respect again, maybe we'll talk about it."

There! She'd said it. Now he'd apologize. She'd accept. Everything would be fine.

Except Corky caught on. "Well then, I guess there's nothing left to say."

"I guess not." Ro-Anne blew the dust from her nail.

"Have a good time." Corky tried sounding cheery.

"I will!" she sang.

They both hung up.

Ro-Anne continued filing until the tears rolling down her cheeks made her reach for a tissue.

Corky called Chuck Troendle. "What's on for tonight?" he asked straight out. "Any plans?"

"Nothing special. Me and Jenkins were gonna get together."

"Fine. Why don't we all take a drive or something. Go somewhere. Get loaded. Still got those fake ID's?"

"Sure!" Troendle was eager.

"Good. Tell Jenkins I'm glad he's coming. We'll need a monster like him, case we get in trouble."

"Right. Maybe I should ask Calvin too. He's always good in a brawl."

"Sounds great. I'm just in the mood. Let's meet here in an hour."

As Corky replaced the phone it rang. A regretful Ro-Anne? He hoped so. "Hell-low?" he uttered seductively.

"Hi, Corky. It's me. Guy the photographer."

"Oh." Deep breath. "What is it, kid?"

Guy made sure his voice carried throaty resonance. "Just wanted to say thanks for referring that reporter from *Newsday*. They're going to run two photos of you."

That cheered Corky up. "Hey! Good work."

"I'm on my way to pick them up now. If you want, I could stop off and show you."

"You wouldn't mind?"

"Mind? No. I'd be glad to."

"Okay. But hurry. The guys are coming over, so we won't have much time for—" Corky stopped when he realized the kid might feel slighted when he wasn't asked to join the boys.

"Hey, Corky. Thanks to you, I'm rich. They're giving me ten bucks."

Corky spoke without thinking. "Well, then, maybe you should come along tonight. Buy us a couple of rounds."

Silence on the other end of the wire. *Me* go with *them?* Stay cool, thought Guy. Don't blow it by getting hysterical. "That'd be swell!" he told Corky.

"Okay, kid. Make it snappy."

"Right." Guy hung up wondering what in the world could have prompted Corky to invite him.

Corky hung up, wondering the exact same thing.

Two hours later there were five of them packed into Corky's Chevy, fast heading out of town, straight for trouble. Four bruisers and a shrimp.

Corky was behind the wheel, Chuck Troendle next to him. In the back, Calvin to his left, Jenkins to his right, Guy sat crammed in between.

Jenkins opened a large brown bag and passed around five bottles of Miller's High Life.

"Where to?" Troendle asked Corky.

"I don't know. What do you guys think?"

"Wantagh?" suggested Calvin, taking a slug from his bottle.

"Wantagh sucks!" Jenkins grunted, and that ended discussion on that.

"Roslyn!" Troendle offered.

"Roslyn sucks!"

So much for Roslyn.

"How 'bout Rushport?" asked Corky, a glint in his eye.

"Perfect!" Jenkins responded with a manly belch. "They've got some clowns there I've been dying to get in a dark alley."

Guy gulped.

Corky pumped the gas pedal.

"I feel like bustin' a few heads!" said Calvin.

"Me too," Jenkins agreed.

Guy cracked his knuckles.

Corky saw the kid's fearsome reaction in the rear-view mirror. "What about you, Guy? You itchin' for a fight?"

Guy shrugged. "You know me. Someone starts up. I deck 'em."

Everyone grinned.

"Let's find us a couple'a faggots to rip apart," said Calvin.

"Yeah!" Guy agreed. "Let's cream a few fruits."

"I'd rather find me some girls," said Chuck Troendle.

156

"Yeah!" The idea appealed to Calvin. "Let's all get laid."

They all agreed that was a terrific idea.

Still peering through the mirror, Corky asked, "Hey, kid? You ever been laid?"

"Sure!" Guy took a roguish sip of beer. "Lotsa times."

"Well then, we don't have to worry about you. It's just these three virgins we gotta take care of."

"I ain't no virgin!" Calvin protested.

"Come off it, Cal." Corky egged him on. "Beating your meat with both hands does not mean you've been laid. It means you got calloused palms."

"Funny, Henderson!" Calvin sneered.

"There's just two secrets to women," Corky boasted. "First and foremost, whenever they say no, they mean *yes.* That's the ladykiller's golden rule. Second, once you're under the sheets—if you got to—say you love 'em. Sometimes it's the only way they'll let you into their pants."

"What if you don't mean it?" asked Guy.

"That's their problem, kid. Serves 'em right for asking once you're too hot to stop."

Calvin belched. Jenkins farted. Everyone roared.

Corky floored the Chevy and sped onto the Southern State Parkway.

By the time they rolled into rival Rushport, forty-five minutes and three beers later, they were indeed a spirited group.

Broadway was crowded with people and aglow with festive decorations of the season. Rows of blue, red and green lights hung suspended from one side of the street to the other; one artificially wreathed lamppost to the next. Rushport was a lot dingier than Waterfield.

Eager eyes roamed everywhere.

When Corky stopped for a red light, a souped-up Ford Fairlane pulled up beside. The car had a couple in front, another in the rear.

Corky looked over at the girl at the window seat, not three feet away. She chewed gum at a reckless pace and

157

her hair was set in rollers and bobby pins. A red scarf circled all this radar.

When she returned Corky's stare, he lowered his window fast and blew her a big kiss.

She giggled and the husky fellow behind the wheel gave Corky a nasty look. The light changed and the Ford took off.

Corky floored the Chevy, trying to catch up. He followed the speeding Ford a mile down the road, until it pulled into the parking lot of a big, thirty-six lane nighttime favorite called Bowl-A-Rama.

"Quick, Jenkins," Corky instructed, turning into the parking lot. "One more fast beer all around. We're stopping. There's good times waiting for us in there. I can smell it."

As the bottles were passed around, Guy hiccupped and said, "I have a confession."

"Go on." Corky gulped his beer.

"Not only have I never been laid," admitted a remorseful, drunken Guy, "I've never even been in a fight."

"Bull!" Jenkins grumbled. *"Everyone's* been in a fight."

"Not me!" said the little fellow.

"Okay, you pansies!" Corky announced. "Enough chit-chat. Chug-a-lug!"

The bowling alley was filled with a young crowd from the local high school. There were college students home for the holidays. Townies milled about.

A jukebox in the bar blasted out, on a doughnut 45 disc, *"Oh I got a girl named Rama-Lama, Lama-Lama Ding Dong."*

The boys followed Corky, walking briskly until he spotted the two couples from the souped-up Fairlane. Stopping at the adjoining lane, he claimed it, announcing they'd park there.

Calvin and Jenkins set out to scout equipment. Corky, Troendle and Guy sat in the curved wooden booth around the huge scorepad.

"Let them play," Corky said. "We'll drink!"

"Bet'cha!" Troendle agreed.

Corky signaled the waitress over and ordered a couple of beers. She asked to see ID's. Troendle proudly waved his falsified draft card in her face. Corky flashed a page of his wallet, a detective displaying his badge.

"What about you?" the waitress asked of Guy.

"Bring him a Shirley Temple," said Corky.

The waitress left. Calvin and Jenkins returned with bowling balls and rented shoes.

Corky caught the attention of the girl with the chewing gum and curlers in the next booth. When he winked at her, she played at being shy and coquettish and looked away.

Her date stood, bowling ball in hands, itchy and agitated.

"He's getting mad," Guy whispered to Corky.

"Christ, I should hope so!" Corky said.

"Aren't you scared?" Guy asked out of the corner of his mouth.

"What's there to be scared about? There are two of them and four or five of us."

The husky fellow threw a fast ball down the lane. Halfway, it dropped into the gutter.

"Nice shot!" Corky waved to him.

The big bowler seethed with anger. Veins in his neck throbbed. Ignoring Corky, he waited nervously for his ball to return, pulling at greasy clumps of dark hair atop his head.

Corky turned to the girl in curlers. "Tell me. Is he always this friendly?"

The girl didn't answer. Just giggled and chewed.

The waitress delivered two beers and a ginger ale with a cherry in it and demanded a dollar-five for the round. Guy quickly handed her his new ten-dollar bill.

The husky fellow was set to bowl again. As he lined up in position, Corky snapped a bill from the change in Guy's hand and held it up, calling, "Five bucks says you can't knock one of 'em down!"

The husky fellow whirled around and grunted with great loathing, "You're on, loud-mouth!"

Then he turned and sent his ball rampaging down the lane. It crashed like thunder smack into the head pin, and one after the other they all toppled over. The big boy beamed as he turned to Corky to collect.

"You owe me five bucks, hotshot!" Corky told him.

"Wadda ya mean?" the fellow protested. *"You* owe *me!* I got a strike!"

"So what? The bet was to knock *one* of them down. You hit all ten! Where's my money?"

The husky fellow panted in place, deciding what to do next. With a snap of fingers, he told his friend and the two girls, "I'll be right back!" Still puffing, he hurried away.

Corky called to the girl behind the scorepad, "Take five points off his score for poor sportsmanship!"

The girl in curlers popped a fresh stick of gun in her mouth and smiled.

Corky summoned his comrades into an impromptu huddle. "Fatty just went for reinforcements, so let's be awake. I think we've hit pay dirt."

"How can you tell?" Guy asked.

"Just be on your toes, kid. It could happen very fast."

Guy was on his toes. And everything else.

Two minutes later the husky fellow returned from the bar. With him were two large boys in black leather motorcycle jackets and greasy D.A. hair styles. One meaner looking than the other.

Guy took a hesitant peek at all that hostile overweight and wondered why the hell he wasn't third row center at the Avalon.

Corky sized up the four prospective brawlers. When he looked to Chuck Troendle, he got back an easy shrug. No problem.

Calvin's eyes were squinting at their enemy. When Corky caught his attention, Calvin nodded affirmatively. No problem.

Jenkins, the more conservative of the gang, balanced open hands up and down like a scale. Fifty-fifty. Maybe yes, maybe no.

And Guy was convinced any one of those beasts could take on his entire entourage for breakfast and still be hungry.

Corky turned to Guy. "This is it, kid. How ya doing?"

"Fine!" Guy answered in the shrillest soprano pitch yet of his mid-pubescent period.

"Okay. Here's what I want you to do. We might get in less trouble afterward if they start a fight with you. You're the perfect underdog, kid. Anyone ever tell you?"

"You kidding? It's the story of my life!"

"Okay. I want you to wait a few minutes. When you're ready, wander over there and strike up a conversation."

"What if they strike me first?"

"I'll be right behind you, so you have nothing to worry about." Corky placed an affectionate hand on Guy's shoulder, and Guy figured what the hell, it was worth forfeiting his life for the comaraderie and attention of the moment.

"Talk to them about anything, kid. You're good at that. Just be sure you somehow eventually get one of them to take a poke at you. That way whatever comes after, *they* started it."

"Swell." Guy tried sounding enthusiastic instead of petrified.

"Okay, kid. Whenever you're ready. Make me proud of you."

Proud? Was he kidding? There was nothing in the whole world Guy wanted more than for Corky to be proud of him.

Turning around, thinking about what to say, how to approach, Guy sized up the four overripe hefties and his stomach turned to Jell-O. "Can I go to the bathroom first?"

"Good idea!" Corky told him, figuring the kid had planned it as strategy. "Better that way. Less obvious that we sent you over. Go, and when you come back, don't come here. Head straight to them."

Guy pointed a thumb in the air, smiled and raced off.

Corky turned to Chuck Troendle. "What do ya think?"

"Here's how it shapes up. Calvin and Jenkins will take the two new arrivals. I'll do the friend and you get Big Greasy since you started with him in the first place."

Corky approved. "Let's have one more beer. We gotta wait till the kid comes back anyway. I told him to start it off and we'd back him up. Tell Jenkins and Calvin to watch out for two things."

"Shoot."

"First, the kid. I don't want him hurt. He can't handle it."

"Second?"

"Second and most important . . ." Corky grinned . . . "whatever else happens, don't let anyone near my face. Anything but the face!"

"Okay, Gorgeous George. Whatever you say!"

"I sure wish I had time for the cutie in the curlers, though. Can't tell you how hot she is for me." Corky winked at the gum chewer even as he spoke about her.

Though she looked away, she also let him know she was at least entertained, if not downright interested.

"Forget it, C-man. We haven't time."

"Why not?"

"Because war clouds are rising."

"I don't know. Bet I could have her and be back in time for the fight."

"Bullshit!" Troendle stated flatly.

"Don't tempt me!" Corky warned.

"Bullshit is bullshit!" Troendle took a sip of beer.

"All right, asshole. Put up. How much you wanna bet I can get her out of here, score and get back before the shit hits the fan?"

"Anything you want, big shot! Name it!"

"All right!" Corky smiled to his prey in the next booth. She secretly snuck him a soft wink, encouraging the bet. "Ten bucks says I can do it!"

"You're on!" Troendle slapped Corky's hand and shook it, consummating the wager.

Corky stood up. Calvin and Jenkins looked at him, bewildered. Where was he going?

"You guys relax. I'll be back in plenty of time."

Calvin shrugged and bowled his heavy black ball.

Corky walked over to the adjoining booth. He knelt down to the girl in curlers and with his piercing green eyes and full smile, whispered, "Follow me in a minute,

162

will ya? I'll be in the parking lot. I've got something important to show you!"

Before she could respond, he placed a gentle finger over her lips, stood up and, looking at her beefy friend, now boiling mad, said calmly, "Nice seeing you, Greaseball. Have a good game!"

Then he walked out of the Bowl-A-Rama.

26

Guy was in the men's room puking his guts out. It was a case of too much beer and not enough balls. Down on one knee, with his head over the bowl, his complexion was yellow, his stomach churned and his mind reeled. He was not a well person.

No time to be sick! he lectured himself, finishing his wretched business. He wobbled to the sink, slurped cold water and splashed it on his face. His stomach calmed and a hint of real color returned to his cheeks.

Nothing like a night out with the boys, he thought.

It was freezing in the parking lot. Corky shivered in his team jacket and rubbed his hands together. He could see his breath.

Where the hell was she? What if she didn't show? Ten bucks and a lot of ego down the drain.

The girl in curlers watched her husky date bowling. This was her second time out with him. He was nice enough company, but what about the guy flirting with her? Naw! It would be wrong to follow him to the parking lot. After all, she was no cheap pickup.

Still, she certainly was curious to know what it was he

wanted to show her. What the hell, she decided. Can't hurt to find out.

She stood up and casually threw an enormous bag over her shoulder. Chewing hard she yawned, "I'm gonna comb out my hair. Be right back."

"I'll go with you, Velma," her girlfriend volunteered.

"No!" snapped Velma. "I mean . . . one of us should stay with the fellas. I'll only be a minute." Without waiting for a response, Velma left.

Guy stared into the bathroom mirror, assuming a threatening boxer's stance and determined he was not in top condition. So he dropped to the floor for a dozen push-ups. Get those biceps pumped to capacity.

As he strained, the door swung open. Two men, truck driver types, walked in and stopped cold at the sight of this kid on the floor of the men's room dipping up and down.

Feeling ridiculous, Guy jumped up and did a quick shadow box, jabbing fists forward, the ole one-two. "Just tuning up," he told the astonished men. "Golden Gloves finals tomorrow morning, you know!" Still jabbing, he danced out of the men's room.

Velma walked over to Corky in the cold. "All right. Tell me fast. What's so important you got to show me?"

"Come 'ere!" Corky took her by the sleeve and led her around the corner into a cul-de-sac alleyway where it was far less cold.

"Where we going?" she whined, having to be dragged along like a stubborn puppy.

After kicking a garbage can out of the way, Corky grabbed her and backed her up, straight against the brick wall.

"What is it?"

He placed his hand on her chin and said softly, "It's you."

"Listen!"—she pushed his hand away—"if you want to ask me out, fine. But you'll have to call first, like everybody else."

He tried kissing her mouth.

She wiggled away. "Stop! I'm in the phone book. You can't just meet someone and expect—"

She was interrupted when Corky's hand gripped the back of her neck. She tried pulling away.

"Don't move!" he instructed, forcibly enough to scare and excite her. Again he brought his lips to her mouth and pressed the length of his body against her.

After sighing softly, she chastised herself. What the hell are you doing? This is crazy! You've got to stop him. Soon.

Trembling but determined, Guy walked toward the O.K. Corral. As he approached the lane in question, he looked over at the home team. His stomach knotted again when he saw that Corky was nowhere around. Maybe it's part of the plan, he prayed.

Corky's hands were under Velma's bra, kneading each of her large breasts.

"We've got to stop. I have to get back," she said half-heartedly into his mouth.

Corky sucked on her neck, whispering, "Got to. Got to have you. I knew soon as I saw you. You drive me crazy."

A chill rushed down Velma's front.

"Here!" He took her hand and put it on his fly. "Feel that? It's so hot for you it could go off right now."

She tentatively squeezed the hardness in his pants.

"That's all because of you, baby. All because of you!"

"Please stop. Please. We can't. It's cold."

Corky unzipped his fly.

"Hi!" said a cheerful Guy to the husky bowler. "I'm your neighbor from the next booth.

The big boy looked down at him. "What of it?"

"Well, I've gotten the feeling there have been some misunderstandings around here. So I'd like to buy you a Coke. Let's have no hard feelings."

"I don't want a Coke," the humorless fellow grumbled.

"Seven-Up?"

"Nothing."

"Well then . . ." Guy slapped his sides and shook his face in a Jimmy Durante palsy. "Dat's dat!" Long pause. "Been downing pins long?"

"Wha'?"

"How long you been bowling?"

The fellow shrugged. " 'Bout five years."

"Oh, a beginner?" Guy laughed.

The bowler didn't.

"Your turn, Pepper!" the other boy called.

"That your name? Pepper?" Guy struggled to make conversation.

"I gotta go." Pepper went to pick up his ball.

Guy followed. "Mind if I watch?"

"Yeah, I mind. Go watch your own stupid friends."

Think fast! "Uhm . . . I'd rather not. You see . . . I work for a television program. 'Monday Night Bowling'?"

"Oh?" The husky bowler was suddenly interested. "I seen that."

"Yeah? Well, I'm sort of a local scout for them. They're always looking for new talent. I liked your style right from the start. That's why I wanted to watch."

"No shit?" The big boy smiled for the first time. "Hey!" —he turned to his companions—"this guy says he scouts for a TV show. Likes the way I bowl."

"Christ, Pepper!" shouted one of the new arrivals, "you'll believe anything. That kid can't be more than thirteen!"

Guy whirled around, angry. His head was spinning, his stomach was rocky . . . he didn't care what he said. "In the first place, I'm sixteen and just happen to be short for my height. And in the second, my old man owns the whole station and I work for him!"

It made sense.

Pepper's bowling ball was in his hands. "Hey!" He got Guy's attention. "Watch this one!"

"Stop! Please stop! No! No more!"

"Got to have you, baby. Got to have all of it!"

166

Velma and Corky were fighting for breath. While her hand caressed his erection, both of his were under her long slip and straight black skirt, then between her legs, trying to figure a way past her panties.

"No more!" she insisted, releasing his cock.

"Don't stop! It feels too good. Can't stop now. Don't say no, baby. Don't do that to me."

"Please. I can't."

"Put your hand on it again. Go on."

He took her hand and led it down once more to his exposed hard-on.

"You can't do it standing up," she complained, suggesting to him she was no novice.

"Wanna bet?" He nibbled her lower lip.

"Stop that, please. You don't even have a rubber."

From his pants pocket, Corky the magician whipped out a Trojan.

Velma gulped. "I don't care. We can't!"

He thrust against her, whispering, "Can I tell you how good that's gonna feel way up inside?"

"Oh no!"

"Oh yes. Gonna be sensational!" Corky found a small hole on the side of her panties and started ripping it open with his fingers.

"No. Not like this. Not out here. Stop that! Cost me seventy-nine cents a pair! Hey, call me. I'm in the book. Please. We'll do it next time."

"We'll do it now!"

"It's too cold!"

"We'll be so warm, baby. I've got the warmest dick in New York State!"

"I don't even know your name—"

Corky shut off further protest by covering her mouth with his lips and easing his tongue inside.

Stop! Velma told herself. Stop him! Then another voice spoke. Stop him? You crazy? So what if you don't know his name. He doesn't know *yours,* dummy! No one will know. He's not from around here. You know all the Rushport boys. So what the hell? He's fabulous looking and I—

No! The first voice returned. This is disgraceful! How can you let a total stranger get away with this kind of . . . *Christ, does that ever feel sensational!*

Guy watched Pepper make his spare. "Good eye!" he told the bowler.

"Think so?"

"I do. Unfortunately not TV material. I mean you shift your weight nicely for someone your size, but there's something missing in your style."

"What's that?"

"Can I be frank?"

"Be anything you want."

"The problem is . . ." Out of the corner of his eye, Guy saw Troendle signaling to him to get on with it. He had no way of knowing Chuck only wanted fast action so he could win his ten bucks. "The problem as I see it, Pepper . . . is that you throw the ball like a fairy."

There was sudden fire in Pepper's eyes as he advanced on the short boy. Calvin, Jenkins and Troendle stood up.

Guy's stomach went into the spin cycle. Where the hell was Corky?

"What'd you say?" Pepper hissed.

"Don't take my word for it. What do I know? I'm really only twelve. And remember what I said about my father owning the station? Well, I lied. I lied because I knew only a dumb-ass slob like you would fall for it. So fuck you, fatty!"

Fatty grabbed Guy's shirt and lifted him high off the ground. It was all too much, too terrifying. Guy felt like a man drowning, and as Pepper was about to punch him out his life flashed before him. He was so scared, in fact, he got sick again. All over Pepper.

The big boy dropped Guy to the ground, screaming in disgust. He swatted at half-digested lumps as if they were invading insects. Wild with hate, he wound up to smash Guy into the ground.

Guy fell over backward. Pepper charged. And Corky appeared out of nowhere, diving onto Pepper's back, strangle-holding him with one arm while his fist rapidly punched away at the big boy's ear.

All hell broke loose. Calvin and Jenkins leaped over the booth and jumped their assigned targets. Troendle let out a savage cry and plowed into Pepper's friend, wrestling him to the ground.

The sound of bowling balls crashing was suddenly drowned out by girls screaming, young men fighting and everyone in the place rushing to investigate the commotion.

Calvin and Jenkins were holding their own with the two who had come in from the bar. Trading shot for shot, they half-boxed, half-wrestled.

Troendle wasn't faring as well. Pepper's friend was pounding him in the stomach and landing punches to his face. One wild shot hit Troendle directly on the nose and blood gushed like a geyser out of control.

Pepper finally flipped Corky off his back. He tripped the quarterback and then bounced on top of him. They rolled over together, fists flailing, punching each other's kidneys.

Corky realized the big guy had a lot more weight, so there was no sense wrestling. He broke out of their hold and scrambled to his feet.

Pepper lunged after him. They swung out, face to face, and Pepper knocked Corky back against the bowling rack. He suddenly had the upper hand and was whacking Corky across the face.

Corky tried covering his face with both hands, but Pepper was going crazy, connecting with every third or fourth shot. One lucky punch split Corky's lip.

Guy, who had been left alone since the fight started, stood there in his dizzy, nauseated state, watching the melee. When he saw Pepper hammering away at Corky's head, his heart pumped so fast he thought it would leap out of his vomit-stained shirt. *"No!"* He hollered. He can't do that. Not to Corky!

A rush of adrenaline drove him to the bowling rack, where he jumped on Pepper, throwing both arms around the bulk of him.

Pepper didn't let up on Corky, but did take the time to elbow Guy and then, when the kid fell, to kick him hard in the ribs.

Guy went out of control. Bouncing back, he darted forward, picked up the nearest bowling ball and dropped the heavy black sphere directly on top of Pepper's foot, smashing his two biggest toes.

Pepper screamed in agony. He lifted his cracked foot and held it while hopping about in place.

Corky had the opening he needed. He grabbed Pepper's shirt, swung back and let the one-legged fellow have it, right in the teeth. He could feel the two front ones breaking, snapping off against the skin of his bleeding fingers. Pepper crumpled.

The manager, two bartenders and assorted others descended on the group, breaking things up, holding fighters at bay.

"Throw 'em out!" the manager screamed. "Throw these fuckin' hoods outta here!"

"*They* started!" Corky gasped for air and pointed to Guy. "They attacked my friend here . . . half their size . . ."

"I don't give a shit! Pepper and these guys play here all the time. I don't know any you punks. You're troublemakers. Out of my bowling alley, and *stay* out!"

"Some democracy!" Corky complained, with mock indignation. "Some fucking democracy. Come on, you guys, let's not stay if that's their lousy attitude. See if we play here again!"

Corky and his friends grabbed their coats. Calvin and Jenkins got out of their bowling shoes. All fought to catch their breath.

Backed up by his enormous bartenders, the manager clapped hands. "All right, let's go!"

Guy, Calvin, Jenkins and Troendle followed Corky.

Pepper sat in the booth, nursing broken toes and busted teeth. "Next time you bastards come around, you're dead!"

"All right, Pepper," the manager intervened, "that's enough."

Laughing within, fighting for breath on the surface, Corky walked past the sea of lanes, past the plastic Santa

Claus with the electric winking eye, toward the exit, watching everyone staring at his disheveled entourage.

Her hair no longer in curlers, Velma traipsed carefree out of the ladies' room. When she came face to face with Corky she looked at him confused, trying to guess how he got so messed up, his lip so bloody.

He snuck her a private wink, letting her know everything was cool.

She stepped forward and in passing, whispered between smiling teeth, "Hey, schmuck. Your fly's still open!"

27

Piling into the Chevy like clowns at the circus, outlaws chased from town by the sheriff, Corky and his band of merrymen made their getaway.

Chuck Troendle held his head back, sniffing in his bloody nose.

Corky pressed a handkerchief to his open lip. "Come on, Jenkins. Get the beer out! What kind of party is this?"

Jenkins opened the bag between his knees and handed out the Miller's. "That's the last of it," he announced.

"First things first!" Corky jabbed Troendle in the ribs. "Hey, Mr. Nosebleed. Where's my ten bucks?"

"You're kidding?" Troendle raised his head. "You got her?"

Corky smiled, nonchalant.

"I don't believe it." Chuck moaned.

"Better believe it, Troendle. That was one for the Guinness Book of Records!"

Everyone took a slug of beer.

"And how 'bout the little one in the back!" Corky looked through the rear-view mirror. "Saved my fucking neck, he did. I owe you a thousand bucks, kid!"

Guy smiled, swilled his beer and came out with a manly belch.

Corky skidded around a corner, back onto Broadway and stopped short in front of a deli. "Okay, Jenkins. I'll keep the motor running. You get a few more six-packs. Let's go, cheap bastards. Everybody cough up."

Spare change and dollar bills were pulled from pockets.

"Not you," Corky told Guy. "I'm chipping in your share." He handed Jenkins three dollars.

The drive back from Rushport was a lively shambles. The boys drank and shouted, comparing wounds, reliving shot-for-shot every detail of the battle.

Back in Waterfield, Corky dropped them off, one by one. Guy was last.

"Some night, huh?" A Corky high on beer pulled up to the Fowler house.

"Some night," Guy quietly agreed. "Jesus. My first fight."

"Three things to remember, kid. Try not to get into a scrap if you can't win. That's suicide. Second, if you gotta fight, make sure you get in that first punch. It's worth fifty pounds on the other fella. Also scares shit out of him. Third, if you lose, you only get beaten once. After that, if the guy isn't your friend, at least he respects you. So keep slugging."

Guy got out of the car. As he was closing the door, Corky's face appeared at the window. "Hey, kid?"

"Yeah?"

"Don't matter what anybody says . . . you're my friend. I want you to know that. And next time someone asks how tall you are, tell 'em Corky Henderson says you're a nine-footer. They don't believe it, tell 'em to check with me."

Guy slammed the door. "Merry Christmas, Corky."

Corky skidded off down the street and Guy watched the car disappear into the night.

Ten minutes later Guy bounced into bed, far too exhilarated to sleep. Lying on his back, he stared at the dark ceiling, hearing Corky's words, over and over again, *"You're my friend."* Christ, he was lucky.

While waiting to fall asleep, ebullient, even proud of himself, he was visited for the very first time with a full, bona fide erection. It was the greatest night of his life.

Nathan Fowler awakened early the following morning in agony. Goddamn cramps, he groaned, hurrying into the bathroom.

The excessive amount of blood in the bowl told him he'd ignored the situation long enough. He would see his doctor.

Guy was devoting Christmas vacation to shaping up. He added to his daily exercise program and increased his intake of leftover turkey and rum-soaked fruitcake.

Four days after Christmas, Corky called. "Got plans New Year's Eve, kid?"

"Nothing special," Guy told him, having no plans at all.

"We're putting a party together over at Marlene the cheerleader's. So get a date and bring a bottle of something expensive. We're starting around eight to make sure we'll be good and blind by 1959."

"A date?" Guy asked like he hadn't heard the term before.

"Yeah. There someone you can ask?"

"Oh . . . absolutely."

"Fine. Thirty-two Temple Road. Bring your camera."

"Corky?"

"Yeah?"

"I take it back."

"What's that?"

"There's no one I can ask. Not really. Couldn't I come alone?"

"Alone? New Year's Eve, kid! Date-night U.S.A.! Everyone in couples. Might as well start making out now. Best way to get to be a C-man, like anything else, is with practice."

"Makes sense," Guy agreed.

"There must be someone you can ask. You want people to think you're queer or something?"

Guy shuddered. " 'Course not."

"School's crawling with available pussy. They'll be lining up for you, kid."

"I doubt it. Hey, Corky, weren't you ever nervous around girls?"

"You kidding, kid? Some of us are born lovers. . . ."

"I guess. Thanks, I'll . . . work on it."

Guy hung up and stared at the wall. A date? *A date?* How was *he* going to scare up a date? Where was that certain someone who might actually accept? He riffled through his mind's file, picturing the girls in his classes, but the only one he knew at all on a first-name basis was Amy Silverstein—

Amy! That was it! He called immediately.

"Hi, Amy. Busy?"

"Yucch! Plowing through my chem term paper."

"How's it coming?"

"It doesn't make any sense, so it must be brilliant. What's up?"

"Up? . . . Nothing. Just calling to say hi."

"Hi."

"Uhm . . . have a nice Christmas?"

"Peachy. Just what is it, Guy?"

"Nothing. Nothing really. You're busy. I'll let you get back to work."

"Whatever you say."

"Right. I'll . . . uh . . . see you down at the *Eagler*."

"No doubt."

"Nice talking to you, Amy."

"Thanks for calling, Guy."

"*Wait!* Don't hang up! There's something else. . . ."

"That's what I figured."

"Listen"—Guy shut his eyes and spoke fast—"if you're not busy this Thursday night, the thirty-first, you know, New Year's, well, Corky just invited me to a terrific party, I mean *the* big one in town, and I know it's kind of sudden, last minute and all, and believe me, I respect you enough to know how rude it is to ask anyone out without

174

plenty of notice, honest, I mean especially for something as important as the last night of the year, but please don't stand on ceremony with me Amy if you're free and wouldn't mind going because Corky said I had to bring . . . no, I mean I *could* ask someone if that's what I wanted, all up to me, and I'd sure like to bring you, seeing how you and I always have such a good time, and you could finally get a chance to meet him and his friends and find out they're a lot more than you give them credit. But don't worry about it, it's okay either way, and if you don't care to go or if you've made other plans I'll shove my head in the oven but I'll certainly understand—"

"Okay."

"Okay what?" Guy was confused by his own convolutions.

"Okay. I'll go with you to the party."

"You mean it's a date?"

"What time?"

"What time . . . oh, eight, I guess. I'll pick you up at eight."

"I'll be waiting."

Guy hung up and did a little dance around the hallway, picking up a sleeping Rasputin for his partner, dancing the cat in circles, hugging and kissing him again and again.

He had a date. He, Guy Fowler, photographer, bowler, street fighter, had a real live honest-to-Injun date. With a girl. Amy. I've been invited to a party New Year's Eve by Corky Henderson himself and I'm taking Amy. My friend Amy.

The Zombie.

Yipes holy Christmas! What the hell have I done?

In his frenzied haste he'd asked the school freak to an all jock-cheerleader gathering. What a crazy, stupid thing to do.

How to get out of it? He called Corky.

"Corky? It's me, again. Guy. Your drinking companion."

"Hi, kid."

"Got a minute?"

175

"Barely. On my way to the gym."

"Then I won't keep you. Just wanted you to know I got a date."

"And in less than five minutes. Not bad. You must be more of a make-out artist than I thought."

"Hardly."

"It's you short smart ones always breaking the prettiest hearts."

"But I have to tell you who I'm taking!"

"Why don't you surprise me?"

"Because you won't like her."

"I don't have to, Casanova. She's your date. Don't worry. I like everyone as long as they're pretty and don't wear metal underwear. Gotta run."

"But Corky . . ."

"What?"

"Metal underwear is the least of her problems."

"How old are you, kid?"

"Fifteen."

"Fifteen? Christ, by the time I was fifteen I was getting it left and right."

"I'm not surprised."

"Neither was I. I'll see you Thursday."

Guy stared at the disconnected receiver, figuring out how he was going to talk Amy into straightening for the one evening, if not her enormous nose, at least her hair. Wasn't there some way she could shrink six inches? Perhaps she'd at least have the good taste and common decency to drape an American flag over her head.

Corky hung up the phone and hurried out of the house. As he drove to the school he wondered if he hadn't laid it on a bit thick, bragging to the kid about how he was a born C-man. Except what else could he have done? Last thing he'd want his number one fan to know was that he'd paid his dues, same as most. Take, for example, that incident . . . several summers past. . . .

Side by side at the Waterfield Country Club, on terry-coated deck chairs, the two women sipped gin and tonics and stared at the lifeguard.

Atop the stand sat fifteen-year-old Corky. His strong arms were folded before him and his long legs dangled lifelessly over the platform. Bored, he watched three monsters thrashing about in the shallow water.

A so-so summer. His remarkable tan and the forty laps a day were about all he had to show for it.

From their cabana the ladies schemed. They'd been keeping tabs for two months, comparing notes.

"One more drink and I'm going over there to talk to him," said the younger of the two.

"Sally, you wouldn't!"

Sally would and ordered another round from a passing cabana boy to prove it.

"This should be interesting!" said the older woman, rubbing her palms in anticipation.

Corky slouched in his lifeguard stand, thoughtlessly stroking the blond hairs on his stomach, just above his bathing suit. His eyes floated along the water and scanned the cabana area.

He saw the two women, awash as usual in gin and tonics, passing the afternoon gabbing under the sun.

They were always watching him, those two, always peering at him over tall frosted glasses. At first it bothered him, making him feel as if he were on display.

But he got used to it. He was, in fact, rapidly adapting to so many eyes staring his way. Looks from fifteen-year-olds and twenty-year-olds, thirty-year-olds and who-knew-how-olds.

He'd grown another inch since Memorial Day when the pool opened for the season. Along with the added height there'd developed a subtle maturity, the suggestion of a deep sensuality behind those large, earnest green eyes; a slow awakening of a powerfully rugged young man suddenly growing out of a boy's body.

When he saw the younger of the two women put her empty drink down and start walking his way, he slouched still farther into his chair and fingered the metal whistle around his neck. He noticed her spirited walk, her provocative figure, despite hips too wide and a stomach gone

177

to excess, too jellied to be exhibited in her two-piece bathing suit.

He put the whistle in his mouth as Sally appeared below.

"Hello!" She smiled up into his eyes.

"Ma'am!" He dropped the whistle and smiled back.

"I was wondering if we could chat. Some place private."

He looked around the pool. The kids had climbed out. "I was going to the pool house to get my sweat shirt."

"Fine," Sally invited herself. "I'll go with you."

She followed him into the pool house.

"I'm Sally Orton." She closed the creaky door. Sunlight filtered in through cracks in the woodwork. They were surrounded by hoses, hooks and gallons of chlorine.

"Corky Henderson," the lifeguard nodded, wondering why she had closed the door, leaving them cramped together in so dark and tiny a space.

"You know the twins?" Sally asked, leaning against the door, hoping the effect of her three gin and tonics weren't showing.

"You mean Gail and Jackie?" He picked up his sweat shirt.

"Gail and *Johnny*. Yes. That's who I mean."

"Sure. Sweet kids."

"They're mine."

"No kidding?" He tried to sound interested.

"No kidding!" Sally mocked his forced enthusiasm.

He looked at her. She winked. He felt very uncomfortable.

"You said you wanted to talk to me, Mrs. Orton?"

"Yes. I wanted to thank you for teaching my kids to swim."

"It's not necessary, ma'am. Really. We're not supposed to accept tips. I was glad to help."

"I wasn't thinking of giving you money. We're not coming back after today."

"No?"

"My husband's flying us to Montreal for Labor Day. We're meeting him there."

"I'm sure you'll have a nice time."

178

"He's been there all summer. Works in industrial diamonds."

"I see." Corky smiled politely.

"Do you?" Sally raised an eyebrow. Look, she told herself, this puppy ain't gonna be the one to light this fire. So it's up to you. Either make the move or let him get back to work. She took a step closer. "Tell me, young man, how old are you?"

"Fifteen."

Sally took a small breath. "Kind of big for fifteen. You play football, or something?"

"Quarterback."

"It figures."

Embarrassed, the six-footer looked away.

"Don't get me wrong. I think you're just the right size." Sally took another step closer. "I think you're perfect."

Their bodies were practically touching. Corky stopped breathing.

"I'm twenty-seven," Sally whispered.

At a loss for words, Corky nodded.

"You think that's old, don't you?"

"Not too old," Corky told her.

"At college I was All-fraternity Dream Girl two years in a row."

"I'm not surprised."

Sally's eyes roamed the well-defined muscles of the lifeguard's chest; his shoulders, arms and stomach. "Can't imagine how anyone could have been allowed so much."

Making her move, Sally pressed a voluptuous breast into him. Then, taking the situation in hand, she squeezed his tight nylon trunks. "That feel good?"

Corky looked down at the floor, saying nothing. The impressive object that sprang to life was sufficient answer.

This is it, big fella, she silently told him. I made the first move. Melted the ice. Now it's up to you.

This is crazy, thought Corky, standing there with a goofy grin. He wanted to kiss her but was afraid she might think him rude. "I wonder if I shouldn't be getting back to the pool, Mrs. Orton."

Sally placed her hands on her hips and stepped back,

sighing with disappointment. "Just my luck, huh? Talk about bad timing!"

"I do something wrong, Mrs. Orton?"

"Sally."

"What'd I do?"

"Nothing. You did nothing, absolutely nothing." She patted the bulge in his trunks. "Lucky for you, you won't have to win Nobel peace prizes, won't have to find a cure for cancer, won't have to do anything but wait. It'll all come. No trouble for you."

"What would you like me to do, Mrs. . . . Sally."

Sally opened the wooden door. "What I'd really like you to do is meet me again in five years because by then you'll know what to do without having to ask."

Twirling her hair, Sally strutted from the pool house. . . .

The minute Amy told her mother about the New Year's Eve party, she was sorry.

You'd think she'd been invited to a coronation.

"I just don't know what you can wear," Evelyn fretted, fingering her way through Amy's closet.

"What's the difference, Mother? It's only a dinky get-together."

"No such thing as a dinky anything!" Evelyn insisted. "Make every occasion a special event and you're bound to be the hit of the party."

"But it's no big deal. Really."

"This looks good!" Evelyn removed a robin's-egg-blue dress from the rack and held it against her own five-foot-four frame. "What do you think?"

"Much too dressy."

"Important thing is to always look your best. Give it your all and we'll soon have invitations we won't know what to do with."

Amy collapsed onto her bed.

Evelyn continued her determined foray through the rack of clothes. "Maybe this yellow outfit. No. Too summery. And your hair, dear. What can we do that would be different?"

"Shave it," suggested Amy, exasperated.

Evelyn let it pass. "Maybe tie it up, huh? Give you an air of sophistication."

Amy got off the bed and joined Evelyn at the closet. "Mother, my 'date' comes up to my waist. The last thing I should look is sophisticated."

Evelyn eyed her daughter up and down, then got lost in the closet again. "How about this green skirt and your silk blouse with the puffy sleeves?"

"Hate!"

"Well, I just don't know." Evelyn scratched her neck. "I think you and I are just going to have to run to town and find something. God knows, parties are important stepping-stones."

"Whatever you say." Amy gave in.

"You've got to feel pretty. A new outfit will stand out and register all over your face, and that's a fact, Amy, dear."

The only thing standing out or registering all over Amy's freshly scrubbed face as she stood in a steaming shower Thursday evening was a stubborn residue of blemishes. Water pellets rained on her flowered rubber cap as she painted herself with Phisohex.

After toweling herself, Amy checked the mirror. No change.

She scrubbed again with the liquid, hoping when the medicated suds popped, her skin would be clear. No such luck.

Damn acne! Taking a scalding washcloth to her cheek, she squeezed at enemy whiteheads, then applied astringent to the area of attack.

Once again she looked in the mirror, and asked the reflection why she had agreed to go to a party with all those beautiful girls? She hardly needed to be reminded of her physical limitations. A fleeting image of Corky answered her question.

She smiled to herself. You're no Sophia Loren, my dear, but you're all you've got!

Corky called for Ro-Anne just before eight. A festive Marian Sommers opened the door. "Whee!" She and

Lester had started their celebration early. "It's the New Year baby!" Marian patted Corky's backside. "How come no diaper?"

Corky smiled politely.

"Wassa matter? Don't I get a kiss for Happy New Year?"

"Sure." Corky leaned forward to kiss the side of her cheek.

Marian shifted her face and greeted him on the mouth. The move stunned Corky and he didn't know which would be more rude—pulling away or responding.

He did neither.

Marian edged her tongue forward, and seemed to leave it there after she withdrew. It was a moment before Corky realized she had transferred the pit from her martini olive.

"Fooled ya, huh?" She took his hand. "Come on, say hello to Lester. He's smashed."

Corky took the olive pit out of his mouth.

"Hap-pee-New-Year!" Lester sang from the couch in the living room. "Get him a glass, Marian. Have a 'tini, Cork. Kick off 1959."

"No thanks. Me and martinis don't mix."

Beautiful and aloof, Ro-Anne walked slowly down the stairs, smoothing on her gloves. Marian and Lester, cackling over some private joke, had no way of knowing what an awkward moment it was for Ro-Anne and her boyfriend, this their first time together since the spat of the week before.

Corky walked over to the bottom of the stairs. "Jesus, you look pretty."

She smiled coolly. What else was new?

He kissed her lightly on the lips, careful not to smear. "Happy New Year."

Ro-Anne stretched fingers into a white kid glove and sighed. "Let's get going."

Amy let Guy help her on with her coat.

Guy shook Evelyn's hand good-by. "Happy New Year, Mrs. Silverstein."

"Call if you're going to be late," Evelyn requested.

"It's New Year's Eve, Mother. We'll be late."

"Just be friendly and warm, don't be afraid to smile and be smart enough not to talk politics or use big words no one will understand."

"Anything else, Mother?"

"No, dear. Just be yourself and have a good time."

28

Hardly the jubilant gala Guy had envisioned, the party was flat when he and Amy arrived.

Eight girls sipped Cokes and gossiped on one side of the living room while their dates guzzled beer and talked sports on the other.

On a coffee table in the middle of the room a colorful selection of silly hats, noisemakers, streamers and confetti sat untouched, festive accessories too childish for these young adults.

Amy took one look around. "Who died?" she whispered.

Guy led her into the room, ignoring guests staring openly, certain this odd couple must have the wrong address.

Corky winced when he saw Amy. He couldn't believe *she* was the disaster Guy had warned him about.

Marlene Sanders, perky cheerleader-hostess, bubbled over. "Appy-ap-pee New Year! Don't you hate it? Poof! A whole year gone, out the window. What happened to 1958?"

Marlene took Amy by the hand. "I'll introduce you to the girls." She looked at Guy and dismissed him. "You join the boys."

Amy entered a discussion of how large an engagement ring could grow before ostentation set in, and Guy arrived to hear predictions of the next day's Rose Bowl score.

The jocks from the Rushport adventure were actually glad to see Guy. His appearance rekindled memories and vastly exaggerated versions of the wild evening fast unfolded. The picaresque tales also reminded them it was time to get drunk again.

Corky surveyed a tray of bottles on the piano and returned with a fifth of Canadian Club. "Okay, fellas. Here's where we separate the men from the pipsqueaks!" He poured a jigger of the whiskey and downed it. "Aaaah! Real firewater!" With half a breath, he passed both bottle and shot glass to Chuck Troendle. "All yours!"

Amy watched the boys draining the circulating bottle, listened to the girls gabbing about hem lengths, and decided she'd never felt more out of place anywhere.

The bottle went around the other side of the room three more times. Everyone passed the test.

As the whiskey found its way into young bloodstreams, Corky brought the bottle over to the girls' side of the room. "Anybody here want a shot?"

No one said anything. The boys across the way shared a hearty laugh.

"Prudes?"

"I'd have a drink if someone would make it for me," Ro-Anne allowed.

"Name it, princess." Corky smiled. "I'll play bartender."

"Can you make an apricot brandy sour on the rocks?"

"I can't even pronounce it without getting sick."

"How about a sloe gin fizz?" asked one of the other girls.

"Come on, ladies. It's New Year's Eve! Isn't there a real drinker in the house?"

Amy raised her hand. "I'll have a slug!" she volunteered.

Silence. Raised eyebrows.

"There's the old Irish spirit!" Corky poured a jigger and handed it over.

What the hell, Amy figured. Anything to break the boredom. Zap! She threw the booze down her throat. Tears came to her eyes. Her insides ignited. She fought for air and when she could finally speak, gasped, *"Delicious!"*

Never to be outdone, Ro-Anne seized the shot glass and thrust it at Corky. "Well . . . maybe just a teensy-weensy one!"

He filled it, she downed it and went into a light convulsion. When her coughing fit subsided, she announced proudly, "It worked, I'm drunk!"

The ball was rolling. The other girls giggled and squealed, suddenly eager to give decadence a whirl.

An hour later everyone was wearing funny hats. The phonograph was piled high with 45's—Elvis, the Platters, Fabian, Dion and the Belmonts. Couples danced the Philly lindy. Guy took photos.

Streamers rocketed everywhere. Confetti blanketed everything.

At ten minutes to twelve someone turned on the television and put out the lights. The excitement blaring from a mobbed Times Square filled the room. Most of the guests crowded around the set.

At the piano, leafing through her younger sister's music sheets, Marlene found what she was looking for. "Can anyone here play 'Auld Lang Syne'?"

Guy was drunk enough to think he could. Walking over, he dismissed the sheet music, telling Marlene he only played by ear. When he tried a few notes, he was amazed he could back up his facile boast.

Someone raised the volume on the television.

"That'll be fine," Marlene told Guy. "Wait for the stroke of midnight." Then she and Ro-Anne, giggling, went off to get more pretzels and beer.

Corky decided to join the crowd at the TV set and made his way through the maze of bodies until he stood next to Amy.

Disoriented, but enjoying her first drunken experience, Amy swayed back and forth in time to Guy Lombardo.

"How come we never actually met before tonight?" Corky asked her.

Amy looked into his penetrating eyes and got lost in the greenery. "Travel in different circles?" she suggested.

"You and Guy dating long?" Corky pinched a confetti flake from her shoulder and held it between his fingers.

Amy smiled nervously. "Guy and I don't *date*. We're friends, is all."

"How nice," Corky whispered, moving closer. "For me, I mean."

Amy wasn't at all sure what he meant by that, but she was suddenly having a terrific time.

Marlene and Ro-Anne returned, laden with reinforcements.

"Last call for drinks in 1958!" Marlene called out.

Guy plinked at the keys, not really hitting them, getting ready for his debut.

Ro-Anne eased her way through the group at the television and stood next to Corky, leaning against him. He put his arm around her, to his left, and winked at Amy, to his right. She winked back.

One minute to midnight.

"Everyone keep your eyes glued to the ball!" someone yelled from down front.

With forty-five seconds left in the year, partygoers busied themselves blowing noisemakers, downing drinks, holding on to each other and chanting numbers in a tense countdown.

As the electric ball on the screen descended, the noise soared. Confetti scattered.

The ball hit bottom. Guy hit the ivories.

Little white bulbs on top of the New York Times Building spelled out *1959,* and the eighteen revelers in Marlene Sanders' living room joined the half a million in Times Square going crazy.

Couples embraced. Long, long kisses, deeply felt.

Amy stared at Guy Lombardo, wishing she were invisible.

Corky kissed Ro-Anne, squeezed her tight and licked her teeth.

"Let's not fight anymore, darling," she whispered in his ear.

"I'm for that," he replied.

Chuck Troendle broke away from his date, turned and

tapped Ro-Anne on the shoulder. She and Corky parted and when Ro-Anne turned to greet Chuck, Corky turned the other way and took Amy away from Guy Lombardo.

As if he hadn't already done enough damage, Corky summoned all his intensity, looked straight into her brown eyes and smiled his winner. Amy fell apart.

Guy played "Auld Lang Syne." Considering the short amount of time he'd been with the instrument and the large amount of alcohol distorting his perception, it sounded pretty good.

He stumbled over a few notes only when, looking up briefly, he was distracted to see Corky taking Amy in his arms before gifting her with the longest, most affectionate kiss of the new year. They kissed forever.

As one year became another, while all around him exchanged affectionate greetings, Guy played the piano. Naturally talented fingers concealed a familiar loneliness.

Ro-Anne was so relieved she'd made up with Corky she felt guilty locking tongues with Chuck Troendle. So guilty, in fact, she might have considered resisting had it not felt so good.

An inebriated Amy dropped her carefully constructed walls and went limp, sagging into Corky's strong arms as they kissed. For her, nothing had ever felt so good.

For Corky, the pleasure was little more than sweet revenge.

THE VENTURE

1959

January

29

Corky and Amy's lips parted.

"Happy New Year," she whispered, eyes still closed.

Corky clipped her chin with a soft-fisted love-knock and turned to give Ro-Anne another extended kiss.

Amy raised her eyelids and stared at Corky's back, trying to put pieces together. They didn't fit. Chemistry and Physics, English Lit and Economics she knew. Those she was good at. But basic emotions was not her game. A novice player, she barely understood the rules.

Corky was satisfied. He'd been ridiculed for weeks after the Thanksgiving skit the Gadflys had put on. The whole school had heard how viciously he and Ro-Anne had been portrayed.

So when Amy—a charter member of those creepy intellectual snobs—dared show her unwelcome, unattractive face at a party on his turf, he made damn sure she'd regret it.

Easy enough. As always. His for a smile. But like too much aftershave lotion, where a few drops would have done the trick, he'd gone ahead and doused her with a whole bottle's worth of charm.

Someone stacked a fresh pile of 45's on the turntable. Couples wandered off finding make-out niches on couches, in darkened hallways, behind living room drapes. Others, not as affection-oriented, still drank and danced, straining to sustain the manic merriment of yesterday's midnight.

Both bathrooms soon had a steady stream of visitors too new to alcohol to have learned restraint. Gagging sounds filled the air.

Marlene's parents arrived home a little after two. Trouble. After stumbling over two sleeping bodies crumpled in the hallway and wading through a pile of confettied debris, they eventually arrived at a place that was once their living room.

The only light came from the piano, where Guy and Amy sat, playing "Chopsticks." Everyone else was scattered about the dark house, wrapped together like pretzels.

"Where's Marlene?!" Mrs. Sanders demanded to know.

Guy and Amy stopped playing. "Upstairs, near the bedroom, last I saw," Amy answered.

Mr. Sanders stalked the room, switching lights back on. "Alcohol!" he observed. "These children have been drinking *alcohol!*"

"Not me!" Guy burped. "Never touch the stuff."

While Mr. Sanders stomped through the house, flicking on lights, Mrs. Sanders followed, collecting glasses.

Scattered about, in various states of unbuttonedness, couples jumped up, faking sobriety.

Awakened, Marlene confronted her folks. "Oh no! How could you do this to me? Home so early? You promised to call!"

"Tell these juvenile delinquents to clear out. Party's over. No one gave any of you permission to drink liquor!"

"It's not yours, Daddy. Everyone brought their own."

"You're a disgrace! I remember when kids were children! You've all had it too damn easy, that's what it is."

The Sanderses soon had everyone roused and on shaky feet. A rush for coats, scarves and gloves ensued, and after hasty farewells, the spirited crowd departed.

Even walking down the hill, laughing, still drunk, partygoers could hear the family squabble raging behind.

Amy and Guy walked along a quiet, icy Quaker Street, hardly looking at each other.

Her quixotic Mona Lisa grin eventually caught his attention. "Well, was I right? Isn't he terrific?"

Amy didn't answer, just nodded several times, yes-yes-yes, Corky was terrific.

Lost in a cloud of euphoria, Amy floated down the block.

"How come Corky gave you such a big kiss at midnight?"

"Corky?" Amy repeated his name as if she wanted to hear the ringing of the two syllables in her ear.

Who, Guy wondered, was this enchanted toad with whom he was walking? Could this mummified Corliss Archer be the same Amy, queen of the cynics, who pushed all that talk about how ugly it was to be one of the chosen beautiful?

"If you like," Guy suggested, "we could get together with him again sometime."

"Fine." Amy smiled. "Where do I sign up?"

"I can't believe you're acting this way!" Guy finally complained.

"What way . . . ?"

"I don't know. Like some love-sick puppy."

"Don't be an ass, Guy"—she snapped out of it—"you wanted me to like your friend and I did. Without reservations. I'd've thought you'd be celebrating instead of stewing."

"Stewing!?" Guy protested. "Who the hell is stewing? I just can't get over the effect he's had on you."

"That's ridiculous. He's a charming fellow."

"Not until he kissed you, he wasn't."

"I'd prefer not to talk about it, Guy, if you're going to act like a fifteen-year old."

They walked home in the cold early hours of the new year without saying another word.

When they got to her apartment, Amy offered her hand. "I didn't mean to get nasty. I never really drank before and I guess I'm a little mixed up."

"I'm a little mixed up, too." Guy twirled a finger at his ear, rolled his eyes and stuck his tongue out like a crazy person.

"I didn't even get to give you a New Year's kiss, Guy. My own date!"

Guy offered his cheek and she pecked it softly.

She turned her face, waiting for him.

"No go. I want the same shot as Corky. Lip service!"

Amy tapped her cheek with a finger. "Smack one in there and cut the smart remarks."

Guy pressed his lips across a row of blemishes. "Happy New Year!"

"Happy New Year, Guy. You're a lovely boy and a good friend." She opened the door and looked back, over her shoulder. "Now if you could only play football, we'd really have something to shout about."

30

Students returning to school after Christmas recess were introduced early Monday morning to the first issue of the *Gadfly*. The newsletter had been secretly run off in the school printshop and then stuffed inside each copy of the *Eagler*.

Dr. Potter came across a copy over his morning cocoa and became enraged. He was not about to permit such yellow journalism within his hallowed halls and immediately organized a meeting to investigate and repudiate.

Leonard Hauser was notified by Dr. Potter personally, making certain the *Eagler* would cover his remarks.

At two o'clock, an hour before the scheduled event, Dr. Potter met with Corky in his office.

"Have a seat."

Corky sat in front of the large desk. Dr. Potter stood at the window. The championship trophy sat on the sill, staring, appropriately enough, onto the athletic field.

"You know, of course, Waterfield has known few students of whom we've been more proud." The principal patted the huge loving cup with affection.

Corky sat back and relaxed. "Thank you, Dr. Potter."

"So it grieves me to have to discuss your English studies."

"Sir?"

Dr. Potter opened a manila file. "Mrs. Bartlett reports

you still haven't handed in your paper on *A Tale of Two Cities*."

Corky said nothing.

"She says you've done poorly on your last two tests and that you've missed classes."

Corky sat up straight. "English came period before practice, Dr. Potter. I needed extra warm-up time."

"We can appreciate that." Dr. Potter leaned against the trophy and cleaned his glasses. "But at Waterfield, studies must come first."

Corky tried remaining calm. No one had said a word about classes, grades or book reports during football season. He assumed they were being lenient, letting him off the scholastic hook in return for nothing less than the trophy now holding up Dr. Potter's elbow. "What happens now?" Corky asked.

"If we didn't have such a high personal regard for you, Corky, I would have let Mrs. Bartlett handle this herself. But you are special to us and we want to see you going on to greater things."

Corky looked at the floor.

The principal continued. "As such, I've convinced Mrs. Bartlett to give you until the end of this week to turn in that book report. If not, she'll be obliged to flunk you."

Corky looked up. *Flunk me!?*

"And if you flunk now, you won't be able to take English Regents in June. You won't graduate on time, won't be able to start college football in the fall, and so on down the line. I'm afraid it's that serious." Dr. Potter put his glasses back on.

Corky's hands were wet.

"So we expect to see that book report right away. Buckle down. Apply yourself."

Corky wanted to punch pompous Potter right in his clean glasses. "I'll take care of it, sir." He stood to leave.

"That's the Eagle spirit!"

At three o'clock, Dr. Potter held his press conference. Those present included Leonard Hauser, Amy, Guy, Ken Crawley and several faculty members.

Standing before the American flag, Dr. Potter announced that the propaganda sheet known as the *Gadfly* would not be tolerated at Waterfield. The articles on America's racism, on the undertaxed rich and overtaxed poor, and in particular the one on Dr. Potter's policy of censorship were clearly the work of misinformed, Communist-inspired agitators.

Dr. Potter then announced he was assigning Ken Crawley to head a committee which would get to the bottom of this radicalism.

Amy wrote as fast as Dr. Potter spoke.

When the oration was finished, Guy was instructed to get a shot of the stalwart principal lighting a match and setting fire to the subversive "rag of filth."

Leonard Hauser smiled. It was going even better than he'd imagined. All this publicity. The *Eagler* would now report the event in banner headlines, creating controversy, and his next *Gadfly* would be even more eagerly awaited.

As the two-sheet mimeographed circular burned in Dr. Potter's crusading hands, Guy took pictures. When he placed his camera case on the principal's desk, he couldn't help noticing an open manila file with the words *Carl Henderson, Jr.* typewritten on top.

While Potter gave his "Let me tell you what makes America great" speech, Guy pretended to put his camera equipment in order. At the same time, he read the report.

Corky had to be alone.

After leaving Dr. Potter's office he ran past the front doors, straight to his Chevy. He cut his last-period class and spent the time racing around the back roads of town.

The car spat and backfired. His fingers squeezed the steering column as if the force of his grip might transfer some of his anger.

Not graduate on time? Impossible. That was for dummies, greasers, rejects.

Eyes straight ahead, he floored the pedal.

The ride didn't help. He was still burning when he pulled into the garage.

"Now we'll see!" Carl hollered good-naturedly from

the living room as Corky walked into the house. "Now we'll see who's the real boss!"

Shit! Corky hung his parka on the coat rack. Monday. The old man's day off. He would be in a playful mood!

Carl hurried into the hallway and put up his dukes. "Let's go!"

Corky held his breath. *Nothing doing. Not now. I've had enough for one afternoon*. He quickly raised both hands above his head, giving up. "No thanks. You win, Dad. You're the wheel of the house. It's all yours."

"One quick tumble!" Carl smacked his lips. "Feeling my oats today, boy. Gonna lick you good."

"Not me, Dad. I'm not going to fight." Corky walked away.

Carl reached out and slapped him across the back of the neck. "Hey, big shot! Wassa matter? I'm not good enough? I taught you to fight and I can still whip your ass! Don't you get uppity with me!"

Corky stood still, his back to his father and closed his eyes, hoping he could contain the dynamite keg smoldering inside. When his father next shoved him from behind, he burst.

Whirling, he grabbed his father by the front of his shirt. "No more!" he shouted. "I don't want you touching me! Not ever again, goddammit!" Without thinking, he pushed the huge man to the floor.

A horrified Dora ran in and went straight to her husband.

Corky looked down at his father, sprawled on the rug, and was immediately sorry. But before he could apologize Carl yelled, "Get out! Get outta my house! You better be the hell out of here before I get up or you'll never walk again, you son of a bitch! That's a promise!"

Corky ripped his parka off the rack and stormed out.

Dora shook her head in confusion. It had all exploded so fast. "You all right?"

"Damn right, I'm all right!" Carl scrambled to his feet. Dora tried to help.

"Get away! I'm no cripple. The day some punk eighteen-year-old can take me is the day I quit living, you understand me? Hell, I would've creamed him, except he took me by surprise. Let him push me again! Let him dare. Big star! He doesn't know who he's fooling with!"

"Carl, you're too excited—"

"I am not!" A vein on Carl's forehead throbbed as he screamed, ". . . *I'm the power of this house!*"

While walking out of Dr. Potter's office, Amy asked Guy to meet her after school.

Guy was sure she wanted to talk about the *Gadfly*. He was wrong.

"Where shall we go?" asked a sprightly Amy, locking her arm around his as they hopped down the front steps.

"How about Teahouse of the August Moon?"

"That dreary spot? Poo. Let's go to Darcy's. Hang out a while."

"Darcy's?" Guy was amazed. "You hate it."

"Says who? It's not without its quaintness. Besides, you never know who you might run into."

Guy shook his head. "Amy Silverstein, just another bobbysoxer. Jesus."

"Well, maybe those dopey girls have more on the ball than I thought."

"Sickening."

"Guy and Amy entered Darcy's. She took a fast look around the crowded hangout. "Gee. American bandstand, Pat Boone and Clearasil. There is a teen-age heaven, after all."

"Get a hold of yourself, Amy." Guy led the way to a window booth in the front.

"It's all so romantic!" She sat down.

"Thought you said sentiment was dead!"

"So I did. Well, I guess it's time for a renaissance!"

"All right. Enough of this boy-meets-girl crap. What about the *Gadfly?*"

"What about it?" Amy was vague.

"Aren't you going to get in trouble?"

"Certainly not," she said, looking from table to table. "Potsy Potter doesn't really care about us. He just wants to hear himself talk. And Ken Crawley knows we're be-

198

hind it, but he wouldn't say anything to incur the wrath of the fourth estate. Like any politician, he needs good press."

"It's all too confusing for me."

"Me too. Let's have a hot fudge sundae!"

"Don't be ridiculous. I'm in training."

"Suit yourself." Amy took a pencil from her purse and was about to doodle Corky's name across the paper place mat when she looked out the window and saw him pulling into a parking spot. "Omigod! He's here!"

"Who?"

"Him-Who! I've got to comb my hair. Fast lipstick job!" Amy bolted from the booth. "It's times like these I wish Greta Garbo had published her beauty secrets."

Corky slammed the Chevy door and stormed into Darcy's.

Guy waved to him.

Corky rushed over. "You seen Ro-Anne?"

"Nope."

He turned to leave.

"Wait! Where you running?"

"Gotta find her!"

"But I have to talk to you!"

"It can wait!" Corky hurried from the shop.

Guy left the booth and ran after him, shouting, "Hold it!"

Corky was jumping into his car as Guy caught up. "Listen. I saw your report file in Potter's office today. You may be in trouble!"

Corky tapped the steering wheel impatiently, then started the engine. "Get in!"

"But I left Amy back—"

"Get in!"

Guy got in.

The Chevy roared off, down Poste Avenue.

She's going to kill me, thought Guy. She'll come out of the bathroom looking her worst best, neither of us will be there and she'll never speak to me again.

"Let's have it, kid!" Corky demanded.

No time to talk in circles, Guy gave it to him straight. "You got English problems."

Corky put pressure on the pedal. "You mention this to anyone, anyone at all kid, it's your ass!"

"Come on. You think I'd ever do anything like that? All I want is to help."

"Help? How, kid? No way I'm gonna be able to get through that dumb Dickens by the end of this week. Impossible. It's a fucking shitty world is what it is."

"*Wrong!* I got the whole thing figured out."

Corky pulled the car to the side of the road. "What the hell you talking about?"

"It's all very simple, really."

"Yeah? How?"

Guy smiled knowingly. He had the answer in one word. "Amy."

31

Evelyn Silverstein opened the door early Tuesday evening and knew it was a miracle. After all these years, the answer to a mother's prayers.

"Hi, I'm Corky Henderson."

Evelyn unleashed her hospitality. "Please come into my living room. French Provincial. Such an elegant style . . ."

In the bathroom, Amy hastily applied finishing touches of a new mascara. It was so easy that afternoon when the woman at the five-and-dime demonstrated.

Amy followed the steps as shown and now looked like a racoon. Damn. Frustrated, she fast slapped cold cream on to remove her blackened eyes. That Corky was already in the living room being devoured by Evelyn sharpened her need to get out there and rescue him.

"I can't imagine what's keeping her." Evelyn smiled

girlishly. "Amy's always punctual. What can I get you while we wait? A cold drink? Fruit? There's still some layer cake—chocolate."

Corky squirmed. "Nothing, thanks."

"I bought it Thursday, so it might be a bit stale, anyway. Cookies?"

"No. Nothing, thank you."

Freshly scrubbed, Amy appeared. "I see you've met my mother."

"Indeed!" Evelyn confirmed, all bright and bubbles. "Such a large, strapping lad, Amy. I was wondering how one starts to feed it."

"One doesn't, Mother. It comes already nourished." She turned to Corky. "Shall we go to my room?"

Unusually neat and organized, Amy had spent the afternoon tidying. She and Corky sat on straight-back chairs, staring across an uncluttered desk.

Amy handed him a pen and pad, opened the book and read aloud, " 'It was the best of times, it was the worst of times.' " She looked up. "What does that say to you?"

Corky shrugged. "Nothing. It's a stupid contradiction."

"Precisely." As she then slowly explained why the author had chosen to begin his story with a series of opposites, the door slowly swung open and in with a trayful of goodies came Evelyn.

"Thinking always makes *me* ravenous. Figured you might want to nosh. Nothing fancy. Two beautiful bananas, peanuts, raisins, and if this isn't enough for hearty appetites, please feel free to go through the fridge yourselves. I can cut open a perfectly ripe pineapple if you'll eat it."

Amy stared at the ceiling while Evelyn placed the tray on her desk.

"I'm watching television with your father, should you need me." Evelyn left the room and, for the first time ever, closed the door tight behind.

"Alone at last!" Amy joked.

Corky pointed to Dickens.

Twenty minutes later Amy had synopsized the plot and social significance of the classic. That was what she'd agreed to do when Guy asked if she would help Corky out of his dilemma.

Now Corky wanted more.

"How will you remember what I've just said?" she asked. "You haven't taken a single note."

Corky placed a hand on her knee. Amy tried to ignore it. "Now tell me something about Madame Defarge."

"I'd rather not."

"Why?"

Corky popped a few peanuts into his mouth. "Bores me."

"That may well be. But you've got to know the story before you can expect to write any kind of—"

She didn't get to finish what she was saying because he put his hand behind her neck and brought his mouth to her.

Their lips met, reunited for the first time since New Year's, mixing her lip gloss with the salt of his peanuts.

He could feel her submission as her back gave in, her shoulders relaxed and, from somewhere deep within, there surfaced a delicate sob of pleasure.

This was it, Amy realized. Ecstasy, no matter how brief, no matter the length of time between encounters, was most assuredly worth the investment. The piper had to be paid.

And when their lips parted, Corky named his price. "Why don't *you* write the report for me?" he whispered into her ear as he nibbled on it.

Amy couldn't. That kind of cheating went against her high principles, and strong moral standards.

As he smiled into her eyes, she looked at him with determination and whispered, "I'd be happy to."

Guy finished his morning exercises and stood tall against the wall, marking off a lead scratch.

He penciled in at five four and a half. A full inch and a half higher than last time. After noting the date on the wall next to the mark, he made an appointment to meet himself there in exactly a month to record the next measurement.

Amy had the best time writing Corky's book report. Wording it as he might, she carefully incorporated his vernacular, his sensibilities. For a time she lived with him through his vision.

Corky dropped by Thursday evening to pick it up. He sat at her desk and read it through without comment. Once finished, he looked to her and smiled. "It sounds so smart. How can I thank you?"

Amy could think of a hundred ways. "Don't be silly."

Corky stood and kissed her. This time, genuine, grateful affection replaced affected passion.

"I better be going, huh?" He broke away. "Got to put all this down in my own handwriting before tomorrow. You won't say anything?"

Amy winked. "Mums de woid!"

When Evelyn heard Amy escorting Corky to the door, she hurried into the hallway to join in the good-bys. "Nice seeing you again, Corky. Sorry your visit was so short."

"Thanks, Mrs. Silverstein."

"Perhaps Amy will ask you for dinner soon. I'm a wonderful cook."

Amy coughed.

"Perhaps." Corky opened the door and kissed Amy on the cheek. Then he was gone.

Amy and Evelyn stared at the door a few moments, saying nothing.

Evelyn finally spoke. "Now that's what I call a lovely boy!"

"Thought you might like him."

"So handsome and tall. So charming, well mannered."

"All that and more," Amy was sad to agree.

"So why hasn't he asked you out?"

Mrs. Bartlett returned Corky's book report with the B + marked in red pencil. A footnote on the last of the three pages read:

> Excellent. This is "A" work,
> marked down due to tardiness.

Nathan sat in the doctor's office, glassy-eyed, staring at illuminated X-rays. When Doctor Zucker finished explaining what all the dark spots could mean, Nathan asked, "What'll I say to Birdie?"

The doctor swiveled in his leather chair. "The more she knows, the easier it will be . . ."

"She won't understand. Doesn't even know I'm here."

"I could speak with her."

Nathan exhaled with relief. "Would you do that, doctor? All those medical terms. She'll listen to you."

The doctor made a notation in his book. "I'll take care of it."

Birdie was washing dishes when the phone rang.

"Birdie? It's Doctor Zucker."

"Hello, doctor." Balancing the phone between her shoulder and chin, she dried her hands.

"Nathan just left a few minutes ago and I thought we might have a little chat before he gets home."

"All right." Slowly, Birdie sat down.

"He's been having problems with his lower digestive tract, Birdie."

"Hasn't mentioned anything to me."

"No. This is true. Didn't want to upset you needlessly, I guess."

"What does it mean?" Birdie was guarded.

"It could be several things. The tests we've taken and the X-rays have not been as encouraging as I'd like. But there's only one real way to find out what the problem might be."

"Problem? What problem?" Birdie balanced herself at the edge of the chair. Back muscles tightened into painful knots.

"What we have to do, Birdie, is a minor exploratory. It's a simple operation which will tell us everything."

"A simple operation doesn't sound serious to me."

"The exploratory itself is not."

Birdie leaned back. "That's a relief. I know anytime you're under anesthesia is cause for concern, but, doctor, for a moment there I was worried."

Doctor Zucker now understood what Nathan meant about having a difficult time explaining the situation. He decided she knew enough. "He'll be reporting to the hospital a week from Monday, late afternoon. Make him comfortable and relaxed until then, will you, Birdie?"

Birdie looked at the receiver with indignation. "Of course, doctor. That's my job!"

Ignoring her shaking hand and the knives in her back, Birdie stiffened her spine and walked into the kitchen.

Everything will be all right, she told herself. A minor operation. So what? Nothing wrong with that man. In nineteen years, he's never been sick. Oh, that Asian flu last year, sure, but everyone had that. Healthy as a horse, that one. I won't allow him to be upset. Not important enough.

She opened the freezer.

I'll cook a wonderful meal. He'll come home and have dinner like always.

From the bottom of the deep freeze, Birdie removed an enormous white paper package: four pounds of ice blue chops. As they defrosted in the sink, she cleaned vegetables, cut up ingredients for a salad, rolled dough for a sage-and-sesame bread and began cutting up apples for her standard apple-cinnamon pie.

I have to be strong, she resolved. No sense getting upset. Why create problems? We'll have a lovely dinner and nothing will change.

Nathan returned home a broken man. He walked without energy.

Birdie greeted him at the door. "Doctor Zucker called."

"I know."

"I've made a marvelous dinner, Nathan. Your favorite vegetables. Lamb chops with mint jelly. Just for you."

Nathan smiled with his eyes and walked slowly to his den. "I'm not hungry, Birdie. Maybe later."

After turning on the television Nathan collapsed into his leather lounger and stayed there the rest of the evening, staring without focus at black-and-white images.

Birdie fed the kids and spent the rest of the night in

the kitchen, keeping Nathan's supper warm, hoping he'd soon be hungry.

What she did not know as she stirred string beans and fought back tears was that the stomach cancer was fast sealing off his colossal appetite, and that he'd already begun the painful, one-way trip to starvation.

February

32

A heavy snow fell on the first day of the new term.

Students had to adapt to more than just harsh weather and the epidemic of mononucleosis sweeping the area. After searching for new classrooms, they struggled to unlock key idiosyncrasies of unfamiliar teachers while putting up with recycled textbooks, marred to incoherency by former owners. None of it made sense. By the second week it was all old hat.

Guy had a new sport to cover. Basketball season was in full flower and the elongated, willowy reeds dribbling up and down court left him cold.

At least his training program was paying dividends. He had gained a few pounds and could feel a definite strength in his arms. Several people noticed the gap between the bottom of his pants and the tops of his shoes and asked if he'd gotten taller. He told them no, he was still the same size, just in training to become a matador.

Ro-Anne wasn't cheering too loudly on the basketball court. Unenthusiastic as Guy, with no champion on whom to focus, even her famed spread-eagle jumps drooped.

She was preoccupied anyway, planning for her Sweet Sixteen birthday celebration the next month. Marian had promised her the grandest party ever seen in Waterfield. They were meeting with caterers and florists, dressmakers and shoe salesmen. The highlight of her life, she could hardly wait.

Corky's arrivals home no longer involved the ritual roughhouse. Ever since their falling out, he and Carl had been coldly cordial. Corky had apologized and his father had accepted.

But Carl had not forgiven.

Dr. Potter looked very dramatic indeed in Guy's photo of him setting fire to the *Gadfly*. The picture appeared in the next issue of the *Eagler,* which just happened to house the second publication of the monthly undercover newsletter.

The irony was circular. The stalwart *Eagler* reported the school's fight against the subversive *Gadfly*. The *Gadfly* reported the fight against Dr. Potter, likening his pyrotechnics to Hitler's burning of the books.

Students normally apolitical were suddenly arguing as to whether or not the doctrines of free speech should allow a publication like the *Gadfly* to exist.

The newsletter, organized to stimulate thought, was proving an astonishing success.

Though football season had passed, Corky stayed in shape, working out with the track team after school.

One Friday, after a long three-mile run, joggers relaxed tense leg muscles in a lively communal shower. The topic of conversation, stall to stall, was the usual. . . .

"If Emily Cordovan had spread her legs any wider in English this morning," announced a dash man, "I'd've creamed in my pants, for sure!"

"Emily Cordovan has the face of a douche bag!" Chuck Troendle yelled across the wet room.

"Maybe so. But her cookie's a beaut!"

"Big C-man! How would you know?" asked a high hurdler.

"I know creamy thighs when I see 'em. Boy, does she want it bad!"

"Bullshit!" Troendle tossed the hurdler a bar of soap.

"It's true!" he insisted, catching it.

"Who cares?" Corky weighed in. "With that face, who would want her?"

"You could do a lot worse," said the hurdler.

"How?" asked another dash man.

"Lots of worse looking girls around."

"Name one."

"Marge Flynn!"

Everyone howled.

"Marge Flynn is a real UGA," claimed the high hurdler.

"What's a UGA?"

"Don't you know anything? Ugliest Girl Alive!"

Roars of laughter amid gallons of water.

Troendle splashed cold water on the fellow next to him.

"Hey, cut it out! I'll tell you one UGA I'd never want to fuck."

"Who's that?"

"Amy Silverstein."

Soaped-up bodies shook with laughter.

"I'd pay ten bucks to anyone who'd fuck her," offered Troendle.

Corky rinsed the last of the suds from his hair and said calmly, "I don't think she's so bad."

The uproar died fast. For a moment water raining on tile was the only sound.

"Oh, come on, Henderson! You mean to say *you'd* fuck Amy Silverstein?"

Corky looked around. They were all waiting. Soaping his crotch, he shrugged. "Sure. She's got a great body. Why not?"

Faucets were turned off and water dribbled down the center drain.

Scrubbed, Corky dashed upstairs to the auditorium.

The sewing club was putting on its yearly fashion show at the Monday assembly. Ro-Anne was one of the models displaying the work of creative fingers.

The rehearsal was half over. Corky asked for Ro-Anne and was directed backstage.

"What're you doing here?!" the alarmed young bride wanted to know. "It was supposed to be a surprise!"

"No one said anything," Corky told her.

All in white, veil pinned to her hair, Ro-Anne pouted.

"It's bad luck to see me before the ceremony. Don't you know that?"

Corky looked to the spotlights. "You're not really getting married, Ro. You're just modeling the gown."

"Still! I wanted to surprise you."

"Look. I only came to say good-by before you left. That such a crime?"

Ro-Anne softened. "I guess not." She whirled around. "Like it?"

"You're beautiful." He smiled.

"They're saving me for the grande finale."

"The best for last."

Ro-Anne lifted her veil. "You may kiss the bride."

Corky kissed the bride.

"I don't know why I ever agreed to go to that stupid health farm with mother this weekend. If it weren't so important I lose those three pounds before my party . . ."

"I know. Just try to make the best of it."

"How? With cucumber sandwiches, steam baths and rubdowns? And not a quarterback in sight." She smiled. "Really, I wish I didn't have to go."

"Me too. You know I hate to be alone."

"You thought about the ring?"

Corky shuffled his feet. "I thought about it."

"And?" Ro-Anne laced fingers around his belt loop.

"And I don't know." He shrugged. "Seems kind of funny."

"What's *funny* about it?"

"Doesn't make sense. I mean, your mother buys you a ring for me to give to you."

"You got it all wrong. Mother's giving me the ring either way. I just thought it'd be a hoot if everyone thought it was a present from you. That's all."

"Who cares what everyone thinks?"

"I care. Plenty. Come on, Corky. Everyone has a crummy old ID bracelet. Please. None of the girls has a birthstone. It would mean so much more. Besides, if the ring comes from you, then you don't have to buy me a present."

Corky folded his arms. "Maybe I want to buy you a present."

Ro-Anne frowned. "On *your* allowance?" She tugged at his belt buckle. "Please, Corky. For me?"

"I'll think about it."

"You're next, Ro-Anne!" the president of the sewing club called from the wings.

"I gotta go." Ro-Anne kissed him quickly on the lips. "Don't watch. You'll make me nervous."

"I'll miss you."

"You better." And then, deeply dimpled, the lovely bride pinched a blush into her cheeks and floated on stage.

Corky went to his fraternity meeting that night and lost nine big ones in as many minutes at the poker table.

He barely had enough change for a glass of milk afterward when they all shifted over to Darcy's.

On Saturday he decided to make plans for the evening. He was not about to stay home in front of the television watching heavyweight wrestling with his father.

Chuck Troendle and Jenkins both had dates with cheerleaders. Calvin was baby-sitting his twin sisters. Everyone was busy.

His last resort, he called Guy. "Hey, kid. Why don't you and me take in a movie tonight?"

It was the best offer Guy had ever received. "I can't," he mumbled.

"What?!" Corky couldn't believe it.

"I've got that dumb basketball game in Valley Stream tonight."

"Oh, crap. Forgot about it."

"Why don't you come along, Corky? I'm sure there'd be room on the bus. . . ."

"No thanks. If I'm not playing, it's no fun."

"What about Ro-Anne?"

"Away for the weekend."

"I'm sorry, Corky. Jeez, any other time . . ."

"Sure. Sure."

"No. I mean it."

212

"Right. Hope it's a good game, kid. You're a real traitor."

Corky hung up and stared at the phone. Saturday night. What the hell was he going to do? He dialed *411*—wrote down the requested information and hung up.

Forget it. The ball of crumpled paper sailed across the room into the trash. Two points.

Corky walked to the window and stared into the gray yard. He stretched and yawned and then went back to the desk and retrieved the discarded paper. Before he could change his mind again, he placed the call.

33

"Hi. It's me. Corky!"

Amy was stunned. "Hello."

"There are a couple of monster flicks at the Midstate tonight. Thought maybe you'd like to see them."

"Sounds like fun," she said without hesitation.

"I'll drop by . . . seven-thirty."

Amy hung up and screamed out her joy. She flung open her closet and searched frantically for something to wear. Thank God her parents were away on their winter vacation. Evelyn would have been impossible.

Too excited to think straight, she called Guy. "Which do you think would be better . . . a pleated skirt with knee socks or a two-piece green and white polka-dot job?"

"No idea."

"I've got terrific legs."

"Then by all means wear them. What's it for?"

Amy was blasé. "Nothing much. Going to a drive-in tonight with Corky."

Guy was amazed. "Tonight?"

"That's right!" she sang.

"Lucky girl." He didn't dare tell her he'd turned down the same offer not three minutes ago.

"I know it's kind of last minute and all, still . . ."

"Don't be silly." Guy made her feel better. "I happen to know Ro-Anne's away for the weekend. He probably waited for her to leave before calling."

Amy's voice reverted to childhood. "You think so?"

"Sure."

"*Yippee.* And thank God my parents are still in the Holy Land."

"Israel?" Guy asked.

"Miami Beach. Oh, Guy. I'm so excited, so excited. If you only knew . . ."

Guy knew.

Corky called for Amy in chinos, heavy sweater and team jacket.

Amy had opted for the mid-calf-length, green-and-white polka-dot outfit.

"A little dressy for the movies," he said, walking in.

Rats! Knew I should have worn the pleated skirt. "I've never been to a drive-in. I could change."

"Don't bother. Get your coat. *I Was a Teen-age Were-wolf* starts at eight."

Amy found both films wretched bores.

Mesmerized, Corky could not be distracted from the wooden screen.

Why doesn't he talk to me? she asked herself. I'm more interesting than this ghastly movie. Look at him sitting there, radiating nothing but waves of gorgeousness. What am I doing here? Maybe I should snuggle next to him? Too forward. Offer to go get more popcorn? Too servile. I'll say something bright, something to remind him there are still two of us in the car. No. This one doesn't go for smart-ass ladies. Okay, relax. Calm yourself. Stop scheming and just watch the movie. If passion is going to strike, let it be spontaneous, through Kismet.

Amy looked to the screen and sighed deeply. *I should live so long!*

The second feature ended and hundreds of headlights flooded the area. Horns honked. Corky started his car.

"Well?" Amy asked, returning the sound box and heater to the stand. "What'd you think?"

Corky yawned. "I don't like movies if they're not in color. You?"

"I think I'd like to be a vampire."

They drove to a seedy Carvel stand outside town. While Corky waited in line she waited in the car, wondering if he wasn't going out of his way not to be seen with her. She quickly dismissed it as insecurity, telling herself he just wouldn't want word getting back to Ro-Anne that he'd been spotted with someone else.

After a round of frozen milk shakes, they drove home. It was eleven-thirty.

"Want to come in?" she asked at the door, her head swimming with expectations of rejection. "Have some tea or something?"

"Your parents asleep?"

Amy took her time and said it slowly. "My parents are in Florida."

They lay together on the couch. A tepid teapot remained untouched on the candlelit coffee table.

Her top was unbuttoned and her bra unhooked. He'd taken off his sweater and the buttons of his shirt were undone to his waist.

They kissed for a long time while he inched his hands up from the bottom of her skirt to the back of her soft thighs.

Eventually, he talked her into taking off both her polka-dot blouse and her Maiden-form bra.

She didn't mind. She was prepared to do anything for him; whatever he wanted. Anything to please.

Corky examined her breasts. "They're small," he commented, "but they're pretty."

When they kissed again, Corky dropped his chinos to his knees. Then he leaned back and lowered his shorts.

Amy was at once petrified and enthralled by the sight of his nakedness. The light from the candle silhouetted his strong physique.

"I want you to do something for me," he whispered.

"I'll try," she whispered back in a shaky voice.

Corky circled his hand around his erection. "You know."

That? Amy reeled in alarm. No one had ever asked her to do that. She was no tramp. "Oh, no, I couldn't."

"Why not?"

"It's awful."

"It's not awful. Go on."

"Please. I don't want to." *What would he think of me?*

"You'll enjoy it."

"I won't. Too ugly."

"It's not. Kiss it."

Kiss it? Was he crazy? Girls just didn't go around kissing boys' stiff you-know-whats. Disgusting!

Corky applied a silght pressure to the back of her neck. Gently he lowered her face. "Go on," he encouraged her. "Kiss it. Do it for me, Amy."

"It's dirty," Amy whimpered from below, "Please, put it away."

Corky sighed impatiently. "It's not dirty. I showered."

Amy poked the obscene object inches from her nose. *Would he maybe like me more?*

"Go on, Amy. It wants you to. Look how it grows when you touch it. Go on. Do it. It'll prove how much you care."

Amy closed her eyes tight and kissed the head of his resilient erection. *See how much I care?*

It responded, rising upward in an arc. "That's nice. Ooh, is that nice. Do it again."

"No," she pleaded. What was this, anyway? In all her love stories, Jane Austen had never once mentioned a thing about cock-sucking.

"Again, Amy. Please." He placed a firm hand behind her neck and eased her face downward.

"No more!"

"Once more," he coaxed.

"It's perverted."

"It's not perverted. It feels great. Go on, Amy. Please. Kiss it for me."

"No. Tasted terrible!" she complained.

Corky cradled her face in his hands. "What'd it taste like?"

"Talcum powder."

Corky smiled. "I told you I showered." He kissed her again. "Let's go to your room."

She carried in their discarded clothing. A light from outside fed through venetian blinds, outlining their bodies as Corky's hands roamed all over her and in the process removed the rest of her clothing.

As much as he could. "Take off that damn girdle, will you?" he demanded after floundering for nearly five minutes.

Amy excused herself and hurried into the bathroom.

Alone, Corky found his pants and took the Trojan out of his wallet. "Women!" he breathed before yelling to the door. "You don't even need a girdle. You got a great ass!"

Smiling, Amy wiggled in the bathroom. At least he noticed.

She came back to him in a pair of white cotton panties. "Better?"

"Much."

He dropped to his knees and planted his mouth in the middle of her panties.

Disoriented, she placed her hands on his shoulders. It was all too foreign, too new. She wasn't ready for such intense intimacy, and pushed him away. He laughed as he fell backward, landing on his rear. Then with a smile he stood and removed his shirt, took off his pants, shorts and only in sweat socks went to her.

They embraced. He removed her underpants and led her onto the bed. Pushing her thighs apart with his knees was not easy. Amy was rigid.

"I don't think we should," she whispered. "I have to be a virgin for my husband."

"Balls."

"It means a lot to me."

"Don't be dumb. You're gonna marry some Leonard Hauser asshole and *you'll* have to show *him* the ropes."

"You're repulsive."

"Might as well learn from the master." He kissed her breast.

Amy erupted, pushing violently against his shoulders.

He grabbed her straining hands. "Hey, cool it. Settle down. Virginity's no big deal. Just do what other girls do."

"And what's that?"

"Lie," said Corky, circling her nipple with his tongue.

Amy stared at the ceiling. "I can't lie to myself."

"Don't be so damn self-righteous." He massaged her thigh. "You want to, don't you?"

"That has nothing to do with it."

Corky arched up, supported by his hands, and looked into her eyes. "Sweetheart, that has *everything* to do with it."

There was no arguing with him. Amy was in silent accord.

"Now relax." He sucked in his words as he spoke. "Do as I tell you. Relax with your legs." While looking at her, he slipped on the rubber.

Please be careful, she thought. Go slow. Please. She closed her eyes in anticipation and grabbed the sides of the sheets. Remember everything, she told herself. Details. She wanted to preserve the experience, savor and cherish this, her first real moment with love.

Corky tried pushing his way in. Nothing.

His erection in hand, he forced it slowly against her and met only with frightened resistance. "Relax," he whispered soothingly. "Loosen up."

"I'm a virgin," Amy whispered.

"I know. Just relax. Relax and try to love me."

Easy. *Oh yes. Yes, I love you.*

She released the sheets and threw her arms around his waist, hugging him tight. Make him care, she told herself. It's not right if he doesn't care. Make him love you.

"Love me!" she cried out. "Tell me you love me!"

Corky brought his face close to hers. "I love you," he whispered.

Amy softened.

Corky eased his way in slowly, forward and up.

Lost to a new and strange intensity, Amy ignored the drops of blood staining the sheets. She had never felt so much warmth and comfort. So much love.

It's not what I imagined, she told herself. But it's no disappointment, either.

As Corky escalated his thrusts into a calculated rhythm she stared into his eyes, thinking only of how much she loved him.

He looked down at her and with each motion tried reaching further inside. When he wasn't thinking of other breasts, other faces, he was aroused seeing how very excited she was by all he was giving.

34

Corky woke up, startled. "We slept too long. Damn it. Knew that would happen."

Amy opened her eyes and looked at the clock. Four-thirty.

"I got to get out of here!" he said, pulling his clothes together. "Hope my old lady didn't wait up for me. She does sometimes. Isn't that crazy?"

Amy slipped into her bathrobe. "You want something before you go? Tea? Coffee?" God, she sounded like Evelyn.

Corky struggled into his socks. "No thanks."

Amy rushed into the bathroom. "Milk?" she called into the other room as she quickly brushed her hair and rinsed with some toothpaste.

"Nothing." He pulled his sweater over his head and started for the front door.

She hurried out of the bathroom and followed him.

"Are you all right? I mean, if you're too tired to drive, you can spend the night."

"Nope. Gotta go. Thanks for everything."

"I had the best time."

Corky kissed her cheek.

She took his hand. "Can we do this again?"

He pulled free. "Hold on a minute. We're getting signals crossed. I like you a lot. I do. You know that. You got a terrific personality and—"

Amy took a step back.

"Now just a minute." He held her hand. "Don't be so touchy. I mean, I'm practically engaged."

Amy pointed to the bedroom. "What about. . ."

Corky cupped her chin in his hand and shook his head. "And you're supposed to be the smart one. Hey, it's late. Don't you see it's late? I gotta run!"

He opened the door, smiled, winked, waved and left.

Chuck Troendle called the next day. "Hey, C-man! I guess you'll do anything for money."

"What're you talking about?"

"Have a good time?"

"When?"

"Come on, sneaky Pete. 'Fess up. Me and Jenkins saw you two lovebirds last night at the Carvel stand."

Oh, shit. "Not me!"

Chuck ignored the denial. "Well, how was she, killer?"

"If you or Jenkins leak one word of this . . ."

"Hold your britches, hotshot. Don't worry about us. It's our dates who'll do any blabbing. They're Ro-Anne's friends. Now tell. Do I owe you another ten or not?"

Corky said nothing.

"Zombie Silverstein. Jesus, you must have really been hard up! How'd you get past the acne?"

Tapping on the phone, Corky finally said, "Keep your money, wise-ass. She wouldn't let me near her. I fell asleep on the couch."

After a weekend apart, Corky and Ro-Anne had no trouble making up for lost time. Kissy-face and huggy-

220

bear and she missed him, no he missed her . . . they'd never part again and that was a promise!

Rather than have it get back to her first, Corky told Ro-Anne about his Saturday night date with Amy, confiding he'd asked her out on a bet but please not to tell anybody.

Ro-Anne waited a full two hours before calling several girl friends. She had to tell *someone*. "Oh, that naughty Corky . . . anything for a laugh. . . ."

On the last day of the month, Guy measured his height and found he stretched to five five and a half.

Another month, another inch. At this rate, he figured, by June of 1961, his graduation, he'd stand seven feet and nine-and-a-half inches. Maybe he should reconsider learning to play basketball, after all.

That same day a white printed invitation, RSVP and everything, arrived in the mail. He and a date were invited to help Ro-Anne Summers celebrate her Sweet Sixteen.

A date? No problem. He'd take Amy.

March

35

It didn't look much like Easter.

An early holiday and still another late winter storm preempted any springtime visions of baby rabbits in lollipop suits rolling colorful eggs down sunny lawns.

Ro-Anne looked out the living room window at the florist's truck skidding up her driveway and winced. "No one will come, Mother! No one! Look at this weather!"

Marian, in rollers and moisturizer, was checking off a long list. "Relax, darling."

"It's the twenty-third of March, Mother. Why is it still snowing? Oh, I hate it here! Why can't we live in California like everyone else?"

"Take a bath and do your nails."

The doorbell rang. Marian looked at her list. "That must be the ice."

"Ice?! Why'd you order ice? Just go outside and shovel it in!"

Marian opened the door and in with old man winter came the florist. "Sorry I'm late. Roads are pretty bad."

"Don't say that!" shouted the birthday girl, dashing up the stairs to drown herself in the bathtub. "Why should I believe in God if this is how he treats my Sweet Sixteen?"

"I think she's a little nervous about the party," Marian told the shivering, wet florist.

Amy had no trouble convincing her mother she should have a new dress for Ro-Anne's birthday. Evelyn was delighted to get lost in the project, shopping daily for an appropriate outfit.

Each evening she'd parade an assortment of dresses and accessories picked up during that day's spree, the relative merits of which she and Amy would then proceed to haggle over.

Evelyn kept returning clothes until she came across a blue velvet dress with long sleeves and a hint of decolletage. It won Amy's instant approval.

Guy felt ridiculous. He hadn't worn his itchy woolen dress-up clothes in months and was sure everyone at the party would think he was wearing long Bermuda shorts.

Amy couldn't believe what Barton had done. Her mother's hairdresser cut her hair, combed it straight back and tied the neat ponytail with a blue velvet ribbon. He plucked her thick eyebrows and applied liner along her lashes. He dotted her cheeks with rouge.

She'd never looked better and was for the first time intoxicated with the potential power of her image.

"I guess I'm ready," said Guy, walking into the den.

"That how you're going?" Butch remarked, gobbling his fourth Hostess Twinkie since dinner. "You didn't say it was a costume party."

"That's enough, Butch!" said Nathan sharply, and the reprimand surprised father and sons.

"But, Dad . . ."

"Your brother looks fine. About time you started treating each other like family, anyway. You're not kids anymore."

Neither Butch nor Guy said anything. Nathan turned off the television. "Let's go, Guy."

Nathan was driving Guy to Amy's, and then Evelyn would take them to the party from there.

"What a rotten night." Nathan wiped the frosted window with his sleeve.

"Some Easter vacation, huh?" Guy assisted, rubbing his side of the windshield.

"I wanted you to have a new suit, Guy. But these doctor bills have really been something. . . . Besides, the way you're going you'd outgrow it right away."

"Sure, that's what I figured."

Nathan turned smoothly around an icy corner.

"Hey, Dad. How come you wanted to lose so much weight?"

Nathan looked at the sprouting pole, not knowing what to say. "I want you to know I'm proud of you."

"Me, Dad? Proud of me? How come?"

"No one reason. I just am."

"How 'bout that? Hey, Dad. Thanks a million!"

Nathan stopped in front of Amy's apartment house. Guy flung his camera bag over his shoulder and started to get out.

"I want you to watch your mother, Guy."

"Watch her what?"

"She doesn't know the real world. I think in a lot of ways, you do."

"What are you talking about?"

Nathan smiled. "Nothing. Go on. Have a good time."

"Wow! Do you ever look good!"

A grateful Amy kissed Guy on the cheek. "And don't you look handsome!"

Guy was smug. "I shaved."

Amy smiled approvingly.

"Here." Evelyn handed Guy an umbrella. "Carry this. And whatever you do, no matter what else happens, don't let Amy get wet."

Evelyn pulled into the Sommers driveway behind two cars depositing young guests at the front door.

"Isn't it exciting?" Amy clapped her hands.

"Just like a movie premiere," Guy agreed.

"Get your umbrella ready, Guy," Evelyn instructed. "Who ordered this blizzard, anyway?"

They were both intimidated when a butler opened the door. After taking their coats and the present they'd brought for Ro-Anne, he pointed the way.

Guy and Amy followed the music of a live five-piece rock and roll band into the crowded ballroom-sized living room. Most of the furniture had been removed.

"Look at these flowers!" Amy elbowed Guy. "It's either a Jewish wedding or an Italian funeral."

A long table with a pink lace cloth was crammed with food. Hams and roasts, turkeys and salads. Pink paper plates displayed Ro-Anne's name and the number 16. Cascading in driblets down a three-tiered electric fountain was a pink champagne-laced punch.

Guy and Amy greeted friends from school. It was strange seeing everyone all dressed up, stiff as boards.

Ro-Anne, Marian and Corky stood in front of a giant fireplace with a roaring blaze. The reception line.

"We should say hello," said Guy.

Amy agreed and squeezed his hand. "Stick close to me."

The tall girl and not-so-short boy joined other couples greeting the evening's hosts.

Marian was in a tight-fitting pink floor-length gown ablaze with hundreds of hand-sewn sequins.

Ro-Anne, also in pink, displayed a plunging neckline held together by the thinnest of spaghetti straps. Semi-circles of her full-rounded breasts were exposed, very grown-up.

Amy and Ro-Anne were icy. One congratulated, the other acknowledged. Glistening lips grazed opposite cheeks.

Moving down the line, Amy said hello to Corky, very handsome in his dark blue suit. He shook her hand and smiled with his eyes. She batted freshly Maybellined lashes. "How nice to see you, again."

It was a good thing, Guy thought, that he and Ro-Anne were now the same height. At his former miniature stature her breasts would surely have hit him smack in the face.

Guy leaned in to·kiss her cheek. Ro-Anne opened both arms, embracing him. "Dearest Guy. How wonderful you look!"

Guy turned red.

"Bring your camera, sweetheart?"

Guy nodded.

"Goodie!" Ro-Anne kissed him again, a short peck on the lips. "Take wonderful pictures, you hear me? It's the most important night ever!"

"I'll try. Happy birthday."

Ro-Anne wrinkled her nose.

The band ended one song, segued into another. Guy and Amy segued out of the receiving line over to the cascading punch.

Marian's boyfriend Lester stood behind the fountain doling out small portions. It was his job to make sure none of the underage partygoers had too much to drink.

He had no idea that some of the boys were sneaking swigs from flasks in the upstairs bathroom.

The champagne flowed downstairs, the whiskey upstairs. Eventually everyone began to relax.

Guy and Amy separated. He roved about, snapping pictures; she stood back, observing. Mostly she watched Corky.

The musicians took a break at ten-thirty and everyone was summoned to sit in the middle of the dance floor. The many presents were piled in front of the band.

Ro-Anne sat on a puffy cushion and opened them.

A girl friend to her left took ribbons and bows as they unraveled and Scotch-taped them to a white box top.

Another girl took pen in hand, recording every word Ro-Anne uttered as she opened her gifts. The living room soon mushroomed into a rainbow of crumpled tissue paper and empty boxes.

Scarves and cuddly stuffed dogs, a fuzzy cotton six-foot cross-eyed snake and stationery; Johnny Mathis record albums, sweaters, a tiny gold-plated charm with "16" embedded in rhinestones for posterity, and more Johnny Mathis.

When finally there were no presents left to open, Ro-Anne was presented with the hat made from the flowing ribbons and wrinkled bows.

She smiled winsomely as Guy snapped a picture.

The girl who had been taking notes then read the list of quips Ro-Anne would say on her wedding night: "What could this be?" "How wonderful!" "Just what I wanted." "That's the biggest thing I've ever seen!" "How does it work?"

The girls snickered and the boys howled at the innuendo.

Amy yawned and went over to the fountain for another pink glassful.

"Oh!" Ro-Anne summoned everyone's attention again as she discovered a small white ribboned box next to her. "Look! One last present!"

She ripped open a tiny envelope attached to the gift and announced mid-blush, "It's from Corky!"

Everyone oohed and ahed, and Corky sat up straight and surprised. Her gift—a quarter ounce of Chanel—was still tucked inside his jacket pocket.

Ro-Anne lifted the delicate bloodstone ring from the velvet box and went into a seizure of joy, bouncing up and down, screaming with delight.

As she threw her arms around Corky, kissing him excitedly, her girl friends, as hoped, turned green.

Corky turned white. Livid, he nonetheless returned Ro-Anne's kisses and went along with the charade.

The band returned. Partners lined up for the stroll. A few did the slop.

Ro-Anne and Marian went upstairs to connect cards with gifts, organizing for thank-you notes.

When the band played a slow dance, a stylized rendition of "Tears on My Pillow," Amy drained the last of her sixth champagne punch and walked up to a fairly inebriated Corky, who was sitting on the bottom step of the stairwell, leaning back on his elbows.

"Pardon me," she asked softly, "is your card filled?"

"You want to dance?"

"Once. If you don't mind. For auld lang syne."

Corky stood up. "I don't mind."

He led her into the living room and they danced. Neither of them said a word, just held each other close and moved slowly around the floor.

Ro-Anne came back into the living room as the song was ending. She glanced from Corky to Amy, and knew there was no bet to explain this. She watched Amy and Corky back away. She saw Amy nodding her head, thanking him. She bit her bottom lip when Corky responded in kind, then stood her ground as Amy rushed past her up the stairs.

Amy hurried into the bathroom as three boys with a flask were scurrying out. She turned on the cold tap water and filled the gold plastic cup above the sink and gulped from it. She filled it again. Looking to the mirror, she saw tears forming in the sides of her eyes. She drained the cup, hoping to hold them at bay.

As she was drinking her third cupful, there was a knock on the door. "What is it?"

"Mind if I come in?" asked Ro-Anne, too sweet.

Amy sniffed, took a deep breath and opened the door. "Hi. Guess I've had too much champagne."

"Who hasn't?" Ro-Anne smiled, going to the other half of the double sink.

Thereafter they talked at each other diagonally, through the long mirror above the sinks.

Ro-Anne applied a fresh coating of lipstick. "Want some sisterly advice?"

I can hardly wait. "Sure."

"I'm thinking what's best for you."

"How thoughtful." Amy forced a smile.

"I think you're making a big mistake." Ro-Anne rubbed her lips together, puckering for her reflection.

"How's that?"

"To be perfectly frank, Amy . . . why don't you leave him alone?"

"Corky?"

"Corky. Once was harmless nonsense. Now you're just making a pest of yourself."

Amy fought to say something. Words were her talent. Where were the words?

"Especially in my house. Tsk-tsk. Bad taste!"

"Who says I'm being a pest?" Amy rose to her own defense.

Ro-Anne shrugged and laughed. "Isn't it obvious, my dear?"

Amy's head was scrambled. She hunted for the appropriate thing to say, came out with, "I have just as much right—"

"Oh, come off it, miss—Where do you get the nerve? Playing Jewish princess is one thing, but let's not get carried away!"

"That's not how it is!"

"Ask yourself honestly. Go ahead, take a long, honest look. What would Corky want with you?"

Amy took a look, and turned away.

"Would it interest you to know you were asked out on a bet? Did Corky tell you that?"

"It's not true!"

"Everybody knows it's true. The whole school is laughing about it!"

Lies! Amy told herself. Lies of jealousy and deceit. Tell her. Go on. Tell her the truth. She asked for it. Taking a step closer, Amy turned her head from the reflection and addressed the real Ro-Anne. "Do you also happen to know that he made love to me?"

Ro-Anne took a deep breath and altered her strategy. It didn't take long. "I'd hate to believe that. For your sake. Only makes you more of a fool. The boys have a name for that kind of sport. Shall I tell you? They call it a mercy fuck, Amy. That's what you got from Corky. A mercy fuck."

Amy brushed past Ro-Anne and fled from the bathroom, well past the point of being able to stop the flow of mascara.

As she approached the bottom of the stairs a flashbulb went off. Following the light to its source, she found, Guy.

"There you are!" he said, trying to be heard above the music.

Amy held his arm.

Guy looked at the dark makeup running down her face. "What's the matter?"

"I want to know something." She squeezed tight. "Promise me the truth."

"You're hurting me."

"Did Corky take me out on a bet?"

Guy looked away. "Jesus."

"Well?" Amy pinched harder.

Guy looked at her, saying nothing.

"I have to know!"

"Hey, I said that hurts!"

"Tell me!" Amy raised her voice.

"First let go."

Amy dropped her hand. "I'm waiting."

There was a long pause before Guy mumbled, "That's what I heard."

Amy pinched her own fingers. "Why didn't you warn me, Guy? I promise I'll never forgive you. You were my friend."

Guy looked her straight in the eye. "Because you were so happy, Amy. I thought for once in your life you should be happy."

She wiped her cheek. "I feel so sorry for you, Guy. Can I tell you that? I wish I knew who got the worse deal. Me because I only had that one night, or you because you can't even touch him."

"That's not true!" Guy's voice broke.

Amy hurried from the room and searched for her coat on the crowded rack in the empty hallway. She pulled it off the hanger.

As she was buttoning up, Corky came in from the other room. "Where you going?" he asked good-naturedly.

"Go to hell!" She headed for the door.

He grabbed her arm.

"Let go, dammit!"

"What's wrong?"

"Leave me alone." She pulled her arm free.

"What is it?"

"You, you bastard!"

He caught on. "Don't believe everything you hear."

Amy laughed and cried at the same time. "I don't care so much that you told her. I can almost understand your feeling you had to justify what we did. But you said you loved me!"

Corky looked down. "You asked me to, remember . . . ?"

"Liar!" She slapped his face. Then, letting loose, she slapped him again and again, harder and harder.

He stood there and took it. Then he caught her hand. "Enough," he said softly.

She turned and rushed out of the house.

He searched for his coat.

Ro-Anne came down the stairs. "What are you doing?"

Corky whirled on her. "What the hell did you say to that girl?"

"Who?"

"Amy!"

"Nothing! That zombie. I told her hands off!"

"Why don't you mind your own fucking business?"

"Don't you yell at me!"

"What really kills me is that I've known it all along. Can I tell you that? I was crazy to think there was ever anything more to it." He went to the door.

"What are you talking about? Where you going?"

"To find her!"

"Now!?" Ro-Anne squealed. "You can't leave now. Not in the middle of my party!"

Corky turned the large brass knob and opened the door.

"Don't bother coming back!" Ro-Anne's stomping foot underlined her words as she pulled the red ring off her finger. "Here!" She extended it to him as though it were infected.

"Don't give it to me. I never gave it to you. Give it back to your mother. You really are dumb. Let me tell you something!"—he pointed a nervous finger at one of her breasts—"the only reason we lasted so long together is because I was afraid people wouldn't think as much of me if I wasn't going with the prettiest girl in school. That tells you what kind of jerk *I* am! So take your crown and scepter, Little Miss Pee Wee Shit, and shove 'em up your prize-winning ass!"

Car keys in hand, he ran out into the snow.

Course I won't forget. I'll never forget." somebody

her mother and you.

she handed Corky a tissue, and there waited a long

before she spoke. "I could Corky. Anything else.

36

Ro-Anne stared at the door. Of all nights, how dare he!

"There she is!" someone shouted from the other room. "Hey, Ro!"

How to explain? What to say? Fresh as the pink rose-buds on her wrist, Ro-Anne pirouetted in place and offered her grandest smile all the way into the living room. The band played "Sixteen Candles."

"Where's Corky?" someone asked.

"Corky? Too much to drink, probably . . . went for some air, I guess."

"He all right?" asked another guest.

"Corky, Corky." Ro-Anne laughed as she fastened sparkling eyes on Chuck Troendle. "Doesn't anybody want to dance with the birthday girl?"

Chuck Troendle was happy to dance with the birthday girl.

After brushing the snow from his windshield, Corky took off in the Chevy, circled the driveway twice, and saw no one.

Coasting slowly down Ridgewood Drive, he scanned one side, then the other. He rubbed the frosted window with his sleeve, turned the corner and went into a skid. Carefully, he eased on the brakes and set the car back on course.

Snow had piled into drifts against doorways and tree trunks. Where the hell was she? She had to walk down Ridgewood if she was heading home.

He reached the end of the street, turned around and drove back up the long block until it ended. No sign of her.

He made a left turn at the intersection and drove beneath the overpass of the state highway. Looking all around, he caught a fleeting glimpse of umbrella. He quickly stretched over, rolled down the window and yelled, "Amy!"

The umbrella swiveled and the old man beneath it, walking his dachshund, looked at Corky. The next instant he screamed, dropped the leash and covered his face.

Corky swung around and the last thing he remembered hearing was the roaring engine of the truck as it ripped through his windshield.

Soaking wet and freezing, her hair limp and ragged, Amy arrived home.

Evelyn left the Late Show and rushed to her. "What happened to you?"

A trembling Amy held her mother's hands. "I want you to call Aunt Bernice, Mother. Tell her we're coming to New York."

The revolving red light of the police car tinted the snow. Orange flares lit up the roadway, warning approaching drivers to turn back—road closed.

The rescue squad from the highway patrol finally arrived. An acetylene torch had to be used to cut through the crushed metal so they could get to the boy pinned behind the steering wheel. Men in an ambulance sat and waited.

The Chevy was barely recognizable. It smelled of Chanel.

The driver of the Seven-Up truck studied the wreckage, piecing together for the police a confused explanation of what might have happened.

One moment he had come off the highway and was making a right turn, the next there was this small blue car below him, folding like an accordion.

After two and a half hours of separating metals, they were finally able to free Corky from his trap. An ambulance attendant squirmed his way in to check if the crash victim was still alive. In a sea of blood he found a weak pulse.

Attendants carefully lifted Corky out from the smoldering, melded dashboard and broken steering column, and it wasn't until they'd laid him down on the stretcher in the snow that they first discovered his left foot had been severed at the ankle.

With the police car leading the way, its siren alarming a stilled countryside, red lights flashing, the ambulance crawled through the deep snow toward neighboring Rushport.

The attendant standing over Corky kept yelling at the driver to hurry. The kid was still losing so much blood so fast, he wasn't sure how long he might last. A red puddle had formed at the bottom of his leg. Blood spurted from the left side of his head.

It was still snowing heavily when they pulled into the emergency room at Rushport Memorial an hour later. The patient had gone into shock and was comatose. The doctors went to work.

Blood was their primary concern. After giving Corky a transfusion, they checked their limited supply and then called a blood bank in Hempstead, ordering a dozen additional pints sent over at once.

The left side of Corky's face had been damaged so as to be medically labeled *comminute*. Hamburger.

At five in the morning Corky was wheeled into the operating room for emergency surgery. Doctors rushed to tie off arteries in his forehead and leg which kept gushing blood as fast as they received it. The left side of his slashed neck was sewn. The bones in his crushed nose had caved in and had to be evacuated so they would no longer apply pressure on his brain.

One surgeon worked on his head, another tied the two arteries at the bottom of his leg and applied a bandaged dressing.

The patient was still losing large quantities of blood, even after the arteries had been connected. The medical team agreed on the diagnosis. Internal bleeding.

Inserting a scalpel just below the chest cavity, the

235

surgeon made a seven-inch incision, down to the navel. A quick examination revealed a ruptured spleen. It was removed.

The police found no identification on Corky or in his car. His wallet had been lost in the steaming wreckage, but they were able to trace the license plate number to Carl Henderson, Jr.

The information was given to the head nurse at the reception desk.

The telephone rang twice before Carl Sr. reached for it. "Hello?" he grumbled.

"Does a Carl Henderson, Junior, live there?"

"What time is it?"

"Carl Henderson. Does he live there?"

"It's Sunday morning! Who is this?"

"There's been an accident. I'm calling from Rushport Memorial Hospital. We're looking for a—"

"Accident? What kind of accident?"

Dora bolted up in bed.

"A car accident," said the nurse.

"Corky? Not Corky!"

"Is this Carl Henderson's father?"

"Corky! Yes, yes it is."

"Your son's been in an automobile accident, Mr. Henderson. Can you come at once?"

"What? . . . yes . . . sure . . ."

"Rushport Memorial. Right off the Southern State Parkway at—"

"Yes, yes. Is . . . is it serious?"

There was a pause. "Very serious."

Carl and Dora drove through the snowstorm to get to Rushport. When they arrived ninety minutes later, pale and numbed, they were told their son was still in surgery. There was no report as yet on his condition, but if they would sign various releases and have a seat, a doctor would speak with them as soon as possible.

Hours later one of the surgeons left the operating room to have a cigarette and talk with the Hendersons. His stained uniform made him appear more butcher than doctor. He apologized for his appearance, saying he would be going directly back to the operating table.

He then delivered a barrage of medical terms and conditions, few of which made sense to either Carl or Dora. He mentioned nothing about the leg. At the time, it seemed the least of the patient's problems.

"But . . . will he be all right?" Carl was finally able to ask.

The doctor dropped his cigarette and ground it into the floor.

"Will he live?" asked Dora in a frail voice.

The surgeon looked at the patient's parents, at eyes pleading to hear something hopeful. "We can't tell anything yet. Right now we're trying to control the bleeding. When we get through that, we'll know more."

Evelyn was having the time of her life.

Everything was falling into place. Arrangements were being made. She called her sister Bernice in the Bronx. Bernice in turn called her best friend whose son was a noted Fifth Avenue plastic surgeon. Though completely booked this Easter recess, he agreed to squeeze Amy into his tight schedule. Amy and Evelyn packed to leave.

After ten hours, the white lights in the operating room were turned off.

Corky lay on a hospital bed, his life connected to tubes sending fluids in, draining them out. Neither receiving nor sending, accepting nor rejecting, if his brain functioned at all, it was in some dark, faraway sleep.

His parents spent the rest of the day in the waiting room. Late in the evening a doctor told them there'd been no change as yet. It might be days before they could assess any permanent damage. For now they were simply doing their best to keep him breathing.

After being given a brief look, Carl and Dora went across the Southern State Parkway and checked into the Howard Johnson's Motor Lodge. It had stopped snowing.

Dora stared out the window, out into the cold, white night. Carl put on the television and sat on the edge of

237

the bed, staring at Dorothy Kilgallen correctly naming the occupation of an opera singer. Then he broke down.

Dora hurried to him and he buried his face in her lap, and cried. "It's my fault, Dora! All my fault."

"Don't talk nonsense." She combed his hair with her fingers.

"I don't want to live, Dora. Not anymore. I want to die."

"Sssssh." Softly, she kissed the top of his head.

"It was me, Dora. Do you know that?"

"What, dear?"

Carl raised his reddened eyes. "I wished for it, Dora. I wished something like this might happen."

The fourth floor hallway of the large Bronx apartment house smelled of burnt pot roast.

Aunt Bernice opened the door, welcoming Evelyn and hugging Amy. "There's my little girl," she glowed. "There's the next Miss America!"

37

Thump. Hurled from the truck, Monday's *Newsday* landed against the front door.

Guy peered outside and was whipped in the face by an early morning wind. The paper rested precariously between two bottles of very cold milk. Bull's-eye.

When Guy lifted one of the bottles from its niche in the snow, the newspaper unfolded.

While bent over, he glanced at one of the front page headlines: WATERFIELD STAR ATHLETE CORKY HENDERSON IN AUTO CRASH. Disbelieving eyes refocused on the large type. Then the milk bottle in his suddenly numb hand crashed to the pavement, dissolving the printed lie in a wave of white.

The Sommers' phone did not stop ringing. Girl friends, classmates, cheerleaders, they all called. They all thought she should know. Ro-Anne knew.

As copies of *Newsday* opened at breakfast tables around town, the calls poured in. Once Marian had heard, she had gone upstairs and broken the news to Ro-Anne.

They dressed quickly and drove to Rushport in Marian's Thunderbird.

Ro-Anne cried the whole way.

Guy called the hospital. They told him Corky was in critical condition and would be receiving no visitors. He said he'd call again the next day.

He phoned Amy. Dr. Silverstein said she wasn't home; didn't know when to expect her.

Ro-Anne and Marian walked into the waiting room and exchanged hugs and tears with Carl and Dora. They sat with Corky's parents for five of the longest hours Ro-Anne could remember.

Once certain she would not be allowed to look in on him, Ro-Anne agreed to return home. She cried most of the way.

On Tuesday morning Corky was rushed back into the operating room, leaking essential brain fluid. Doctors feared the possibility of infection or permanent memory damage.

A nurse prepared him for surgery, shaving the hair from his head.

Amy sat in a soft powder-blue chair at the House of Revlon on Fifth Avenue. Tilting her backward, an attendant washed her hair. A hairdresser then applied a sticky white substance over every strand, straightening her wet, kinky curls. Hair done, she was passed on to another salon, where, her foot in an attendant's hand, she submitted to her first pedicure. "Tip to toe," Evelyn was describing the overhaul.

After another five hours of surgery Corky was wheeled back into his room. A nurse changed the dressing on the bottom of his leg.

He was returned to the operating room on Wednesday. Bone implants were set in his cheeks, giving the unsupported eye something to lean against.

In the office of a Park Avenue dermatologist, Amy winced as the stinging dry ice burned into her cheeks. The doctor dabbed gently at her skin, scaling off an outer layer, removing her acne.

The doctors would have preferred to wait a few more days, but by Thursday Corky's breathing was so erratic they decided to operate at once.

A neurosurgeon dissolved the blood clots under his skull and then bone surgeons spent five hours restructuring his nose.

"This may hurt a little, Amy," said Aunt Bernice's best friend's son, the plastic surgeon, as he brought a large syringe to the base of her nose.

The two injections Amy had received prior to her arrival in the operating room made her drowsy and relaxed. Still, when the doctor stuck her nostril with the long needle, she moaned.

Men and women in white loomed over her under blinding lights.

Once the local anaesthetic took, the plastic surgeon began. Amy could feel something on her nose. Hands? Instruments? Though there was no actual pain, she uncomfortably sensed the bone being fractured, broken down before being built up again.

A sculptor working in crushed ice, the surgeon's highly paid fingers molded and shaped. The sound of bones being rearranged sickened Amy as she drifted in and out of sleep.

Someone said, "Smile, please."

The lids of Amy's eyes opened and she smiled. Voices around the operating table approved.

She was wheeled out to the recovery room as the next patient was wheeled in.

The operation had lasted twenty minutes.

After spending four days at Doctors Hospital, Amy went back to Aunt Bernice's apartment in the Bronx. She spent most of her time staring out onto the Grand Concourse, watching cars drive by, by day and night.

The rims of her eyes were black and blue. Clotted blood clung to stitches in her nostrils. A small plaster cast covered her nose and she was bandaged from cheek to cheek. She had trouble breathing and was instructed *not* to sneeze. It hurt when she laughed.

Fortunately for her, she found little that was humorous.

Two things especially annoyed Dr. Silverstein. One was working inside a mouth that had recently hosted onions; the other was being disturbed while watching prime-time programming.

So when Guy placed his fourth call that week, at the very climax of "77 Sunset Strip," the good doctor abandoned his chairside manner. "How many times do I have to tell you, young man? *Amy is not at home!*"

This time Guy would not be bullied. "I can understand her not wanting to speak with me, Doctor Silverstein. Honest."

"What are you talking about? Once and for all, she's not here!"

"But doesn't she know about Corky's accident?"

"What accident? She knows nothing. She's in New York with her mother."

"New York?"

"That's right."

"What's she doing there?"

"Visiting her aunt."

"But she said nothing to me about any visit . . ." Guy

stopped when Dr. Silverstein breathed impatiently. "Never mind. I'm sorry. When you speak with her will you tell her I called? It's important."

"I will," said Dr. Silverstein, forgetting the message as soon as he hung up.

Complications set in. Fluid built up in Corky's lungs and he contracted pneumonia. The accompanying high fever prevented the doctors from operating again for ten days. Impatiently, they waited.

As Amy sat in one of five rooms of the doctor's busy office an assistant removed stitches, pulling them from her nostrils like thread from an unwinding button.

The plastic surgeon breezed in for a minute and sat down in front of Amy.

Evelyn stood against the wall.

"Well, Amy . . ." The doctor slowly peeled off the adhesive. "How do you feel?"

"Lousy."

"Your eyes are still a bit discolored."

"You should have seen her a week ago, doctor!" Evelyn said.

The surgeon smiled. "Small price to pay for beauty, don't you think, Amy?"

Amy didn't answer.

"Don't move now." The doctor tugged at the last bandage before lifting the small cast off her nose.

The surgeon leaned back to get a better look. Evelyn stepped forward.

"Well?" Amy asked nervously. "I feel like Claude Rains in *The Invisible Man.*"

The doctor handed her a face mirror. "See for yourself."

The tender skin was swollen out of proportion. The black and blue around the eyes was distracting.

But the Fanny Brice baked potato was gone.

"Oh . . . doctor," Evelyn gasped with reverence. "She's beautiful!"

242

April

38

On Sunday, the day after she and Evelyn returned home, Amy went with her father to his office. She sat there with her mouth stretched open while he tugged, pliered and removed the braces from her teeth.

Halfway through polishing her enamel, he paused to ask her tonsils, "Isn't all this better than a trip to Europe?"

Guy sat in the Silverstein living room sipping a glass of milk. Across from him, barely resting against the edge of a velvet chair, was Evelyn. She chatted nervously, careful to mention nothing about the past ten days. Tense, expectant, she was poised to gauge his reaction.

When Amy finally walked through the front door she was sliding her tongue across a row of non-metalized teeth.

Guy jumped up. "About time!" he said, joining her in the foyer. "Where've you been?"

Evelyn followed, bursting with anticipation.

Amy didn't know quite how to react to the sight of Guy. Though still annoyed, part of her wanted to show off the improvements. She opted for nonchalance as she walked into the living room. "I've been to the dentist."

"I mean all week." Guy pursued her. "Don't you believe in returning messages? You have any idea what kind of time it's been? Didn't your father tell you I called?"

"Never mentioned it." Amy sat down on the blue couch.

"I don't believe it."

"Believe what you like." Amy smiled, affording Guy a view of her pearly-whites.

Guy sat down next to her. "Well, where were you?"

Amy combed her silky straightened hair with her fingers. "I was away."

Evelyn watched intently from the foyer.

"And what about Corky?" Guy banged the coffee table with a fist.

"What about him?" Amy frowned.

In a sudden dawning, Guy realized she actually still knew nothing about what had happened. Then his mouth dropped open because he first noticed how she'd changed. Studying her, he said at last, "Then you don't know?"

"Don't know what?"

Guy leaned forward. "What have you . . . done . . . to . . . yourself?"

Amy pointed to her nose.

"Omigod."

Amy pointed to her hair.

Guy bit his tongue.

Amy pointed to her teeth.

"Where are your braces?"

"No more hardware."

Guy was dumbstruck.

"Well . . . ?" She smiled. "What do you think?"

Guy reached out, took both her hands and said, "Corky's been in a terrible car accident!"

Monday morning the new Amy went to school.

Three other altered noses returned from Easter recess that day, equally anxious. Nervous and still shaken by the news about Corky, Amy walked through the halls between classes, risking reaction. Two girls asked if that wasn't a new hair style. One thought she'd found a new makeup. The boy sitting next to her in English noticed a change in her profile. "Didn't you used to wear glasses?"

Amy nodded.

"Thought so. You look better without 'em."

For weeks everything was black. When Corky's brain began transmitting again, nothing but bile came forth.

Still in a light coma, he dreamed. Unending, horrible dreams. The snakes were back, crawling over every part of him. A vicious water moccasin oozed up into his nose and in his stupor he pulled at it, ripping the intravenous tube from his nostril. Whenever a nurse injected him, Corky felt razor fangs sinking their thick venom into his system.

A penned animal, he went wild, ripping tubes from his nose, from his arms, kicking at reptiles; lost in a traumatized coma, screaming for help.

They strapped him down. Subdued with leather tapes on his wrists and thighs, unable to fight back, Corky was devoured by the snakes.

Though still uncertain about his future, the doctors agreed they'd never seen so strong a patient, so fierce a fighter.

"I gave him that!" Mr. Henderson told them proudly.

Carl went back to work. The people at Sears Roebuck had told him to stay out, on pay, as long as necessary. But after three weeks he could no longer put up with sitting around all day to hear a thirty-second report of little or no progress. Grateful his company insurance plan would cover most of the medical bills, he lost himself in his work, selling dishwashers, toasters, vacuum cleaners, making only infrequent visits to the hospital, trying to forget he had a son in a coma. Trying to forget he had a son.

Dora didn't miss a day. She'd read in the waiting room until told she could look in. After staring for three minutes, she'd drive home to Waterfield.

When Corky's temperature finally dropped low enough, the doctors operated again. This time the teeth in his broken jaw were wired together.

Letters arrived at the Hendersons' notifying Corky he'd been granted full athletic scholarships at both Michigan State and Syracuse. With each announcement, Carl got blind drunk.

When he finally stirred from the horrors of his long sleep, the first thing Corky perceived was dark blue. As in that suspended moment when night offers its first hint of another day, so did the blackest of Corky's nightmares come to an end.

The snakes stopped hissing, stopped biting. Slowly dissolving, they retreated into the recesses of his mind.

During the day he saw oranges, yellows. At night, blues.

When at last he opened his eyes, a frightening, blurred vision of bizarre surroundings forced him to shut them again.

A nurse was washing him at the time. She jumped back at the sight of eyelids opening. "You've been in an accident," she told the unfocused gaze. "You're in a hospital."

Corky's eyes closed again and the nurse hurried to find a doctor.

As darker shades grew lighter and lighter shades became blurred images and blurred images came into focus, Corky could see. But he could not remember.

The doctors spoke to him and he responded, either through clenched teeth of his wired mouth or by squeezing their hands.

Yes he was uncomfortable. Yes he would like another shot of Demerol to ease the pain. No, he didn't remember his name. No, he didn't know who the big man and the short woman crying in front of him were.

The doctors asked the Hendersons to be patient. Since the damage was in the brain's frontal lobes it was personality that was affected, not motor skills. If Corky had been hit in the back of the head he would now be paralyzed. The medical team hoped his disorientation was temporary.

After another week Corky knew his name. He recognized his parents.

Sketchy elements returned. He remembered football. He remembered a red crew-neck sweater. He remembered breakfast that morning. He remembered nothing about the night of the accident.

A giant oak tag get-well card was constructed in art class and everyone in school put their signature to it.

The three-foot greeting with eleven hundred names was hand-delivered by student body president Ken Crawley. Corky did not remember Ken.

The doctors decided it might help if closer friends stopped by for a very brief visit.

The following Saturday, Guy and Ro-Anne took the bus to Rushport. Whatever they had been expecting in no way could have prepared them for what they found.

With only intravenous feedings, Corky had lost close to forty pounds in five weeks. Frail, he lay in bed, eyes closed. His muscles had atrophied and his face belonged to a horror film.

Ro-Anne could not watch. It was too awful, to unreal and repulsive. Biting her fingers, she groaned and ran from the room.

Corky opened his eyes. Guy stepped forward and stood next to the bed. Corky looked up and thought the visitor even taller than his five-foot-seven height.

Corky remembered Guy. *"Camera,"* he uttered softly, through clenched and wired teeth.

"That's right," said the visitor. "It's me. Guy."

"Guy." Corky shook his head.

"I think that's enough for now," said the nurse.

Guy leaned over and smiled. "I'll come back and see you soon."

Corky closed his eyes.

"What happened?" Ro-Anne grabbed Guy's arm as he drifted into the waiting room. "Did he wake up?"

"For a minute."

"I couldn't stay. I couldn't. I don't know that person in there. That wasn't him. Not my Corky!" She flung her arms around Guy and cried. "How could that be, Guy? How could that . . . person in there still be alive?"

Guy held her tight. "Don't cry."

"Will he forgive me, Guy?" Ro-Anne raised her head and sniffed. "Will he ever forgive me?"

"Of course," Guy assured her. "He doesn't remember a thing."

They rode the bus home in silence, staring blankly at telephone poles whizzing by. As they turned onto Poste

Avenue, back in Waterfield, Ro-Anne came out of her daze and turned to Guy.

Her hand had drifted onto his knee, and Guy patted it and smiled. She smiled back.

They walked in the chill, hardly speaking. Ro-Anne had her arm in his.

It was dark by the time they reached her driveway. Cocoon buds, green and bundled up on naked shrubs, were ready to unwind; small promises of spring.

"Please come in," said Ro-Anne. "My mother's out with Lester. They're never home till late. I'd hate to be alone 'til then."

"Me too."

"I'm a very deep person, Guy. I got a lot of feelings, you know."

"I can tell."

"What if I throw a couple of TV dinners into the oven?"

"Sounds fine."

Throughout their Swanson's meal they talked only of Corky. Once the aluminum trays were cleared, Ro-Anne took Guy into the television room. They sat next to each other on a large pink and white couch, watching "Gunsmoke." James Arness shot an ornery outlaw and Ro-Anne cried.

Feeling helpless, Guy held her hand. She wept and wrapped her arms around him. He didn't know what to think. What to do.

Then they kissed.

No. Please. Don't! A frightened voice cried from inside. *Don't touch her. You can't.* He put his arms around her.

Drawn to him by the trauma of the afternoon, Ro-Anne made some crazy sense out of his consolation. Reassuring warmth replaced vacant words.

What is she doing? Stop her. Just let go. Drop your arms and lean back.

Their tongues touched; for Guy, a weird new sensation.

More than anything he wanted to stop. What the

249

hell's going on? Slowly he brought a tentative hand to her breast.

"No. Don't do that!" she whispered, removing it.

Guy heard Corky's voice as loud as the television: *Rule number one—whenever they say no, they mean yes!*

Dutifully, his hand returned to her breast, refusing to let go. Ro-Anne didn't resist. She recognized the technique. Ignoring all sense of reality, she lay back. He followed. It wasn't as if he had a choice.

Each move of the hand was calculated. Every caress and kiss. Each next step was as he imagined Corky would have handled it. Guy Fowler would never have dreamed of lying on a couch with anyone as untouchable, as beautiful as Ro-Anne Sommers; lying there half naked, their tops thrown to the floor. Guy Fowler would never have known where to begin.

But as Corky, he proceeded to make love to her.

It was a fine arrangement. For a while.

By the time they had struggled out of all their clothes, and he was lying on top of her though, too much confusion, too much guilt had set in.

He could no longer pretend. The sight of her lying there naked, longing not for her surrogate lover but the genuine article, was too jarring.

He went soft. Sitting up, he hid his face in his hands.

She sat up too and all sugar-sweet asked, "Is there something wrong with you?"

Wrong? Of course not! He'd show her there was nothing wrong. What kind of man did she think he was, anyway? No real man could refuse her.

He turned and kissed her again. Hard. As he was biting her lip, Amy's voice suddenly came from nowhere, telling him again he could never touch Corky. Guy sent the uninvited cruelty away, admitting into the movie playing behind his eyes more appropriate visions.

He saw Butch's dirty postcards. He thought of the half-naked girl in a *Playboy* centerfold, her amazon tits, her alluring lips. Nothing.

Amy's nagging voice returned, and even as he tried erasing it, a tormenting image played on his mind; a triumphant Corky sitting on a locker bench in jockstrap and shoulder pads, pulling Guy toward him, encouraging an embrace.

No. Guy fought it, replacing the sick, erotic fixation with a pair of voluminous breasts.

Ro-Anne blew in his ear. "Oooh," she moaned, recalling how much Corky liked that done to him.

Corky, Corky, Corky, she thought, lying down again, twisting her head left to right.

Guy read her mind and went stiff again. Like a pro he mounted her, pushed his way in and, his face buried in a cushion, pounded away.

"Yes!" she cried, once again in the back seat of Corky's Chevy. "Yes, my darling . . . that's it!"

And now as he thrust at her violently, he was himself. Guy. Little Big Guy Fowler—one of the fellas—doin' it! Joining the ranks. Sowing his wild oats, tossing off his virginity and his boyhood with the school's hottest piece of ass.

One minor problem.

At the height of passion it was no longer Ro-Anne, but the recurring image of a half-naked Corky in the locker room, responding to his touch, that carried him through the long, abandoned ride home.

When it was over Ro-Anne wept and Guy shipped his disturbing thoughts straight back to a dead spot behind his brain, from which he promised himself never to summon them again.

Ro-Anne pushed him off, sobbing, "Oh my God, are you crazy? What have we done?"

39

"You won't tell anyone about this!" Ro-Anne pointed a reproving finger at Guy.

" 'Course I won't."

They stood at the door, saying good-by.

Ro-Anne baby-talked. "Corky would feel just awful if he knew you'd bird-dogged him."

Now she tells me. "I know."

"And besides. . ." She waved a frivolous hand in the air. "Oh, never mind."

"No. Go on. Say it."

"Well, besides that"—she giggled—"who would believe it?"

Guy smiled stupidly, knowing she was right. "My lips are sealed."

"I'm not going back there, Guy. Never again."

"To see Corky?"

She nodded. "I can't. It's just too devastating, isn't it?"

"Devastating." Guy stared at his shoes.

"Besides . . ." she pouted. "We'd just broken up when he ran out on me looking for Amy, that ugly witch."

That was it! Guy finally linked the missing piece to the puzzle of Corky's accident.

"So if he could go after some UGA like her, maybe I never really knew him anyway."

Guy shook his head. "Maybe not." Turning to leave, he kissed Ro-Anne's cheek. "By the way, have you seen her lately?"

"Who, Amy?"

"Yeah. Next time take a close look."

"Why would I do that?"

"She's not so UGA anymore is why. Good night."

Guy returned home in a daze.

Clippity-clop, Birdie descended the stairs. Paying no attention to her son, shivering in the doorway, she rushed directly into the kitchen.

"Where's my pie pan?" she hollered at the refrigerator.

Barging her way back out of the kitchen, she approached Guy. "Where have you been?"

"Hi Mom," said Guy, preoccupied.

"Do you know what time it is?"

Guy looked at her blankly. "I went to Rushport to see Corky. Remember?"

Birdie threw both hands high in the air and barreled back upstairs. An unusual welcome.

Guy unbuttoned his parka.

Nathan, thin and slow, came down the stairs. "Why didn't you call or something? Where's your mother's pie pan?"

"I went to Rushport today. To the hospital."

Nathan didn't hear him. "We haven't time for any jokes, Guy."

"I just walked in the door, Dad. I've had a very rough day."

"None of us have had it easy, so don't tell me your troubles. You know your mother and her superstitions. Says she won't go without it."

"Go where?"

Birdie traipsed down the steps again. "You know what it is, Nathan. I shouldn't be leaving. You're not well enough yet for me to travel."

"Travel where?" Guy asked.

"I'm fine!" Nathan insisted. "You're going and that's final!"

"Going where?" Guy asked again, feeling part of some strange merry-go-round for which he held no ticket.

"You stay out of this. Your mother's made it to the Pillsbury Bake-Off finals. She's leaving for St. Louis tonight!"

"I am not! How can I go?" Birdie argued.

"That's wonderful," said Guy, subdued, trying to sound cheerful.

"She didn't even tell us about it. If Rose hadn't found the telegram. . ."

"Which recipe did they finally accept, Ma?"

Birdie fussed at her dress and blushed. "You know that lemon-rhubarb glazed crumb-cake with raisins and the anise flavoring?"

Guy nodded.

"Well, I mailed it in on one of my index cards as this

year's entry, not knowing that on the back was the recipe for my cinnamon-apple pie, the one I've been baking for almost twenty years, and *that's* the one they picked!"

"Apple pie? Plain ole apple pie?"

Birdie nodded with pride.

"Not in the pantry!" yelled Butch, bounding down the steps.

"Well, I'm not going without it." Birdie moped into the living room. "Disappeared right under my nose. Can't you see it's an omen?"

"Cut it out, Birdie, you'll miss your train!" said Nathan, following her.

"Who cares?" Birdie collapsed onto the couch, folding her arms in frustration.

Nathan sat next to her. "I want you to go upstairs and finish packing."

Birdie turned away.

Butch went to the couch. "Come on, Ma. One pan's as good as the next."

"I'm not going. Period. Your father needs me here."

"About time you got home!" Rose came up from the basement and reprimanded Guy on her way into the living room. "Anyone find the pan yet?"

As Guy remembered where indeed the pie pan was, Butch snapped his fingers at him. "Corky? How's Corky?"

Everyone looked to Guy. "Better. The nurse said he was feeling better."

"Good," said Butch, and everyone nodded silently until Guy said softly, "I know where the pan is."

As everyone came to a stunned silence, Guy hurried into the kitchen, opened the oven door and removed the pie pan. He'd put it there that morning when he'd seen it on the counter, freshly scrubbed, and without thinking had simply returned it to its customary storage spot on the bottom shelf of the oven.

In their frenzy no one had bothered to check there. Too obvious.

The Fowlers stood huddled together as Guy delivered the sacred pan into Birdie's open arms.

"All right. Enough!" Nathan clapped his hands. "We haven't time for any mushy stuff. Finish packing, Birdie. You'll be leaving for the station in five minutes!" Exhausted, he sat down.

"Yippee!" Butch raced from the room. "I'll start the car!"

"I'll help you finish packing, Ma!" Rose took the stairs two at a time.

Birdie regarded her pie pan with loving fondness, as if she'd just picked up the Oscar for Best Cook. She placed an open hand on Guy's cold cheek and kissed him. "Remember when you were a little boy and we took that car trip to Uncle Arthur's in Albany? All alone in the back seat, remember how you tied a handkerchief around your mouth and signaled to other cars for help?"

"I made believe I was being kidnapped," Guy recalled.

She nodded. "And then the state police pulled us off the road and took out their guns. Remember?"

"It took ten minutes to convince them I really belonged to you.'

Birdie sighed. "You've always been a strange and wonderful child."

Guy smiled a goofy grin and performed his bogus tap dance. "Hey, Ma. You better get going. You and your pie pan are on your way to fame and fortune!"

May

40

"You have a visitor," said the nurse.

Corky opened his eyes.

Amy walked into the room. "Hello." She went over to the window and placed the plant on the sill. "I brought you these. Azaleas. It's finally getting warm out. They're playing baseball—"

Corky tried turning his head toward the window. It hurt.

"Move closer, miss," said the nurse. "He can't see you over there."

Amy went to the bed, fighting to retain composure. She decided it would be better to get right to it. "I know what you're thinking. You're wondering why I'm here, right? Fair enough. Well, it's like this. . . . Guy said you were looking for me when you got hurt. I wanted you to know how sorry I was and that I understand things better now. I'd like to be friends. . . ."

Corky still remembered nothing about the night of the accident. His eyes opened and closed.

Amy cleared her throat. "Azaleas aren't very hardy. Still, it's spring, you can't go out yet so I thought I'd bring the mountain to you. . . ."

He looked at her. Nothing registered.

"It's Amy, Corky. Amy Silverstein."

"*Ro-Anne?*" he asked through wired teeth.

"No. It's Amy."

He shook his head. It wasn't Amy. He would have remembered Amy. Was his mind still distorting reality? Nothing in his limited computer had any data stored on this attractive stranger.

Amy smiled nervously. "Well, I just wanted to drop

257

by with this. I'll let you get back to sleep." She touched his hand. "Feel better. Feel better soon. Okay?"

Corky thanked the nice girl and went back to sleep.

Wiping her Anglofiled nose, Amy hurried from the hospital.

As Corky's concussion healed the doctors began to hope there would be no permanent memory damage. Soon they could begin fittings for an artificial limb and the additional reconstructive and superficial operations required on his face.

On the third Saturday in May, Guy again took the bus to Rushport.

Corky was sitting up in bed. Though bandages still covered most of his face, his eyes were wide and alert.

In a chair next to the bed Dora thumbed through *Life* magazine.

"How's the star today?" Guy asked, walking in.

"Better," Dora answered, standing up. "Will you stay with him a few minutes, Guy? I'm gonna run to the cafeteria, get some lunch. Want anything?"

"Nothing for me, Mrs. Henderson. Take all the time you need."

Dora left the room.

Guy smiled at Corky. "Well . . . what's new since I was last here? Let's see. My mother didn't win any prizes or money at the Bake-Off. She got a consolation Hotpoint electric range, though. That interest you any? She had a terrific time. Imagine being locked up with hundreds of foodaholics like herself? She returned fatter and wiser, says she's baking her way to the top next year." Silence. "How are you?"

Corky opened his eyes and signaled with his finger for Guy to come closer. Through locked teeth he grunted into Guy's ear the words *Rough Ferrow.*

Guy didn't understand. "Say it again."

Pursing his lips, Corky tried. *"Rough Ferrow."*

"What about it?"

"ROUGH FERROW!" Corky made a fist.

"I can't understand what you're—"

Corky's eyes strained with frustration. "Help . . . me," he uttered in a pathetic whimper.

"Help you?"

"Help me!" Corky tried lifting his head.

"Hey, relax. 'Course I'll help you. Don't get excited."

Corky lay back and closed his eyes. "Phomas?"

"What?"

"Phomas?"

"Promise? . . . Yes. Yes, I promise."

"Come. Two weeksh."

"You want me back here in two weeks?"

Corky nodded.

"That's all? Sure. I'll be happy to. Easy. I was coming anyway."

"No wiresh," said Corky, pointing to his teeth.

"Great. When you can talk without all that interference you can tell me better what you want."

Corky nodded.

Dora came back into the room with a white paper bag and a container of coffee. "How about half a chicken salad sandwich, Guy?"

"Mmm." Corky grumbled with great yearning.

"No thanks," said Guy.

Dora sat on the chair next to the bed. Guy struggled for something to say. Corky fell asleep, and after a few minutes Guy told Dora it was time he got going.

As the bus sped through Long Island, Guy wondered what it was he had promised to do for Corky.

The Hendersons have really been through it, he thought. First the fight to see if Corky would live, then if he would see, then if he would walk, then if he would remember. But now, thank God, it looked as if everything might be all right.

Still . . . if everything was so hunky-dory, what the hell was *Rough Ferrow?*

June

41

It wasn't love, but it sure was fun. Ro-Anne and Chuck Troendle had teamed up.

The bond of distress they shared while Corky was in critical condition made them realize how much they'd always really been meant for each other.

First they met at Darcy's, after school. Then on Fridays after his fraternity meeting. Every Saturday night they went to the movies. He was crazy about her, always saying how terrific she looked, always buying her stuffed animals. She enjoyed the attention, liked his sense of humor and there was one other thing.

He had a car.

She was greatly relieved when he asked her to the senior prom at the Waldorf-Astoria. For a while she'd been scared there'd be no one to go with now that whatshisname wasn't around. She wasn't about to miss seeing Connie Francis at the Copa, before heading for the beach at five in the morning, trying to stay awake through the sunrise.

One Friday night, Chuck dangled his ID bracelet before her eyes. She wasn't ready to accept it. They weren't *that* serious. Still, she didn't want to appear ungrateful. So what the hell, they were going steady. It wasn't as if she had anything better to do.

The *Venture* came out. Photo to photo, it was a yearbook filled with Corky.

On the personality page he was voted Most Popular, Best Athlete, Best Looking and Most Likely to Succeed. . . .

"Hey! Look at you!" Guy was pleased to find Corky sitting in a wheelchair. The wiring had at last been removed from his mouth.

Corky exercised his jaw for Guy. "They've had me on farina for a week."

"Terrific . . . beats living off a tube, I bet." Guy widened the partially open window. "Aren't you hot in here?"

Trees in the distance were covered with blossoms. A warm breeze scattered flowers to the ground.

Guy crossed the room and stood over Corky. "Brought you a surprise." He took the *Venture* from his briefcase and offered it to Corky. "Picked it up this morning."

Corky looked the other way.

"It's your copy." Guy extended his arm.

"Get it out of here."

"You're on almost every page."

"Who cares?"

"Oh, come on. You're just feeling rotten because . . ."

"*Take it away!*"

"All right. Relax. Don't get your balls in an uproar." Guy didn't know what to do. "Tell you what. I'll leave it here on the night table and if you change your mind—"

"*I said! . . .*"

"Okay, okay, I heard you. Forget it. Don't look at your yearbook. See if I care."

Guy returned the *Venture* to his briefcase and stood there, counting the silence. "Hey . . . I didn't tell you. Got a summer job."

"Doing what?"

"Afternoons down at the camera shop. Selling equipment."

"Nice."

"Yeah." Guy moved his visitor's chair and sat next to Corky.

Corky studied the sprinkler system on the ceiling. "How's Ro-Anne?"

Guy looked down. "Fine. Fine."

"Never came to see me. Not once."

"Sure she did. Lots of times. You were off in never-never land. She was here."

"What do I care? Dumb bitch. And what about the rest of them? The guys on the team? Petrillo?"

"It's not as if they didn't care, Corky. They all ask about you, all the time. Rushport's a long way from town. People have their own lives."

Corky looked out the window. "I guess."

"Hey!" Guy sat up. "You should see Amy Silverstein! She's really different now. . . ."

"Big deal. She was always really different."

"Yeah." Guy dropped the subject. "I guess so."

"Now *she* can ask *me* out on a bet."

"Don't talk like that . . . it's not healthy feeling sorry for yourself."

"What makes you think I want to be healthy?"

"You'll be fine soon enough."

"Never," Corky said bitterly.

"You recovered better than anyone expected. The Seven-Up truck miracle. You're just unhappy. . ."

" 'Course I'm unhappy, you idiot. You think this is some kind of joy ride?"

"I didn't mean. . ."

"You think it's some great thrill being a cripple?"

"Come on, you're no cripple Your leg was just. . . ."

"You wanna live behind this face a while? You wanna go through the rest of your life the phantom of the opera?"

"Stop. It's temporary. They're going to fix all that."

"Never! They can't. No way. Too far gone. You said you'd help me, Guy. Remember? Last time you were here. You promised to help."

"I will. You know that. Anything."

"You better. I'm counting on you, kid. You're the only one I can trust. Been planning this a long time and believe me, I know just what I'm doing. We have to work fast. There's not much time."

"Fine. Name it."

"Seconals."

263

"Huh?"

"Little pink pills. Coach gave 'em to me last season to help me rest up before a game."

"Seconals?"

"Yeah. There's a bunch of them in the medicine chest in my bathroom at home. I want you to bring them to me."

"But what for?"

"Got it all worked out. I want you to stop by the house. Pick up something. Drop something off. Doesn't matter. Yearbook. Perfect. Deliver my *Venture*. They'll love it."

"I don't understand."

"Once you're in the house, say you have to use the bathroom. They're on the top shelf of the medicine cabinet. All the way to the right. Little plastic bottle."

"But if you can't sleep the doctor can give you something."

Corky said nothing, and Guy stood up as he realized what Corky wanted. "Are you crazy? I'm not going to listen to this!"

"You said you'd help me!" Corky started to get out of the wheelchair.

Guy rushed over and gently pushed him down. "Stay still, will you? You can't get up yet."

"I can!"

"I'll get the nurse in here if you don't stop. You want them to tie you down again?"

"I want nothing. All I want is to die. You've got to help me, Guy. You're the only one."

"You have your whole life in front of you!"

"Not like this! I won't live like this. Not this face. I hate this face!" Corky started crying. Tears ran over his bandages. "No foot, Guy. They chopped off my fucking foot!"

"Come on now. It'll be all right."

"You better not go back on your word, kid. You'll pay for it. You said you'd do anything for me. *Anything*. You promised me after I fixed things straight with your brother. Did you forget?"

" 'Course I didn't forget. I'll never forget."

"Then do like I tell you."

Guy handed Corky a tissue and then waited a long time before he spoke. "I can't, Corky. Anything else. Anything at all. But you can't just kill yourself."

"Why the hell not?"

"I don't know. Lots of reasons. It's a sin."

"So is living like this!"

"Nonsense."

"Look, Guy. You promised. You keeping your word or not? I have to know."

"Of course I'm good for my word. I'd do just about anything for you. Anything. But you're my friend and I won't let you take the cowardly way out."

Guy's words sparked the fuse.

Corky's eyes went wild as he exploded. "Cowardly? You out of your fucking mind, kid? Who the hell you calling names? You of all people, you fucking little fruitcake!"

"Hey, come on. Don't."

"Get outta here! You just get outta here right now before I have you thrown out!"

"Take it easy. You're gonna bust something."

"Damn right!" Corky hollered as he reached out and knocked the water pitcher off the night table.

The plastic bounced and ice flowed across the linoleum.

"Jesus," Guy mumbled.

"Leave! Scram! Get out of here!"

A nurse hurried in. "What's going on?"

"Nothing," said Guy.

"I want him out of here! Away from me!"

Guy turned to the nurse. "He was fine a minute ago."

"You better go," the nurse said sternly.

Guy started toward the wheelchair. "I'm sorry, Corky."

"Out! Get out of here!" cried Corky, tears all over. "I don't want your pity! How dare you! I'll tell you what kind of loser *you* are! Even your own brother knows it. It was Butch who blackballed you, your own brother, did you know that, fruitcake?"

Guy looked at the floor. "I didn't. Not until now."

"Good! I hope it ruins your day. Hope it ruins everything."

The information came too late and was now unimportant. "Corky, I . . ."

"Whoever said you were my friend, huh? You ever hear me say it? Never! I never said it, kid. Never. You think a little creep like you could ever be a friend of Corky Henderson's? You think it's possible? I pitied you, is all. You never stood a chance. Corky Henderson doesn't have any faggot halfpints for friends . . ."

Guy could only feel sorry for Corky. He stood in the doorway and said calmly, "As it happens, I'm three inches short of reaching six feet. I'll forget all you've just said because I know you're upset. Have a nice afternoon."

Then he turned and walked out of the hospital, into the June heat.

42

"Guess what?" an ebullient Evelyn interrupted her daughter's studying for her finals.

Amy looked up and recognized the look on her mother's face. "If it's about a boy, I'm not interested."

"Listen to this." Evelyn leaned against the desk. "Marilyn Snyder just called. Saw you at the supermarket yesterday. Thinks you look simply divine, couldn't get over it. Wants you to go out with her son Eric, when he comes home from Philadelphia this weekend. He's got a cousin's wedding to take you to."

"Forget it."

"What do you mean, forget it? He's in college, Amy. Penn State. Economics. Maybe he'll ask you down for a weekend next fall."

"I'm not going."

"I already told Marilyn yes."

Amy threw down her pencil. "Why'd you do that?"

"Now just hold on a minute, miss. With what it cost to get you to look like something . . ."

"Oh, shit!"

Evelyn opened Amy's closet. "Let's see now . . . what can we wear?"

Guy returned to Rushport Memorial the following Saturday. The nurse at the front desk went to see if Corky was awake.

She returned with Dora.

"I'm sorry, Guy. Corky hasn't been feeling well. He doesn't want to see anyone. I think he's a little depressed."

Guy smiled through his disappointment. "I understand."

"The doctors said it was to be expected Corky wanted to know if you'd changed your mind about your promise to him."

Guy stared at Dora.

"I didn't understand it either, but that's what he said."

"No, Mrs. Henderson. Tell him I haven't changed my mind. Tell him I'll come back again to see him soon."

"Good idea. Maybe next time he'll be up for some company."

"I hope so."

Two weeks later, on the afternoon of the last day of school, while others inaugurated summer freedoms, Guy returned to the hospital, greeting card in hand.

He decided not to announce himself and went straight to Corky's room. Clean and vacant.

Guy stopped a nurse in the hallway. "What happened to Corky Henderson?"

"Who?"

"Patient in two-twenty-nine."

The nurse peered into the empty room. "Discharged."

Guy was stunned. "When?"

"This morning."

"But he's still recovering. They take him home?"

"Front desk has all that information." Shaking a thermometer, the nurse continued down the hall.

"Buffalo," said the nurse behind the typewriter at the front desk. "Transferred to the Prosthetics Institute there."

"Buffalo?"

"You a relative?"

"Friend."

"Left by ambulance yesterday. Fine rehabilitation center in Buffalo."

"But no one said anything about . . ." Guy stopped when it hit him. *Rough Ferrow*. That was it . . . *Rough Ferrow*—Buffalo. Now he understood.

The nurse went back to work.

Guy walked down the hall again and stared at the tidy bed. Corky in Buffalo? Transferred. Just like that. Guy felt like crying, but there were no tears. Corky had depended on him, had considered him his last chance before being sent away.

On his way out of the hospital, Guy dropped the greeting card into an ashtray outside the elevator.

He knew it without knowing it.

He would never hear from Corky Henderson again.

THE VENTURE

1963

Homecoming

43

While the sun went down, Amy stood at the top of Edson Hill and stared at the school.

It was another place. Even the name had changed.

Workmen on a scaffold high above the main entrance rubbed out old letters with a noisy buffing machine. As light faded into a dark, cold night, they put tools away and climbed down.

The barren sky offered little chance of snow before Christmas.

Amy strolled through the main lobby, down to the Delaney Gymnasium, finding everything smaller than before.

The softly lit basketball court-ballroom was partially filled with returning alumnae. Red and yellow crepe paper intertwined around basketball hoops.

She looked around at vaguely familiar faces, wondering why she had come. Then she spotted Leonard Hauser and ran to greet him.

Guy and Rose found a parking spot in front of the school. While he spun the Oldsmobile into the tight space, she babbled about how nervous she was seeing old friends again and how grateful she was to Guy for accompanying her.

"How do I look?" She flipped the rear-view mirror toward her.

"Fine." He flipped it back into position.

"I don't know when I've been more excited!"

Together they walked into the school.

Rose nudged Guy. "Seems like yesterday, doesn't it?"

"No," Guy told her.

They passed under the WELCOME HOME, CLASS OF '59 banner and were in the gymnasium.

The four-piece band was at full blast. Zealots danced the twist.

Guy watched a huge roomful of strangers drifting in and out of groups, and couldn't imagine why he had agreed to come.

Rose yelled, "There's Harriet!" and disappeared into a thicket of bodies.

Guy walked to the bleachers and sat. He glanced at his watch, leaned back and exhaled. Bored stiff. Then he saw Amy.

She looked terrific. Tall, confident, vivacious. Though her hair was again frizzy, a natural kinkiness was fast becoming the accepted look. He walked over to say hello.

She let out a whoop and embraced him warmly. "Who be this tall oak which towers before me?"

"Hello, Amy."

"You may not believe this. I used to know a fellow looked just like you, only he was half your size."

Guy smiled. "Not quite."

"Jeez, you look good."

"And you!" Guy told her emphatically.

"Sure." She laughed. "Not the Grace Kelly my mother expected, but not Zasu Pitts either."

"It's nice to see you, Amy."

"Listen to that voice! When did you start sounding like Ronald Colman, and what are you doing here? Your homecoming's not for two years."

"My sister didn't want to make her entrance alone. How would it look? I haven't seen her since we arrived."

"How is Rose?"

Guy shrugged. "Some things never change. She and her husband still live at home with my mother. He works with Barry."

"Who's Barry?"

"Barry. My brother."

"Butch," Amy corrected him.

"No. Barry. He hasn't been Butch for years. Ever since

I told him it was a choice homosexual expression. He wasn't wild for the association."

"I see. What does *Barry* do these days?"

"Inherited my father's Olds place. Runs it with an iron fist."

"And you?"

"Me? Junior year at Boston U."

"Studying what?" Amy asked in a familiar snappy editorial tone.

"Haven't picked a major yet."

"What are you waiting for?"

Guy put his hands in his pockets. "Guess I haven't decided what I want to be when I grow up."

Amy smiled. "I know how you feel."

"Do you?"

"I've been spending a lot of time finding out about myself. Cornell is an amazing place."

"In what way?"

"Well, for one thing, when I got there I was suddenly being asked out left and right. A little confusing at first, all those bright, Jewish, eligible men. I just wasn't prepared. When guys told me I was pretty, I was theirs. So I got lavaliered to a Phi Ep in my freshman year. He wasn't ready to name a date for us to get engaged, so I broke it. How dare he take advantage of my pretense of honor! Then when I was a sophomore, I hit bottom. True! Got pinned a Zebe. Thankfully he'd given duplicate pins to two other girls and a lavalier to a fourth. Learn from my mistake. Promise you'll never go to a Rutgers weekend."

"I promise."

"Let's see. I went with a Sigma Chi WASP my senior year—my big rebellion—and just before I came home last night, I broke my engagement with an ex-A. E. Pi. My mother was bereft!"

"Engaged!"

"Yep. Diamond ring. Bridal shower. The works. I was the envy of the graduate dorm. I think his name was Henry. I remember accepting his ring for a very good reason."

"What was that?"

"He was the first to offer."

"Didn't you love him?"

"Love him?" Amy grimaced. "I didn't even know his political affiliation. As it turned out he was a Fascist."

"I see."

"And that was his best feature."

"So you finally made it."

"Finally. Took about a month for the bubble to burst. Somehow he'd talked me into doing his laundry—'women's work'—so while scrubbing his soiled boxer shorts I suddenly thought, for this I gave up working on my thesis? For this my mother dedicated her life, to get me here, up to my elbows in dirty suds? I'm in the same lousy state she's complained about forever. So I returned the ring with his clean laundry and here I am, free and crazy. Want to marry me?"

"Sure."

"I adore falling in love with love. I've already got a date with my ex-fiancé's roommate first night we get back."

"Busy girl."

"Making up for lost time. For a while I was determined to have my M.R.S. before my P.H.D."

"So it seems. You smile different."

"Do I?" Amy's eyes widened.

"Not as self-conscious as I remember."

"Isn't it amazing what the assorted jewelry of a few burly fraternity men can do for a girl's ego?"

"Apparently. How goes the journalism? Still the wiz kid?"

"Still trying. That's one of the reasons I'm here. Going to do a 'How Things Have Changed' piece for the school literary rag."

"Have things changed, Amy?" He grinned.

She stared at him. "Haven't they?"

Both nodded their heads at the same time.

A shrilled cry of recognition went up as two girls behind Amy found each other.

"Don't turn around!" warned Guy.

"What?"

"You won't believe what just walked in."

"Why won't I?"

"Too late!" said Guy just as a happy voice behind Amy screamed out, "Oh, God! I don't believe it! Guy Fowler! No!"

Amy didn't have to turn her head to remember who went with all that enthusiasm. "Oh-Oh." Amy bit her lip facetiously. "The expensive aroma of Chanel choking the air tells me Ro-Anne Sommers must be near."

"You got it," Guy whispered as Ro-Anne plowed into him with overwhelming affection.

"No-no-no!" Ro-Anne squealed, looking up and down. "Don't tell me. Little Guy Fowler! What happened to you?"

"Finished my Wheaties."

"My dear, had I but known you'd be growing into such a hunk, I never would've tossed you to the wolves."

Guy looked over to Amy and winked.

Ro-Anne turned around and threw her arms around Amy, as if greeting a long-lost friend. "I don't believe it! This really is a reunion! Hail, hail, gang's all here! Why, Amy Silverstein, just look at you! Thin as a rail and prettier than ever. What's your secret?"

"I found God."

"So sharp, this one!" Ro-Anne laughed. "A tongue of steel. You guys have simply got to forgive me, looking so dreadful. Catch this haircut, will you? I could kick myself." Ro-Anne whirled in place. "Had it done day before yesterday in Chicago. Serves me right. What do they know in that hick town? My supervisor was after me, though. Passengers kept finding golden curls in my TWA tea!" Ro-Anne elbowed Guy to make sure he caught the pun.

"I think it looks nice," Guy offered.

"You like it now, you should've seen it before the scalping."

"How are things going?" asked Amy.

Ro-Anne sighed. "Let me tell you guys something. I don't think I ever really knew what living was before riding the air waves. Talk about fun! We just finished a five-day layover in L.A. Longest party ever. Great crew. What a blast! I had to come home for Christmas to dry out. But I'm not sure I ever will. Cocktails with my mother can wipe you out as bad as a couple of Bloody Marys before breakfast at thirty thousand feet."

Ro-Anne laughed, and Amy suddenly realized she was a bit drunk.

"Anyone interesting show up?" Ro-Anne's eyes covered the room. Guy and Amy stared at one another. A short drum roll interrupted their knowing gaze.

"Hello, and may I have your attention!" barked a young man through a microphone on the band podium. "I'm Harvey Levinson, student council president, and it's my great pleasure to welcome you, the class of 1959, back to John F. Kennedy High School. How does it feel being back at the alma mater? One thing you can't forget is memories!"

"Get the hook!" Amy whispered to Guy.

"Before we go on, the student council has asked that we devote sixty seconds of tribute to our recently fallen leader."

A reverent silence stilled the entire room.

"Ladies and gentlemen, if you will . . . a minute of prayer and reflection in memory of John Fitzgerald Kennedy."

Two hundred heads dropped to study the high shine on the wooden floor. A white pin-spot signaled out the American flag on the podium.

Sixty seconds is a long time. After a third of a minute, nervous heads lifted, anxious eyes wandered, other thoughts raced through active minds.

Guy looked up at Amy. She smiled.

Ro-Anne half-giggled to herself.

Guy turned his head to the metal doors at the entrance and saw a tall figure standing there, silhouetted against the illuminated hallway. He stopped breathing for a moment and looked down again. Couldn't be.

Amy's eyes also came upon the big man in the shadow of the doorway. She squinted to get a better look and at the same time told herself to stop playing games. He wasn't going to come.

"Thank you very much," said a voice over the microphone. Everyone breathed in relief and resumed moving about.

The band broke into another twist and couples made their way to the middle of the floor.

"Anybody care to dance?" Ro-Anne looked at Guy. Before he could answer, Guy saw the sides of Ro-Anne's mouth slide from joy to doubt to discomfort as she looked past him, toward the door. And he knew without having to turn who it was she had seen.

A wave of recognition swept the room. Heads turned, bodies stretched, hands even clapped.

"Corky!" was the cry and it echoed all over the gym. Scores of people left intimate circles, hurrying to greet him.

Neither Guy nor Amy nor Ro-Anne moved as a stream of alumnae flowed past them.

"I've been looking forward to this night for a month," said Ro-Anne. "Now I'm scared as hell."

"Relax," Guy told her.

"But what'll I *say* to him?"

"Start with hello," Amy said. "Let him take it from there."

The center of attraction, Corky could not have been happier. It had been years since he'd commanded this sort of reception, and the hope of it was one of the main reasons he'd decided to come. He craved a hero's welcome. Now he could relax.

"He looks so marvelous," Ro-Anne said quietly. "I never dreamed. . . . How do you suppose they did it?"

"Mirrors," snapped Amy.

"Should we go over to him?" asked Guy.

"What, and join the multitudes? Never. He's had enough time in the limelight. I'll get his attention." With a wave, a smile and a loud "Yoo-hoo," Ro-Anne signaled to Corky.

"I should've brought my whistle," said Amy.

A smiling Corky heard a shout and turned to see Ro-

Anne. His stomach dropped and for a brief moment he shook all over.

Then he waved back. "Excuse me," he said to the dozen people around him as he made his way across the room.

Walk slowly. Take your time. Maybe they won't notice. Make sure your left side faces the wall.

Amy, Guy and Ro-Anne watched Corky walking casually toward them, and each of their nervously wide, anticipatory smiles stiffened as one by one they spotted his limp. Slight. Barely obvious, but hardly the robust gait they remembered.

First he hugged Ro-Anne, who screeched out his name and threw her arms around him, forcefully kissing him on the lips.

He turned to Amy.

"Hello, Corky." She extended a long arm. He took it and brought her to him. It was an affectionate embrace and she could feel all his warmth.

Guy was next. Corky shook his hand. "Jesus, kid. How dare you grow up so handsome. You sure you're not on stilts?"

Guy smiled. "Positive."

Corky took a step back. "Let me look at all of you."

He looked at all of them. They looked at all of him. Not a dry eye in the bunch.

"Hell, I thought reunions were supposed to be happy!" Ro-Anne complained.

"Absolutely right!" Corky snapped his fingers. "Guy, let's hear a joke!"

"I haven't any left," Guy said in all seriousness.

"Well then," Corky suggested, "let's just break down right here on the floor." Forcing a laugh, trying to keep things light, Corky smiled. He smiled his guaranteed dazzler for them and they each felt even sadder because they knew how hard he was trying and it just wasn't there. The sparkle in the green eyes, missing. The controlled nonchalance, gone. The wavy hair seemed straighter, receding a bit.

When he happened to turn to look at the band, they all noticed. The surgeons had done an amazing job. The plastic work, the cosmetic surgery and the planing of the skin; all of it done wonderfully well, almost covering the remaining superficial scars.

"How have you been?" asked Amy.

"Never better!" Corky winked, praying to devastate as before.

"What'cha doing?" Ro-Anne wanted to know. "I mean with your life?"

"Things couldn't have worked out better!" Corky beamed. "Buffalo's a terrific place. Real sports-minded. Play everything from ice hockey to tetherball. Can't get their fill. My dad got himself transferred after the accident to a big Sears just outside the city. Beautiful store, smack in the middle of a giant shopping center. Turned out to be a real step up. Anyway, some guys in the sporting equipment department knew about a big firm looking for a rep, someone to cover the tri-state area. Who was better qualified? So I took the job. Love it. Harley Sports. We make skis, basketballs, baseball mitts, all that jazz."

No one said anything. The band started a slow number.

Corky took out his wallet. "Show you my card! Let you see what a big deal I am."

Trying to appear excited, they each accepted:

HARLEY SPORTS EQUIPMENT
CARL HENDERSON, JR.
SALES REPRESENTATIVE

"Very nice," Amy said quickly.

"Yeah. I was selling over in Hempstead this morning, so I figured, why not drive by, catch the Homecoming."

"I'm glad you came," said Guy.

"Me too!" Corky lied. "I see nothing's changed."

"How can you drive?" asked Ro-Anne. The icy reception of the question made her realize what she'd said. An open hand covered her face. "I'm sorry. Always putting my foot in my mouth!"

Guy and Amy looked away.

"I didn't mean . . ." Ro-anne realized she'd goofed again.

"Relax, huh?" Corky told her. "First of all, I drive with my right foot, like most *normal* people. And second, outside of running the hundred-yard dash in record time, I can do most anything."

Ro-Anne breathed in relief.

"I'll prove it. Let's dance." He reached for her hand and led her to the dance area.

Guy looked at Amy. "Shall we?"

"With great pleasure. How nice to be able to put *my* head on *your* shoulder."

Guy and Amy danced.

Corky and Ro-Anne danced.

Someone lowered the lights further and switched on the spinning mirrored ball. A blizzard of snowflakes circled the gymnasium.

"You look beautiful," Corky told Ro-Anne as they danced. "More beautiful, if anything."

"I'm not so sure." She frowned. "It used to take me three-quarters of an hour in the morning to get ready. Now almost an hour and a half."

"You'll never lose your looks."

"I better not. I'll kill myself."

Corky smiled.

"You look wonderful too, Corky. Handsome as ever."

He moved closer. "It's easier meeting new people who didn't know me before. They don't expect as much, if you know what I mean."

Ro-Anne kissed his cheek. "You ever miss the old days?"

"Too often," Corky said. "Can I tell you something crazy? Remember some of those outrageous touchdowns I scored that sent everyone in the stands wild?"

"Of course I remember."

"It made me feel so . . . well, so high inside, I got depressed."

Ro-Anne didn't understand. "But why?"

Corky stopped dancing. "I guess because I knew that

no matter whatever came afterward, I was never going to be happier than right then."

Ro-Anne felt too saddened to respond. She rubbed the small of his back and they resumed their slow dance.

Guy whirled Amy around in a fast spin and then leaned her over into a French dip. She laughed and looked at him. "And what about you, tall stranger? What's going on in your life?"

Guy shrugged. "Not much."

"No romantic interest?"

"Naw. I've got plenty of time for that once I sort out the rest of me."

She looked at him with affection and asked warmly, "Still confused?"

Trust Aunt Amy to get right to the bottom of things. Guy hugged her tighter. "Let's just dance, okay? I didn't come here to be analyzed."

"Right you are!"

"I can tell you one thing."

"What's that?"

"I do what I want nowadays."

"Smart boy."

"Yeah. I guess I have you to thank for making me stop living for the neighbors."

"Did I convince you of that?"

"You started it."

"Splendid. Now how do I convince myself?"

"Jeez, you feel good next to me," Corky whispered into Ro-Anne's ear.

"Mmm."

"Hey! Can I take you to dinner tonight? Name the spot. I got a nifty expense account."

Ro-Anne couldn't. Too upsetting. "I'm sorry, Corky. Wish I'd known. Made other plans. I'll take a rain check, though."

Corky couldn't look at her, so he pressed her head into his chest. "You got it!"

A student, sixteen and cynical, disapproving of sappy old-timers laboring over lost history made his way to the top of the bleachers with his camera and, looking down, snapped for the coming yearbook a picture of the elderly gathering.

Amy watched Corky dancing with Ro-Anne. "Tell me, Guy, who was the villain of our piece?"

Guy also looked over at Corky and Ro-Anne and said softly without sarcasm, "The villain was growing up."

"In a way I'm sorry I came."

Guy kissed her forehead. "Me too."

Above them the shining mirrored ball spun, fragmenting reality.

Below, couples danced into the fourth dimension.

BESTSELLERS

☐	BEGGAR ON HORSEBACK—Thorpe	23091-0	1.50
☐	THE TURQUOISE—Seton	23088-0	1.95
☐	STRANGER AT WILDINGS——Brent	23085-6	1.95
	(Pub. in England as Kirkby's Changeling)		
☐	MAKING ENDS MEET—Howar	23084-8	1.95
☐	THE LYNMARA LEGACY—Gaskin	23060-0	1.95
☐	THE TIME OF THE DRAGON—Eden	23059-7	1.95
☐	THE GOLDEN RENDEZVOUS—MacLean	23055-4	1.75
☐	TESTAMENT—Morrell	23033-3	1.95
☐	CAN YOU WAIT TIL FRIDAY?—	23022-8	1.75
	Olson, M.D.		
☐	HARRY'S GAME—Seymour	23019-8	1.95
☐	TRADING UP—Lea	23014-7	1.95
☐	CAPTAINS AND THE KINGS—Caldwell	23069-4	2.25
☐	"I AIN'T WELL—BUT I SURE AM	23007-4	1.75
	BETTER"—Lair		
☐	THE GOLDEN PANTHER—Thorpe	23006-6	1.50
☐	IN THE BEGINNING—Potok	22980-7	1.95
☐	DRUM—Onstott	22920-3	1.95
☐	LORD OF THE FAR ISLAND—Holt	22874-6	1.95
☐	DEVIL WATER—Seton	22888-6	1.95
☐	CSARDAS—Pearson	22885-1	1.95
☐	CIRCUS—MacLean	22875-4	1.95
☐	WINNING THROUGH INTIMIDATION—	22836-3	1.95
	Ringer		
☐	THE POWER OF POSITIVE	23499-1	1.95
	THINKING—Peale		
☐	VOYAGE OF THE DAMNED—	22449-X	1.75
	Thomas & Witts		
☐	THINK AND GROW RICH—Hill	23504-1	1.95
☐	EDEN—Ellis	23543-2	1.95

Buy them at your local bookstores or use this handy coupon for ordering:

FAWCETT BOOKS GROUP, 1 Fawcett Place, P.O. Box 1014, Greenwich, Ct.06830

Please send me the books I have checked above. Orders for less than 5 books must include 60¢ for the first book and 25¢ for each additional book to cover mailing and handling. Postage is FREE for orders of 5 books or more. Check or money order only. Please include sales tax.

Name_____ Books $_____
Address_____ Postage _____
City_____State/Zip_____ Sales Tax _____
                                        Total $_____

Please allow 4 to 5 weeks for delivery. This offer expires 11/78.

SHORT STORIES

- ☐ THE WIND SHIFTING WEST—Grau   23349-9   1.95
- ☐ PASSIONS—Singer   23399-5   1.95
- ☐ THE MUSIC SCHOOL—Updike   23279-4   1.75
- ☐ PIGEON FEATHERS—Updike   23356-1   1.75
- ☐ CONTEMPORARY AMERICAN   30832-4   2.25
  SHORT STORIES—Angus
- ☐ THE WHEEL OF LOVE—Oates   C2923   1.95
- ☐ THE GODDESS AND OTHER   C2774   1.95
  WOMEN—Oates

Buy them at your local bookstores or use this handy coupon for ordering:

- -

FAWCETT BOOKS GROUP, 1 Fawcett Place, P.O. Box 1014, Greenwich, Ct.06830

Please send me the books I have checked above. Orders for less than 5
books must include 60¢ for the first book and 25¢ for each additional book to
cover mailing and handling. Postage is FREE for orders of 5 books or more.
Check or money order only. Please include sales tax.

Name_____   Books $_____

Address_____   Postage _____

City_____State/Zip_____   Sales Tax _____

   Total $_____

Please allow 4 to 5 weeks for delivery. This offer expires 11/78.

A-34